## She hadn't expected him

She crossed the threshold and wished she could perform a disappearing act when she saw the man who sat near the stone fireplace. He was holding a book in his hands, and sunlight spilled over his face as he turned toward her.

He rose slowly, the fingers of one hand curving around the book's spine and drawing her attention to it. Her heart swelled with pain as she recognized the jacket, and her gaze shot back up to the face that hadn't changed since the last time she had seen it, two years ago. His eyes, too, were the same—blue-green and mysteriously deep.

Everly knew that someone would have to say something, so she spoke, and was amazed that her voice stayed steady. "Were you critiquing my latest effort?" she asked. "I don't mind—as long as it's unqualified praise."

Dear Reader:

Romance offers us all so much. It makes us "walk on sunshine." It gives us hope. It takes us out of our own lives, encouraging us to reach out to others. Janet Dailey is fond of saying that romance is a state of mind, that it could happen anywhere. Yet nowhere does romance seem to be as good as when it happens *here*.

Starting in February 1986, Silhouette Special Edition is featuring the AMERICAN TRIBUTE—a tribute to America, where romance has never been so wonderful. For six consecutive months, one out of every six Special Editions will be an episode in the AMERICAN TRIBUTE, a portrait of the lives of six women, all from Oklahoma. Look for the first book, *Love's Haunting Refrain* by Ada Steward, as well as stories by other favorites—Jeanne Stephens, Gena Dalton, Elaine Camp and Renee Roszel. You'll know the AMERICAN TRIBUTE by its patriotic stripe under the Silhouette Special Edition border.

AMERICAN TRIBUTE—six women, six stories, starting in February.

AMERICAN TRIBUTE—one of the reasons Silhouette Special Edition is just that—Special.

The Editors at Silhouette Books

# ELAINE CAMP
# After Dark

Silhouette Special Edition

Published by Silhouette Books New York

**America's Publisher of Contemporary Romance**

SILHOUETTE BOOKS
300 East 42nd St., New York, N.Y.   10017

ISBN: 0-373-09316-0

First Silhouette Books printing June 1986

America's Publisher of Contemporary Romance

Printed in the U.S.A.

## ELAINE CAMP

dreamed of becoming a writer for many years. Once she tried it, she quickly became successful, perhaps due to her reporter's eye, which gives her a special advantage in observing human relationships.

THE FLORIDA KEYS

Underlined places are fictitious.

FLORIDA

Gulf of Mexico

Everglades National Park

Florida Bay

Key Largo

Plantation Key

Cudjoe Key

Key Vaca

Upper Matecumbe Key

Boca Chica Key

Lower Matecumbe Key

Cabot's Key

Grassy Key

Marathon

Sugar Loaf Key

Key West

Little Bit Key

Straits of Florida

## Chapter One

The heron, which had been named "George" by the residents of Cabot's Key, landed on spindly legs. He eyed the flock of pelicans as he dropped the flopping fish to the sand. The pelicans waddled closer, drawn by the smell of the fish that George was preparing to devour. George stood over it and, when the pelicans got too close for comfort, turned his white feathers inside out and opened his beak in a blatant threat. The feathers on his long neck created a bristling crest as George flapped his wings and took three charging steps toward the interlopers.

His squawk floated on the sea breeze and through the open window to where Sebastian Dark stood and watched the test of courage. George was outnumbered, but fierce in his attack. The pelicans unfolded their gray wings and lifted themselves into the air, away from the quarrelsome heron. George speared the fish, worked it around until its head was pointed toward his gullet and the scaly morsel disappeared. George's long neck moved with a great gulping swallow and the lunch was history. The pelicans floated off with incredible grace now that they were airborne. The show was over.

"That's telling 'em, George," Sebastian said, touching two fingers to his forehead in a jaunty salute. "Still ruling the roost. I'm proud of you."

Sebastian's aquamarine eyes took in the idyllic scene beyond the preening heron. It was another sun-splashed day in the Florida Keys, the type of day taken for granted in the Keys, but envied by those living in the northern United States—blue skies, cirrus clouds stirred by the sea breeze, flocks of sea gulls and sandpipers and the rustling of palm fonds. This paradise never failed to rejuvenate him and reaffirm his decision to remain in the southern climes. He'd lived through enough bitterly cold winters and he never wanted to see another frozen vista again. Not after Siberia. Not after the demoralization of the work camp.

Cabot's Key had a charm all its own. Privately owned, it offered seclusion and uninterrupted peace and quiet. Less than ten miles from Key West it was nevertheless far removed from the bustling, tourist-packed Key where Sebastian Dark had recently made his home and had opened his new architectural business.

His first job as an architect had been on Cabot's Key. He'd been hired by Cabot Viverette to design and construct a writers' colony on the northern half of the ten-square-mile property. Construction of the twenty cabins and central recreation building had been completed a year ago, and the colony was attracting authors of all kinds who sought tranquillity and refuge from telephones, agents, booksellers and editors.

Sebastian knew all about refuges, and the desperate need to get away from everything and everybody before you exploded into a million bits of nerve endings. Yes, he knew about that... intimately.

A tall man, he had an erect bearing that he had developed as the son of an air force commander and had further honed during his own six years in the U.S. Air Force. The air force was a Dark family tradition. Every Dark male had served since the birth of aviation, and Sebastian hadn't once entertained the notion of breaking with tradition. After receiving his architectural degree he had joined up, eager to fulfill his family obligation.

Having inherited the lean, lithe build of his Dark ancestors, he had excelled in swimming and track as a teenager and had lettered in swimming during college. His silky, straight brown hair belonged to his mother's side of the family, but the peculiar blue green of his eyes was a Dark family trait. Everything about him was long: long limbs, long waist, long neck, long face. Even his hair was a little too long for the current styles, falling negligently to his shirt collar and across the tops of his ears. His visage was brooding, helped by the full poutiness of his lips and the hooded intensity of his gaze. His voice was as smooth and potent as brandy, rich-toned and warming.

Still concentrating on the sun diamonds strewn across the ocean's surface, Sebastian reached up one long-fingered hand and absentmindedly touched the gold eagle suspended on a strip of leather around his neck. He had worn the eagle ever since his release from the Russian prison where he had spent fourteen horrific months. It had been given to him by Cabot, and to Sebastian it represented the freedom he had lost and regained.

Sighing away the wavering images that threatened to haunt him, he turned from the window and his gaze fell on a book resting on a table near him. Furrows appeared between his eyes as he picked it up and read the words on its cover: *Mango Tango* by E. B. Herring.

Everly... The lines between his eyes deepened. He'd go to his grave regretting what he'd done to her. It was for the best, he told himself for the hundredth time. He'd done her a favor, but he was sure she didn't see it that way.

"Sorry to keep you waiting," Miss Martha apologized as she entered the sunny drawing room and immediately noticed the book he held. "I haven't finished it yet, but it's good. It's no wonder that it's still on the best-seller list."

Sebastian replaced the book and held out his hands to the tall reed-thin woman. "I know. I've read it." He grasped her hands and placed a kiss at her temple where strands of her ebony hair had escaped the confines of her severe chignon. She smelled of cedar and furniture polish. "Let me guess. You've been cleaning closets this morning."

Miss Martha's sloe eyes widened. "How did you know?"

"Lucky guess." He sandwiched one of her hands between his. "I wonder if Cabot realizes that he happens to have the best household supervisor in the South?"

Miss Martha's thin lips pressed together to keep back the sound of her laughter. She was a woman who found it difficult to indulge in frivolity. "Will you take tea with me?"

"Of course. I've been dreaming of your butter cookies ever since I left. It's funny the things you miss, isn't it?" He released her hand and waited for her to sit on the medallion-back sofa before he sat across from her in one of the two Louis XV chairs. He slanted his ankle over his knee, adopting a comfortable demeanor in front of this woman who had become more than just a household supervisor to him. Miss Martha—did she have a last name? he wondered—was the person he'd come to depend on when he needed a calm head and reasonable words of advice. One look at her serene face could assuage his most troubled thoughts. The effect of her presence was already working on him, and Sebastian let some of the stiffness leave his shoulders.

"I miss you . . . we all do," Miss Martha said, smoothing the long dark skirt over her crossed legs. "But I'm glad you've opened your own business in Key West."

"So am I."

"Where are you living?" she asked in her melodious voice.

"Behind the office. There's a small apartment back there with a side courtyard. It's all I need."

"Have you had any clients yet?"

Sebastian smiled indulgently. "I've only been in Key West ten days, Miss Martha. I've hardly unpacked."

"But you already have a fine reputation as an architect. Everyone in the Keys knows that you designed the writers' colony." She grew silent while one of the maids brought in a tea tray. "Thank you, Ginger. That will be all. I'll pour." Miss Martha lifted the silver teapot and filled two delicate china cups, adding cream and sugar to one and only cream to the other. "Here's yours. You have such a sweet tooth," she said, smiling warmly. "And here are your cookies."

"Ah!" Sebastian took three of the cookies and wasted no time in biting into the buttery goodness. "My dream has come true." He took another bite and rolled his eyes in ecstasy, drawing another stifled laugh from Miss Martha.

"You're easy to please," Miss Martha commented with a lift of her slender brows. "All the cabins are occupied now," she said, moving the conversation to the writers' colony. "Sean O'Shaunnesey arrived yesterday. He told me that he's working on a novel about an Irish priest, but he's secretive about it."

"I think all authors are secretive about their work," Sebastian said, finishing the first cookie and starting on another. "I'm going to make a glutton of myself on these."

"Go ahead. Your secret is safe with me." Miss Martha's eyes shone with amusement, but her lips were unsmiling. "Are you glad that your own author days are over?"

"You know I am. Granted, my share of the royalties from *Wrong Place, Wrong Time* made me financially solvent, but that book was a lead weight around my neck in many ways." In frustration, he drove his fingers through his hair. "The publicity tours, the talk shows, the radio interviews, the speeches, the lectures...it went on and on until I thought I'd go stark raving mad if I had to recount my prison experiences one more time."

"I know." Miss Martha set her cup and saucer on the tray, then sat back against the couch. "It's time to put the past where it belongs—behind you. I don't think that Mr. Cabot realized the strain you were under when he asked you to accompany him on the publicity tours. He adores promoting his books. The limelight is his favorite place."

"Not me," Sebastian said with a firm shake of his head. "My preferred place is in the deep background."

"Not too deep," Miss Martha cautioned. "Don't shut yourself away from everything."

He smiled, noting her concern. "I don't think that's possible, even though it sounds wonderful to me. Have you heard from Cabot?"

"Not since before you left. He's laying groundwork for his next book, but I don't know anything about it. All I know is that he's staying in the New York City penthouse."

"The penthouse..." Sebastian grew silent as he sipped the cinnamon-flavored tea. Cabot's penthouse overlooked Central Park and Sebastian could remember it in vivid detail, although he hadn't been inside the apartment in two years. The penthouse was where he'd met Everly, and in those spacious, lavishly appointed rooms they had taken tentative steps toward each other until they had finally fallen into each other's arms, clinging tightly, as if they both knew that this ecstasy couldn't last for long.

"Sebastian..." Miss Martha's velvety voice pulled him away from the memories. "Are you living in the past again?"

"Yes," he said with a self-conscious laugh. "Force of habit, I suppose." He took another cookie from the platter and barricaded his mind against the desire to remember.

The coauthor of the current best-selling murder mystery, *Mango Tango*, was having trouble keeping her eyes on the ribbon of highway that stretched over the Atlantic Ocean. Brilliant blue water sparkled on either side of the Overseas Highway, and gulls called to her, dragging her attention from the two-lane highway to the dots of land scattered across the water like so many emeralds.

The bridge traffic was light, affording her the opportunity to drive below the speed limit and indulge in spurts of sight-seeing. It had been more than two years since Everly Viverette had driven along this winding roller-coaster stretch of engineering genius. To the north was the variegated blue of Florida Bay and to the south, the teal blue of the Gulf Stream. Ever since she'd driven through Key Largo, she had been stunned with the commercial growth of the Keys since her last visit. Making her way through the Lower Matecumbe Keys, she slowed the rented midnight-blue Corvette as she entered the city limits of Long Key. Her favorite restaurant was still in business, but it was surrounded by other businesses that were new to her. Shell shops, a new post office, insurance agencies, bait shops and diving schools lined the highway along with fishermen who had dropped their lines over the bridge and waited patiently for a massive grouper or small shark to take their bait.

Everly switched off the air conditioner and cranked down the window to let the sea breeze flow over her. Her curly, bobbed, chestnut hair blew into her eyes.

Her eyes—large and brown, and surrounded by dark thick lashes—widened as she struggled to see everything at once. Sun rays tangled through her hair, picking up the red highlights among the short mass of shimmering curls. With her close-cropped hairstyle and enormous eyes set in a small heart-shaped face, she had a elfin quality. She had been told more times than she could count, perhaps because of her gamine features, that she had a little-girl-lost look that made men adopt a protective manner toward her. This never failed to irritate her, since she felt like a female Goliath inside, although she was only a couple of inches above five feet on the outside.

Her father had called her "Little Bit," but had known from the time she was old enough to talk that she was a dynamo. She had proved it by falling out of trees, skinning her knees, roughhousing with the neighborhood boys and breaking her arm twice and her ankle thrice—all while indulging in her favorite sport of baseball, which she had played with the gusto of a major leaguer. Stealing bases had been her speciality, and she had been fearless when sliding into a protective baseman, bent on tagging her "out" or doing bodily harm.

When she was sixteen she had directed her energies from the baseball diamond to the many-faceted world of writing, following in her father's footsteps. Her school essays had received high praise, and she had realized that she had found her niche, her life's work. It wasn't easy work, but it was gratifying and absorbing. It wasn't, however, until she began plotting books with her cousin Blaire Thomlin that she had felt the touch of greatness. Their first finished novel had been praised by their literary agent and bid on by three major publishers. Once published, it had propelled the coauthors known as E. B. Herring into best-selling orbit.

The jagged outline of Knight Key joggled her from her reverie, and Everly realized that she had zipped through Marathon Key, the very heart of the Florida Keys, without even being aware of it. The famous Seven-Mile Bridge loomed before her like a silver ribbon spanning yards of blue satin. As the car tires sang along the hot pavement, Everly loosened her grip on the steering wheel and stared ahead at the irregular sprawl of the land in the distance. The Spanish had called the string of disconnected land *Los Martires*, the Martyrs, because of their twisted shapes. The little islands had been called *cayos* back then, which had eventually evolved into the word "keys."

Everly sucked in her breath as the Corvette climbed the highest point on the bridge, some sixty feet above the Moser Channel. She grinned, remembering a summer when she had brought Blaire with her to her father's estate. Blaire had been white with fear when Everly had driven her rust-bucket Mustang over the bridge.

As the Corvette skimmed along the Seven-Mile, Everly watched two cormorants leave the water's surface and sail into the air and over the stunted red mangrove trees that covered the Saddlebunch Keys. Spanish bayonet and salt-bush grew alongside the highway, swaying with the Gulf breezes. The smell of salt water was strong, bringing with it memories of lazy afternoons spent fishing or shell hunting. Soon she would reach Similar Sound, and then she'd be able to see the outlines of O'Hara Key, Shark Key and Cabot's Key. Ah, yes, she thought with a wistful sigh. Cabot's Key and her very own Little Bit Key.

Nostalgic feelings wove through her for a few moments before being dispelled by the reason that had kept her so long from her beloved Florida Keys—Sebastian Dark.

Her fingers tightened around the steering wheel until her pink-tinted nails pricked her palms. She wiggled higher into the bucket seat as tension snaked around her spine, but she held on to her decision to come back to the Keys where she planned to build a house on Little Bit, a mere stone's throw from Cabot's Key where her father's estate was nestled. The threat of seeing Sebastian again had kept her away for two years and that was long enough. She knew the possibility of not seeing him again was remote, but she clung to it for a few moments until she discarded its foolishness. She'd see him again. It was inevitable. He'd finally moved from Cabot's Key to Key West, but Key West was less than ten miles from Cabot's Key and she assumed that Sebastian would visit from time to time. After all, he'd lived on Cabot's Key for two years and probably thought of it as his second home. Her father had kept her abreast of Sebastian's comings and goings, although she had feigned indifference.

How would she react when she saw Sebastian Dark again? she wondered. How would *he* react? He should beg her forgiveness for dropping her from his life like a bad habit, but she knew somehow that Sebastian Dark wouldn't get down on bended knee before her. He would probably play it cool, act as if nothing had happened between them, and that, she knew, would add salt to her wound. He'd used her and thrown her aside like an empty beer can and that was something she would never forget nor forgive!

Calming herself, she concentrated on the beautiful scenery as her eager gaze focused on the lush vegetation of Cabot's Key. Little Bit looked overgrown, having not been used for years, but Cabot's Key was well cared for. The red-tiled roof peeked up above the lower treetops, beckoning Everly as she turned off the main highway onto the strip of asphalt that wound through groves of royal palms and royal poinciana trees in full crimson bloom. Two gigantic bayan trees stood before the Cabot Estate, their off-shoot roots dripping from the lower branches like long gnarled fingers seeking the warm soil.

The house had two stories and a full attic. Sugary pink with white accents, it glistened like a sand castle in the sun. Everly parked the car in front of the house and stretched her legs as she climbed out of the low-slung vehicle and stared up at the fanlight above the front door. Graceful fluted columns supported the second-floor balcony that ran around the house, and eyebrow windows let sun pour into the attic rooms where Cabot Viverette worked on his novels when in residence.

Staring up at the attic windows, Everly recalled times when she was a precocious child of eight and had viewed her father's office as a wonderland. Shelves upon shelves of books were up there and had towered over her diminutive figure. It was in Cabot's work area where Everly had discovered *Treasure Island*, *Black Beauty*, and Nancy Drew mysteries. When she was fifteen she cut her literary teeth on Agatha Christie and Dashiell Hammett and had felt the onslaught of inadequacy when she read Lillian Hellman and F. Scott Fitzgerald.

"There will always be better writers than you," her father had told her when she moaned that she would never be as good as Steinbeck or Hemingway. "But there will always be worse writers than you, too. And *that*, my dear Little Bit, is what keeps scribblers like you and me behind the typewriter."

"But I don't have any confidence in what I write," she'd groaned.

"Show me a writer with self-confidence and I'll show you a damned fool," he'd barked, laughing at her forlorn expression. "Lack of self-confidence goes with the territory, Everly. Get used to the terrain and avoid it whenever possible."

Smiling at the sweet memory, Everly mounted the six wide steps to the porch and started to ring the doorbell, then stopped the motion. This was her home, she reminded herself. She didn't need to ask permission to step inside it.

Opening the door on its silent, oiled hinges, she walked into the foyer and let the rush of memories flow over her. The freestanding stairway curved up to the second floor, its cherry wood banister shining and unmarked. The place smelled of passion flowers that grew outside the door and of lemons and limes from the groves nearby. Everly tucked her flat purse under one arm and smoothed the wrinkles from her red cotton shirt and navy-blue twill slacks. She patted her hair, feeling its curling disarray and surrendering to the orneriness of it. Should have worn a hat, she thought.

Voices reached her, soft and lilting, and she went toward the sound that came from the drawing room. Crossing the threshold, she wished she could perform a disappearing act when she saw the man who sat near the stone fireplace. He was holding a book in his hands—hands that she knew so well—and sunlight spilled over his face and lit his eyes as he turned toward her. Everly was barely aware of Miss Martha standing up with a sharp gasp of surprise. The only person in the room as far as she was concerned was Sebastian Dark.

He rose slowly, the fingers of one hand curving around the book's spine and drawing her attention to it. Her heart swelled to painful proportions as she recognized the red-and-black jacket and her gaze shot back up to the face that hadn't changed since the last time she had seen it two years ago. His eyes were the same, blue green and mysteriously deep. His lips, full and generous, parted and he mouthed her name—Everly—and there was a question mark at the end of it that registered in the furrowing of his wide brow.

Everly glanced at the book again, knowing that someone would have to say something eventually and that it might as well be her. Forcing a half smile to her lips, she met his gaze boldly.

"Speak of the devil and look who walks in," she said, amazed that her voice was so steady and full-bodied. "Were you critiquing the latest effort by E. B. Herring? I don't mind, as long as it's unqualified praise."

"Everly!" Miss Martha rushed forward and clutched her shoulders in a rare display of emotion. "Why didn't you call and tell me you were coming? I would have made special preparations for you."

"No need for that," Everly said, finally managing to look away from Sebastian's shocked expression. "I'm just home folk. You look wonderful, Miss Martha. You never change."

"Well, you have changed. You cut your hair!"

"Oh, yes." Everly shrugged and laughed softly. "After years of trying to tame my hair into a straight long style, I surrendered to Mother Nature and let it curl all over the place. Keeping it shorter makes it easier to manage."

"It looks delightful." Miss Martha slipped one bony arm around Everly's shoulders and turned to face Sebastian. "Doesn't she look delightful, Sebastian?"

Sebastian cleared his throat and placed the book on the table beside the tea tray. "Yes, uh, delightful."

His obvious discomfort tickled Everly and she could barely keep the grin from her lips. "I thought you lived in Key West now, Bastian."

At the sound of her nickname for him, he straightened as if he'd been speared and his mouth turned down at the corners.

"I do. I'm here visiting Miss Martha."

"Oh, I see." Patting Miss Martha's hand on her shoulder, Everly turned sideways to shut out Sebastian. "I can't believe all the changes in the Keys! New businesses are everywhere!"

"Yes, progress is well upon us." Miss Martha glanced toward the door, then gestured with one hand. "Come in here, Lewis, and have a look! Our Everly has returned to the fold."

Lewis, stooped and round-shouldered from his hours of pruning and weeding, ambled forward. His leathery face folded into a mass of wrinkles as he smiled and shook Everly's extended hand.

"Land sakes," he said, his voice deep and foggy. "If this don't beat the world! It sure is good to lay eyes on you again, Miss Everly."

"Thank you, Lewis. How have you been? The grounds look lovely, by the way. Just as I remembered them."

"Kind of you to say so. I've been fit as a fiddle." He pressed a callused hand to his side and gave a little wince. "The old arthritis acts up on me every so often, but I get around okay for a cantankerous seventy-six-year-old."

Everly laughed and let go of his hand. "Cantankerous? Why, you've always been a dear around me." Everly sniffed the air that blew in from the open door. "I can smell the lemon and lime trees. It always smells heavenly on Cabot's Key."

"Is your baggage in the car?" Lewis asked as he mopped his balding head with a colorful handkerchief.

"Yes. In the trunk." Everly held up the keys and Lewis took them.

"I'll bring them in for you."

"Thanks, Lewis." She glanced at the door as Lewis shuffled in that direction and saw that Sebastian was moving unobtrusively toward its escape hatch. "Leaving so soon, Bastian?"

He stopped and compunction thinned his lips. "I—I need to get back to my office."

"You don't have to leave on my account," Everly said as an inner voice cautioned her to keep a civil tongue but went unheeded. "I'm not going to make a scene in front of witnesses." She felt Miss Martha's keen regard and Sebastian's slow burn, but she kept her gaze averted from both of them by pretending to examine the foyer and drawing room.

"I've got to go." He turned on the threshold and directed his next comments to Miss Martha. "Thanks for the tea and cookies, Miss Martha. I'll drop in again soon. Next time you're in Key West come by and I'll play host."

"I'll do that. Take care, Sebastian."

Everly glanced sideways to catch his hurried departure, and with his absence she relaxed, only then realizing how tense she had been in his presence. She smiled, feeling the strain of it on her lips, and turned to Miss Martha.

"Will you take me on a tour of the house? Is my old room still available?"

"Of course, Everly. We haven't touched a thing in your room. Everything is just as you left it." Miss Martha lifted a hand, indicating the staircase. "Does your father know you're here?"

"Yes," Everly said as she mounted the stairs. "He said he'd join me in a week or so." She paused, hearing the roar of an engine, and glanced over her shoulder to see a dove-gray M.G. zip past the front of the house with Sebastian at its wheel. "Does Sebastian visit often?"

"He's only been living in Key West a couple of weeks. He's a fine young man."

Miss Martha's tone was protective and Everly abandoned the subject of Sebastian Dark. The worst was over, she told herself. She had faced him without being reduced to a shrew and she was proud of herself. She wondered if Sebastian was weak with relief now that the ordeal was over.

On the road to Key West Sebastian slipped on a pair of mirrored sunglasses and guided the convertible with one hand. The wind poured over the top of the windshield and swept his hair straight back. The strong current of air felt good as it stung his face and made his eyes water. The ball of fury that burned in the middle of his chest began to dissolve and, in the patches of sunlight that bounced off the hood of his car, he could see her face briefly.

That face! It was captivating. With her shorter hair she looked like a French waif. So much like those paint-by-number pictures of enormous-eyed children that had been popular a few years back. She still had that aura of melancholy that had always tugged at his heart and made him want to shelter her from harm. But, strangely enough, it was her hands that had created a wellspring of emotion within him when he had recovered from the shock of seeing her again. Those hands—those tapered, small fingers—had soothed the savage beast within him when he'd returned to the States. Like a magic salve, they had coated him with unconditional love that had slowly brought him back to the living.

Displaying the patience of Job, she had endured his tirades of bitterness, his black moods, his mumbled confusion, and she had given him focus and purpose again. For someone so young—she had been twenty-three then, five years his junior—she had been remarkably wise and infinitely understanding of his state of mind.

However, once he was back on the straight and narrow, he had become frightened of his need for her; afraid that he had come to depend on her too much and would never be able to face the world on his own power again. The fear grew into panic and a desire to escape the easy life she offered him. He had rebelled at first by trying to gently disengage himself and when that didn't work, he tore himself from her and bolted for freedom.

His exit could have been more graceful, he knew, but he'd been in no physical or mental state for graciousness. After fourteen months of surviving in a Russian prison, he had been single-minded about getting away from responsibilities and emotional ties. He had wanted no confines, no parameters, and most of all, no commitments to anyone but himself.

The M.G. sped up and over a small incline and toward the city of Key West. One corner of Sebastian's mouth twitched in appreciation as he recalled Everly's curvy figure and shining eyes. It's too bad we can't be civil to one another, Sebastian thought with a sigh of regret. She's so pretty. Always has been, always will be. His grin became one of self-recrimination.

One thing hadn't changed between them. With little effort on Everly's part, she could still turn him inside out.

## Chapter Two

Approaching the southern edge of the Key where the writers' colony was sequestered, Everly stood on tiptoe a moment to peer over Lewis's stooped shoulder.

"The colony has become quite popular, hasn't it?" she asked.

"Land sakes, yes!" Lewis shook his head, paused to pinch a yellowed leaf from a rosebush, and continued his shuffling walk. "We usually have a waiting list of folks wanting to spend some time here. I guess 'bout near every big author's been here since it was opened. I would'a never thought so many writers would have a yen for solitude."

Everly laughed, moving to his side when the paved lane widened. "It's not that we have a yen for solitude, it's that we must have peace and quiet at times to meet our deadlines or to think through a particularly troublesome plot." She laughed again at a flash of memory. "Once I noticed that Dad seemed more preoccupied than usual and I asked him what was troubling him. He said, 'Not much. I've just written two hundred pages on my new book and I haven't got a plot yet.'"

Lewis made a harrumph sound and Everly realized that this bit of insight was lost on him. He was a grounds keeper and knew nothing of plots and characterizations.

"How's Miss Blaire getting along? She ain't been here in years!"

"She's fine," Everly said, stopping for a moment to pluck a particularly fragile wild rose. She pressed it to her nose, but it had no scent, so she tucked it behind her ear.

"She married off yet?"

Everly counted to ten before she answered in dulcet tones, "No, Lewis. You're one to talk, you old bachelor."

"Let me tell you, missy, if I had it to do over I'd a married me a good woman, I would."

"You still could."

"Naw!" He ran a hand over the hairless top of his head. "Nobody'd be a wanting an old geezer like me. In my prime . . . well, I could'a had me a woman then. Take Mr. Sebastian—"

"No, thanks." Everly smiled to take the edge off her words and directed her gaze to the clearing ahead. "Here we are! My, my! These cabins are beautiful. I don't know why, but I thought they'd look more rustic. These are downright sophisticated!"

"Sure are. Fancy, ain't they?"

Everly nodded absently as she moved to the front of the first cottage and stared up at the sandstone wall and peaked roof. The windows were either round, square or triangular.

"Can we go inside one or are they all occupied?"

"Number three is vacant until this afternoon," Lewis said, moving toward it as he selected a key on his massive key ring. "Some poet is checking into it. We get a lot of them poets."

"Dad was inspired when he thought of this," Everly said as she waited for Lewis to unlock the heavy wooden door.

"I'm glad he kept the cost down so that struggling writers could afford to stay here."

"He don't make no money on this, that's for sure." Lewis went inside, leaving Everly to follow him. "This colony just breaks even."

"Oh, Lewis!" Everly stood in the center of the living room and turned in a slow circle, tipping back her head as she did so to take in the beamed ceiling. "This is fabulous!"

The living room was immense, divided into a living area and a work area, the latter being closed off by an Oriental screen. Decorated in soft shades of tan and ivory with splashes of apricot and teal blue, the effect was soothing to the eye and disposition. The irregularly shaped windows let sunlight pour in, creating strange patterns on the coffee-colored carpet.

Everly went to the kitchenette, which was small since meals were provided by the estate staff. The area was bright with pastel tiles that climbed the walls and covered the floor. A table for two sat in one corner under a small skylight. The next room she discovered was the bathroom—peachy and warm with a claw-foot tub and old-fashioned shower. The bedroom adjoining it wasn't large, but large enough for the double bed, dresser, night table and walk-in closet. A skylight broke the ceiling above the bed.

And *everywhere* there were shelves! Every nook and cranny was utilized. Bookshelves, whatnot shelves, concealed shelves, corner shelves! Even one end of the bedroom closet contained shelves from floor to ceiling. It was heaven!

Everly went back to the work area and ducked around the colorful silk screen. The built-in furniture was made of knotty pine. The desk was tucked into a corner; it was L-shaped with wide slabs of polished knotty pine that provided ample room for a typewriter or word processor with plenty of room left over for a printer. Above the desk were shelves of every shape, height and width. Below the desk were more shelves and plenty of leg room. The chair was on rollers and it was roomy enough for a big man and cushiony enough for a petite woman. The armrests were wide and the seat and back were adjustable to fit any stature. A circular window to the right of the chair provided a view of the colony's main house, which stood in the center of the circled cabins. A triangular window on the other side gave a view of the glittering Gulf Stream. There was no carpeting in this area; wood floors made it easier to roll about in the chair.

Rounding the screen, four steps took her into the kitchenette and six took her into the living room.

"Perfect," Everly announced with a definite nod. Considerable thought had been expended on the floor plan. This cabin had been designed expressly for writers by someone who knew what writers needed most—easy access from the office area to the coffeepot and the living-room couch.

"Like it, do you?" Lewis asked as he examined the hanging ferns in front of the living-room window.

"I adore it. Oh, I've been looking for a place just like this. I can't believe all these shelves! It's fantastic."

Lewis chuckled. "That's what everyone says. They love them shelves. The women usually talk about the closets, too. There's four of 'em, you know."

"Four closets?" Everly sighed with exaggeration. "In a place this size? One is usually the norm. Oh, Lewis! I could move right in here and never want to leave."

"Sorry, missy. This one's rented for the rest of the month and there's a waiting list for the others."

"I know." Everly shrugged helplessly. "I guess it doesn't make any difference that I happen to be related to the landlord?"

"Nope." Lewis grinned and motioned to the front door. "Want to take a look-see at the community house?"

"Yes. What's in it?"

"Games and stuff. There's a couple of television sets in there and one of those machines that shows movies."

"A VCR?"

"Yeah, I guess that's what it's called." He flung open the double doors and stepped back to let her enter. "Once in a while we throw a party and use this place for it."

Everly went in and examined the game tables, pool tables, video game machines and big-screen televisions. Picnic tables and benches took one side of the room while comfortable couches and chairs were arranged on the other side. The center held the game tables. The roof was a skylight, giving the room an open-air feeling since it also had numerous windows.

"This is cozy," Everly said, turning back to glance at Lewis. "Do the writers eat their meals here? I thought that—"

"The meals are taken to their cabins, but once in a while we have a cookout and we use those tables then. Once a month we throw a bingo party and those tables are full. Not only with the residents, but with outsiders."

"Really? I didn't think Dad let outsiders onto the Key."

"Only on bingo nights. The money from it goes into a scholarship fund for local college students."

"Oh, I see." Everly smiled, thinking that her Dad had become quite the philanthropist. "Lewis, will you go over to Little Bit with me?" she asked, turning back to him.

"Little Bit?" He rubbed his whiskered jaw. "It's all grow'd up over there. You sure you want to?"

"Yes, please? I want to see the old house on it."

"Mmm." He wiped his face with a red handkerchief. "What's left of it, you mean. It's fallin' down."

"It is?" Disappointment wilted her spirits. "Well, I'd like to see it anyway."

"Okay. Tide's out so's we can walk over there."

"Good." Everly led the way toward the strip of land that formed a natural walkway when the tide was out. She picked her way across it, stepping over puddles and patches of mud while Lewis plowed through them behind her. "This was always a special place for me," she said, raising her voice to be heard over the ocean and screeching birds. "My place. My own island. I'm thinking of living here."

"Here? Why not in the main house?"

"Because that's my father's house. I want my own place. Little Bit is my very own Key."

"Won't be able to live in the house on it," Lewis grumbled. "One good wind and that thing will fall into the ocean."

It can't be that bad, Everly thought. She remembered the house. It was old, but a new coat of paint and a little repair work would do the trick. She was sure of it. All the old place needed was a little tender loving—

"Oh no!" She stopped in her tracks and Lewis bumped into her. "I don't believe it!"

The house had no roof to speak of, just gaping holes surrounded by loose shingles. One side of the house had crumbled to the ground like a ruined house of cards, leaving the interior exposed to nature's damage. The picket fence she recalled was gone; the charming porch, crushed by a fallen tree.

"Told you it was a mess."

"Yes, so you did." Everly stumbled forward, her numb mind still rejecting the truth before her eyes. "What happened to it? It used to be so lovely."

"Don't recall it ever being much more than an abandoned house," Lewis said. "Nobody's lived in it for 'bout twenty years. If something's not taken care of it goes to pot."

"Well, I guess I'll have to tear the rest of it down and start all over again." Everly set her fists on her hips and tried to imagine her dream home standing where the dilapidated cottage had fallen to ruin. "Nothing can be saved of this one."

"Nope. Nothing to save. You really thinking of building a house here?"

"Yes." She grinned over her shoulder at Lewis. "Did you think I'd pitch a tent and rough it?"

"Just didn't think you'd ever live here, that's all. Thought you'd eventually take over the New York penthouse."

"Oh no!" Everly shook her head in a vehement denial. "Anywhere but there! Besides, I love the Keys."

"Me, too. Onliest place I want to be." He motioned for her to follow him. "Come on, Miss Everly. I'll walk you back to the main house and then I've got to get back to my work."

"Okay. Thanks for the tour, Lewis."

"My pleasure."

They walked back to the main house in silence, broken only by Lewis's mutterings when he saw a wilted flower or bug-infested vine. By the time they'd reached the house, Everly felt like one of Lewis's wilted flowers and longed for a tall glass of fruit juice.

"I'm not used to this tropical climate," Everly said, laughing a little as she entered the house and saw Miss Martha's worried scowl. "It's sort of humid today."

"I think it might rain this evening," Miss Martha observed. "I'll get you something to drink after I answer the telephone." She hurried to the tall stand in the foyer where the telephone clicked like a cricket. "Cabot's Key Estate," she answered in her melodious voice that spoke of her upbringing in Bermuda. "Oh, hello! Yes, she's right here. I'll put her on the line." She extended the receiver to Everly. "It's your father, dear."

"Oh great!" Everly grabbed the receiver and pressed it to her ear. "Hi, Dad!"

"Hi there. How's my girl?"

"Fine. I just got back from Little Bit. The house is ruined, Dad. I'll have to build one from scratch."

"That's too bad, but I thought the place was pretty run-down. How do you like the colony?"

"It's beautiful!" She leaned back against the banister and smiled her thanks when Miss Martha handed her a frosty glass of pineapple juice. "Wait a second." She took two long swallows and sighed. "I'm back. Had to quench my thirst. Dad, the cabins are wonderful. Just what a writer dreams of. I'd like a house just like them, in fact. Except bigger, of course."

"Of course." His resonant chuckle tickled her ear. "How do you like all those shelves? I told Sebastian that they were top priority and he came through with flying colors."

"He sure did! He's got a knack for—" She chopped off her raves and swallowed more of the pineapple juice to douse her enthusiasm. "Anyway, I like the cabins. I'll keep the floor plans in mind when I hire someone to build my house on Little Bit."

"Well..." Her father drew out the word for dramatic effect. "Why not hire my architect? I highly recommend him."

"No way."

"You've seen his work and—"

"No, Dad!" She clamped her teeth together, angry that her father continued to attempt to rebuild the bridge between herself and his best friend, Sebastian Dark. "There are other architects around here."

"But Sebastian has just opened his own business. He'd love to design a house for you. I'm sure of it."

"Please, Dad. Don't start." She clutched the receiver and her eyes closed wearily.

"Have you seen him yet?"

"Yes, and the reunion was unpleasant. I don't want to be around him. He's untrustworthy."

"Now Everly," Cabot scolded gently. "Don't be mule-headed. Why not bury the hatchet? I'm sure that Sebastian would like nothing better than to be on friendly terms with you."

"Friendly terms," she said with a derisive laugh. "That's a hoot! *He* left *me*, Dad. Not the other way around."

"But that was two years ago, Ev. He wasn't himself and—"

"Oh, who was he? Anyone I know?"

"Don't be a smart-mouth, Everly Suzanne." His voice held a note of impatience. "I'll be there in a few days and we'll iron this out. You need to make peace with Sebastian."

"Fat chance." She could feel his crackling anger on the other end of the line, but she didn't care. How dare he defend Sebastian! "Are you still in New York?"

"Yes, and I've got to run. I'm having lunch with a friend." His sigh whispered to her. "Be civil, will you?"

"Yes, I can do that."

"Good. Who loves you, Little Bit?"

"You, Dad." She smiled and repeated the lines they had said to each other as far back as she could remember. "And who loves you, Mr. Viverette?"

"Miss Viverette," he answered. "See you soon, honey."

"Bye, Dad." She replaced the receiver and continued to lean against the banister until she'd finished the glass of juice, then she picked up the telephone again and dialed a long-distance number. The phone rang four times before it was answered.

"Hello?" Blaire sounded preoccupied.

"Greetings from the sunny Florida Keys."

"Everly!" Blaire's voice sang across the line. "You sound like a postcard."

"What are you doing? You sounded foggy when you answered."

"Oh I was reading a letter from our dear agent."

"What's the latest from Monica Feber and Associates?"

"She writes that a high-and-mighty fellow author has declined to provide advance notices on our book for the jacket. Can you believe that Ben Butler would be such a cad?"

Everly winced at Blaire's agitated voice. "Oh, well. It's a free country, cuz. If Butler doesn't want to endorse our book, that's his right."

"What's with him?" Blaire asked. "I hate writers who give other writers the cold shoulder."

"Blaire, calm down! It's no big deal. Our book will sell without his endorsement."

"That's what Monica says in her letter."

"See? What did I tell you?"

"It still gets my goat!" She was silent a moment before asking in a calmer tone, "How are you doing? Getting plenty of sand and surf?"

"Not in the Keys, Blaire. Beaches aren't plentiful here. Remember?"

"Oh, that's right. The coral reef cuts off the big breakers. No breakers. No sand."

"Right. I went over to Little Bit and my house is hopeless. I'm going to have to hire an architect to build a new one."

"Oh that's too bad. Or is it? A new house would be super, wouldn't it?"

"Yes." Everly twisted the curly telephone cord around her index finger. "Dad suggested that I hire Bastian for the job."

"That's a good idea."

"*What?* Whose side are you on?"

"Are we taking sides? Sorry. I didn't know we were going to do battle over this."

"You know what I mean," Everly complained then added sarcastically, "After what Bastian did to me, I'm sure I'd hire him!"

"Well, why not?" Blaire said with a lilt to her voice. "That was years ago. Let bygones be bygones."

"Physician heal thyself," Everly shot back. "Why not forgive Butler while we're at it?"

"That's different."

"Is it?"

"Oh I hate it when you throw logic in my face!" Blaire laughed, letting Everly know that she was only kidding. "Do what you think is best, Everly. But if Sebastian Dark is a good architect, I don't see the problem. You don't have to be around him. He'd be hired help."

"I don't know . . ."

"Hey, Everly! Lighten up. After all, he's just a man."

"Right. Well, I guess I'll talk with you later. Are you still going to take a vacation?"

"Yes, I've booked a flight to Canada. I thought I'd visit an old college friend who lives in Quebec."

"Gloria?"

"Yes. Have you met her?"

"No, but you've talked about her. Sounds like a good idea, Blaire. Quebec is beautiful."

"So I've heard. Thanks for calling. You've brightened my otherwise gloomy day."

"Buck up, cuz."

"Right!" Blaire giggled. "Bye now. Give my love to Uncle Cabot."

"Okay. Good-bye." Everly hung up the phone and tugged at the bangs that curled on her forehead. Just a man, she mused, then laughed harshly. What a joke! Sebastian could never be "just" anything to her. He had been her first lover and a woman never forgets her first affair. She had tried—tried *hard*—to put him out of her mind and out of her heart, but she never could banish him entirely. He was a hurt that wouldn't heal.

Cabot Viverette stared at the telephone for a few moments, his salt-and-pepper brows meeting at the bridge of his nose in a frown.

"Trouble, Cabot?"

The lilting accented voice turned him toward the woman who sat queenlike on the divan. The sight of her oval face framed by silvery hair that flowed over her shoulders never failed to make his heart swell with devotion. Her luminous gray eyes reflected her every emotion and she never tried to hide her feelings. She wore them openly, courageously.

"My daughter," Cabot answered, moving from the telephone to sit beside Katra Kamenski on the divan. He took one of her delicate hands in his. Blue veins could be seen beneath her lily-white skin and Cabot traced one with his thumb. "She's holding a grudge and it worries me."

"What grudge? Explain, please."

"Oh I shouldn't burden you with this," he said, lifting her hand to place a kiss in its palm. "It's family, you know."

"I know, and that is why I'm interested. You see?"

He smiled, thankful for this woman. What had he ever done to deserve such a jewel? he wondered. "I see." He unbuttoned his suit jacket and crossed one leg over the other. When his arm slipped around Katra's shoulders, she rested her head against the curve of his neck. "I've told you about Sebastian Dark."

"Yes, the young man who spent time in the Gulag."

"Yes, a Russian prison."

"I read the book, of course. It brought back . . . well, it made me remember the times in the concentration camps when I was young."

Cabot grew silent, knowing how horrible those memories were for her. He'd read several of her books about experiences she'd had during the Holocaust and they had moved him deeply even before he'd met Katra a few months ago. He'd never before met such an engaging woman and he had fallen in love with her within twenty-four hours of their first meeting.

"Tell, me, Cabot," she urged. "What troubles you about your daughter and Sebastian?"

"Well, they had an affair a couple of years ago."

"Oh yes? That's hard on a father."

"Yes, it is." He frowned, remembering how upset he'd been when he'd realized what was going on under his nose. "But I've come to grips with what happened. Everly hasn't."

"The affair ended unhappily?"

"Yes." He sighed and tipped his head back to stare at the ceiling. His fingers made lazy circles on Katra's shoulder. "Sebastian was short on patience and Everly wasn't ready to handle a misguided affair. Once Sebastian got back on his feet, he wanted to stand alone, but Everly clung to him stubbornly until he finally blew his top and said some . . . well, some ill-chosen remarks."

"Ah, the things we say when our hearts are involved," Katra said softly.

"How true," Cabot agreed, dropping a kiss on top of her head. "I had hoped that time would heal the wounds, but that's not the case. Everly is bitter. I don't know about Sebastian. He plays his cards close to the chest."

"I don't understand that last part, Cabot. 'Close to the chest'—what does this mean?"

"It means . . . well, he's secretive."

"Understandable," Katra said, a smile in her voice. "He learned not to trust while imprisoned."

"Yes, I suppose so. You'd know more about that than I would."

"What were the exact circumstances of his imprisonment? I can't recall . . ."

"He was an aide-de-camp; worked for an air force commander and accompanied the commander on a trip to Russia. It was a time of strained relations. Our governments weren't talking to each other because there was talk of spy infiltration on both sides. The commander—man by the name of Herbert Forrester—was suspected of spy activity, which was a crock, it turned out. Anyway, somehow through paranoia, the suspicion switched to Sebastian."

"Typically Russian," Katra said with a slur in her voice. "They love to point the finger."

"Yes, well, Sebastian was acting as courier and had access to files and top-secret information, although he was kept on the fringes by Forrester. The Russians didn't know this. They began to think that Sebastian was meeting secretly with some of their top officials who were working on a space weapons project—"

"Star wars," Katra interjected. "Such a frivolous name for such a destructive project."

"I agree."

"Continue, Cabot. I'm sorry for the interruption."

"It boils down to Sebastian being at the wrong place at the wrong time with the wrong person. He was in a watering hole in Moscow and he met a man who spoke English, so naturally they became pals for the evening. It was innocent stuff like playing a game of darts and lifting a few lagers. But unbeknownst to Sebastian this friendly Russian was a suspected informer. All of a sudden men rushed in and arrested Sebastian."

"That's how it happens," Katra said, nodding her head against his shoulder. "Without warning or reason."

"They interrogated Sebastian, and when he didn't answer their questions, they applied mental and physical torture. In the end, they had him sign a 'release' paper that was supposed to be a pledge that he was telling the truth, but turned out to be an admission of guilt."

"Guilty of what?"

"Conspiring against the Soviet Union or some such rot. By the time the American embassy got wind of it and all the red tape was sorted through, Sebastian spent fourteen months in a Siberian work camp before he was released."

"Pity...such a pity to disrupt a life so."

"He told me that he had felt forsaken. Forsaken by everything he had been brought up to believe in."

"Yes, yes." Katra nodded and sat up, leaving the circle of his arm. "If you are a good, honest person you will be rewarded. That's how it's supposed to be, no? Then everything blows up in your face and there is nowhere to turn. Nowhere to run."

"I'm sorry, darling Katra," Cabot said, sitting up and kneading her tense shoulders. "I shouldn't have spoken of this...the memories..."

"It's fine. I'm fine." She rested her hands on his at her shoulders and leaned one cheek against his fingers. "And how is this Sebastian doing now?"

"Better, but I have no real comparisons. You see, I didn't know him before the catastrophe. I tend to think, however, that he used to be more outgoing...more open with his feelings."

"Yes, you're probably right. It takes time to get over such a violation. And your daughter? She hasn't forgiven him?"

"No, she hasn't. I'm not sure she should, but I think she should try to settle this thing between them."

"Perhaps she still loves him?"

"I...I don't know." Cabot let his hands slip from her shoulders and down her back. Her cranberry blouse was silk and tailored to perfection. Cabot's fingertips skimmed across the material as a thought bloomed within him. "Could that be? Do you think she could still love him after all of this?"

"Why not? What is that American expression? There's a thin..."

"Line between love and hate," Cabot supplied with a smile. "Yes, you're right. It could be possible, but that's the last thing Everly would want to hear from me."

"You might stand on neutral ground," Katra suggested, "and let this thing work itself out."

"Yes, I'll do that for the time being. It's none of my business, really. I'd like to see the two of them settle their differences since they both mean so much to me." He turned her to face him and was struck by her regal beauty. "Where would you like to go for lunch, my lovely Katra?"

"Here." She leaned forward and kissed his lips. "I want to spend the day in this penthouse with you. No interruptions."

"That sounds wonderful." He kissed her full lips then added, "Will you come to Cabot's Key with me?"

"I'll join you there in a week or so. I have a few things to do and I think you need some time alone with your Everly."

"You're right." He framed her exquisite face in his hands. "She'll love you just as I do."

"What's in this box?" Maribelle Aimsley asked as she peered into the cardboard container. "Looks like books."

"Hmm?" Sebastian glanced over his shoulder and confronted Maribelle's rounded derriere as she bent over at the waist. The view made him grin devilishly. "Oh those are extra copies of *Wrong Place, Wrong Time*. Just put them on that lower bookshelf."

"Okay." Maribelle dropped to her haunches and began lining up the volumes. "Will you autograph one of these for me? I've never read it."

"Sure." Sebastian's teeth sank into his lower lip and he fought off the urge to tell Maribelle not to bother reading it. More than once he'd wished he hadn't agreed to that book project. It wasn't pleasant having his life spilled out for all the world to read. He especially hated it when his women friends read it to glean insight into his personality. It was a waste, since he held no resemblance any longer to the Sebastian Dark in that book. That Sebastian had been born and had died in a Russian work camp. "You sure you want to read it?"

"Why not? It's about you."

"Well, not really." He finished dusting the Oriental vase and set it on the low marble table. "It's about me during a stressful period. I'm not the same person now."

"Oh, well, if you don't want me to read it..." She looked at him and her green eyes glinted with amusement. "Will you still autograph it for me?"

"Yes. It'll cost you five bucks."

She smiled and shook a finger at him. "If you're going to be that way, I'm going to charge you by the hour for helping you move into this place."

"Your point is well taken." He fitted his hands to the small of his back and twisted sideways to relieve his kinked muscles. "This place isn't so bad, is it?"

"It's small." Maribelle sat on her rump and ran a hand through her long strawberry-blond hair. "Are you sure you want to live in back of your business? Sometimes it's good to get away from the work area."

"No, I think I'll like it. That's why I leased this place— because it had living quarters in back. Wouldn't you like to live in back of your hair salon?"

"No way, Jose!" She wrinkled her pert nose at him. "I have to smell permanents all day long and I sure don't want to smell them all night long, too! Phew!" She patted the floor beside her and flashed a suggestive smile. "Take a load off, handsome."

"No, there's still too much to do," he said, resisting the temptation she offered. He'd only been dating her for two months but liked her easygoing attitude. She never pressed for promises. She just took what he offered...however light and temporary it might be. Maribelle was easy to please and pleasingly easy.

He studied her for a moment while she turned back to the box in front of her. Her short-shorts were snug and her polka-dotted blouse had a scoop neckline that tantalized. He'd met her in a club and had enjoyed the way she had talked to him as if she'd known him for years instead of minutes. He enjoyed her body, but feelings were lacking. He liked her, but he didn't truly desire her.

"What about these?" Maribelle asked, lifting one volume of a set of Shakespeare tragedies.

"Up there," Sebastian said, pointing to the top shelf. "I'll steady the ladder and hand them to you."

"Okay." She held out a hand and let him haul her to her feet then she wrapped her arms around his neck before he could get away. "One kiss, handsome? One kiss for your helper?"

Sebastian grinned and lowered his mouth to hers. Sebastian indulged her for a few moments then he set her away from him.

"Enough!" He placed a hand over the steady beat of his heart and then touched his wet lips. "You take my breath away, Maribelle."

"Well, isn't that the point?" she asked with a laugh before putting her foot on the lowest rung of the ladder. "Hold on to this rickety thing, Sebastian."

"Got it." Sebastian stood behind her, bracketing her body with his arms as she climbed up the ladder. When she was ready, he handed her the first book. "Here you go."

"Okay," Maribelle said, reaching for it and lifting it to the shelf. When all four were in place, she turned sideways and grinned down at him. "Ready?"

"For what?"

"Here I come."

He had only a moment to realize her intentions and he acted instinctively, holding out his arms and catching her lithe body as she fell from the ladder.

"You're nuts!" he admonished as she rained kisses across his face. "You could have broken your neck."

"I didn't, though." Her green eyes sought his. "To bed, Sebastian."

"No, Maribelle. You promised to help me unpack. Remember?"

"I have, and now I want my payment."

"We're not finished."

"I am." Her lips pursed into an invitation. "Go ahead. Make my day."

In spite of himself, he laughed and she joined in. Her hands moved up the back of his head and added pressure that Sebastian resisted, thinking of all the work he still had to do before his living quarters were livable.

The bell over the front door of the shop tinkled and Sebastian turned with Maribelle in his arms.

"Yes? Who's there?" he called as he let Maribelle slip down his body. She kept her arms around his neck and her long fingernails scraped against his scalp. "Cut it out, Maribelle!" He glanced at her mischievous smile then back to the open door that led into the front offices. His heart slammed against his ribs when he saw Everly step over the threshold.

"Everly!" His voice broke on her name and his hands came up to grip Maribelle's wrists in an instinctive motion.

"Sorry if I'm interrupting," Everly said, her gaze on the woman beside him. "I was told that you were open for business."

"He is!" Maribelle chimed in, letting her hands float down Sebastian's chest.

"So I see," Everly said with a smile that could have frozen boiling water.

## Chapter Three

If Sebastian hadn't looked so stricken, Everly might have been angry, but his wide eyes and bobbing Adam's apple as he swallowed convulsively sent amusement spiraling through her. She pursed her lips slightly to keep from out-and-out grinning, but she saw Sebastian's brows lift and she knew that he'd caught the amusement in her eyes as they drifted over Maribelle, who seemed oblivious to the crackle of tension in the air.

Leggy, Everly thought with a twinge of envy. The strawberry blonde's legs went on and on, displayed to the hilt by her skimpy shorts.

Well-endowed, Everly mentally added as her gaze swept up to the woman's bust, then moved self-consciously to her own. She tucked her suede clutch purse under her arm and wondered what to say next.

"Uh . . ." Sebastian swallowed hard again as he brushed aside the woman's wandering hands. "Maribelle Aimsley, this is Everly Viverette. She's Cabot's daughter."

"That so?" Maribelle extended one hand and shook Everly's. "Glad to meet you. Who does your hair?"

"My hair?" Everly repeated, thrown completely out of kilter by the question. "I do. I mean, I style it. I had it cut in New York."

"Oh, I love it!" Maribelle circled Everly to get a view of the entire creation of loose mahogany curls, topped by a small pillbox hat of suede. "It's perfect for your face."

"Well, thank you." Everly shook her head a little and threw Sebastian a baffled look.

"Maribelle runs a hair salon," he explained with a shrug. "She's helping me unpack these boxes." He tapped a tennis-shoed foot against one.

"How nice," Everly said, taking a moment to survey the clutter.

The living room was long and narrow with bookshelves lining one wall and a bay window fitted into another. The walls were painted a light oyster and the carpeting, more serviceable than plush, was hunter green, which picked up the color of the draperies. Sebastian's furniture reflected his taste in understatement; a big six-cushion couch to accommodate his six-foot-plus frame, a leather recliner, an old-fashioned rocker, low glass-topped tables, ginger-jar lamps and a high-tech stereo system. She could see through the doorway into another room which, she assumed, was the bedroom. Was there no kitchen? she wondered, then noticed a hot plate and portable refrigerator in a far corner of the living area. Dismal, she thought with a slight frown and then recalled that Sebastian had admitted once to being all-thumbs in the kitchen.

"Hey, I've heard about you!" Maribelle said, snapping her fingers as if she'd suddenly pieced a puzzle together. "You write books just like your Dad!"

"Yes, but mine are better," Everly said with a teasing smile.

Maribelle laughed and Everly noticed how pretty she was with her sparkling green eyes and friendly disposition. Was she good for Sebastian? Were they lovers?

"I've...I've come at a bad time," Everly murmured, feeling like the odd woman out.

"No, not really." Sebastian shoved the tips of his fingers into the front pockets of his jeans. "What's up?"

She didn't answer immediately. Her attention was caught by his casual stance and attire, which made her remember a time when they had treated each other as more than passing acquaintances. The way he tucked his fingertips into his pockets was endearingly familiar as was the way he rocked slightly on the balls of his feet. She wondered fleetingly if he still ran a hand down his face when he was frustrated.

"Are you here on a visit?" Maribelle asked when the silence became suffocating.

"No, I'm here to stay."

"You are?" Sebastian asked, clearly surprised by her answer.

"I am, and that's why I've dropped by. I want to hire you."

"For what?"

Everly grinned, shaking her head a little at him. "Well, there's a nasty rumor going around that you're an architect. I want you to build a house on Little Bit Key." She laughed softly when he blushed. "But if you're occupied with something else, I can make an appointment and come back later."

"No, no." He looked at Maribelle, arching one dark brow. "Do you mind, Maribelle?"

"Mind? Heavens, no!" Maribelle shoved him in the back with ten sharp nails. "Go on. This woman is talking money! I'll finish unpacking these boxes while you conduct business." She smiled warmly at Everly. "Nice to meet you. Welcome to the Keys."

"Thanks." Everly turned and went back into the office area, thinking that she'd feel less uncomfortable if Maribelle Aimsley wasn't such a delightful woman. She sat in the chair in front of Sebastian's desk, crossed her legs and flicked a loose thread from her dark slacks. "I bet you never thought I'd hire you for anything, did you?"

"I admit that I'm stunned," Sebastian said, his gaze following the movement of her fingers as he eased himself down into the chair behind his desk. He shoved aside a stack of books and crossed his arms on top of the desk. "Are you sure you want to do this?"

"What? Hire you or build a house?"

"Both."

"I'm sure I want to build a house on Little Bit." She faced him squarely, hoping he wouldn't detect her qualms. "And I'm reasonably sure that you can meet my demands. I saw the writers' colony and I like the floor plan."

"Thank you," he said, dipping his head in a brief acknowledgment. "Did you want a cottage or a house?"

"A house—a two-story one with a great view of the ocean."

"You're really going to move here?"

"Yes. Why shouldn't I?"

"Oh, I just thought you'd want to live closer to New York. I didn't know you liked this area so much."

"The Keys have always been special to me. I used to spend lots of time here until . . ." She glanced away, pretending to study an arrangement of framed seascapes while she berated herself for almost giving away too much.

"Until I moved here?" Sebastian finished quietly, watching her face tense and her hands clutch her purse too tightly.

"Yes." She raised a hand to fluff her curling bangs. "But that's silly. The Keys are big enough for both of us. Right?"

"Right." He sighed with uneasiness. "It's good to see you again, Everly."

Her gaze swept to him and her eyes widened with astonishment.

"I mean it," he added quickly then looked down at his clasped hands when her large eyes became too much for him to bear. Any time he looked too deeply into them he felt as if he were drowning in memories.

"Well," she said, laughing, "I didn't expect *that*. I thought that you'd be anything but glad to see me."

"I see no reason not to be friends," he ventured, still staring at his long fingers.

"Friends." She said the word as if it were an insult.

"Something wrong with that?" His gaze lifted briefly to hers.

"I don't want to be your friend again, thank you. I just want to hire your services. Is that clear?"

A sense of regret plummeted through him as he lifted his lashes to meet her frosty glare. "I'm sorry to hear that, Everly. I was hoping that we could . . . well, become—"

"Pals?" she asked with a definite sneer in her voice.

He lifted one shoulder in a careless shrug. "Yes."

"Hah!" She tossed back her head and glanced at the ceiling. "You have your nerve, Bastian."

Leaning back in the chair, he propped one elbow on the padded arm and stroked the lower half of his face. "I didn't mean to be unkind."

"Unki—" Her lips pressed together to chop off the word. "I think we'd better change the subject before I tell you exactly what I think of you, Sebastian Dark!"

He ran a hand down his face in abject frustration and the gesture didn't go unnoticed by Everly. She swallowed hard and looked away from him to stare blindly at the water cooler.

"Why *did* you come by here?" he asked in a biting tone. "If you don't want to bury the—"

"I came here on business," she interrupted, whipping her head back around to face him. "While I have no respect for you on a personal level, I do admire your talent. I've found that I don't have to like someone to hire him and that's why I'm here. *Capisce?*"

He refrained from screaming at her at the top of his lungs to quit being so damned self-righteous, and the muscles in his jaw writhed as he ground his teeth together. Placing his hands flat on the desk, he pushed himself up and paced to the window behind Everly and looked out at Whitehead Street.

"I don't see how we can work together if we can't talk civilly to one another."

"I will if you will. I'm mature enough to deal with you this time around."

"Mature," he whispered with a short laugh.

"What did you say?" she asked, turning in the chair to look over her shoulder at him. He stood with his weight shifted to one leg, the other bent at the knee. One hand was propped high against the windowsill and the other rode his waist. As she looked on, a memory imposed itself and the office window became the picture window in the penthouse...

*"What's wrong, Bastian? You seem edgy."*

*"Everly, I... I can't go on like this."*

*"Like what?"*

*"Platonic." And he had turned from the window to let her see the dark fire of desire in his eyes. "I want to make love to you. How do you feel about that?"*

*"Relieved..."*

"...if that's okay with you. Everly? Yoo-hoo, Everly!"

"Wh—what?" She blinked away the vision and felt her face flame with embarrassment. "I'm sorry. What did you say?"

He studied her for a moment, wondering what had put that sad sheen in her eyes. "I said that I could come by tomorrow and look at the property if that's okay with you."

"Oh, sure. There's an old house there."

"Yes, I've seen it. It's a shambles." He turned around and leaned his shoulders against the plate-glass window, bowing the rest of his body away from it.

Everly nodded. "It will have to be torn down."

"Is that where you want the new house built?"

"I . . . guess so."

"Well, we'll have a look. How about ten o'clock? Too early?"

"No, that's fine." Suddenly the unspoken comment he'd implied registered and she stood up too quickly...too stiffly, but she couldn't help herself. He remembered her penchant for sleeping until noon on weekends, she thought as she looked everywhere but at him. What other things did he remember about her? It seemed that she remembered everything about him down to the smallest detail and it galled her. A woman's mind was a catchall for foolish sentiments, Everly thought, moving slowly toward the door.

"Would you like a cup of coffee or—"

"No, I can't stay." She placed one hand on the doorknob and pulled it toward her. "See you tomorrow."

"Everly . . ."

She glanced at him, but he was too close for comfort so she crossed the threshold before facing him again. "Yes?"

"Thanks for the business." He held the door open with one hand and leaned closer. "You're my first customer."

"It was Dad's suggestion," she said, then wished she hadn't. It sounded childish...petty. She looked down at her hands, which were shaking. "You'd better get back to your guest."

"Yes . . . well, I'll see you tomorrow around ten."

"Right."

Sebastian let go of the door and the bell tinkled at her parting. He glanced up at it, and when he looked out the window again she was already in her car, pulling away from the curb.

She can't wait to get away from here, Sebastian thought, turning aside and walking slowly to the back of the building. Why the sudden decision to hire him of all people? It was obvious that she couldn't be in the same room with him for more than a few minutes at a time.

"Is she gone?" Maribelle asked when he entered the living area.

"Yes."

"Did you get the job?"

"Not yet, but I think I will."

"Great!" Maribelle kissed his cheek. "Aren't you excited?"

"Thrilled." He shoved his fingers into his back pockets and frowned at the packing boxes. "You can go ahead and leave. I'll do the rest."

"Well, if you're sure—"

"Yes, it's okay. Thanks for your help." He stroked her hair and pulled her closer to drop a kiss on her forehead.

"Have you known Everly long?"

"Long enough." He turned away and lifted one of the boxes onto the coffee table.

"Were you two... well, close?"

"Why do you ask?"

"You acted sort of... tense around each other, like there was a lot of water under the bridge."

"There is." He sighed heavily, wishing she'd drop it.

"Uh-oh." Maribelle grabbed his shoulder and pulled him around to face her. "You're doing it again."

"What?" he asked in a bored tone.

"Shutting me out. You do that when I start talking about something you don't want to talk about. Why don't you just tell me to shut my trap? I'd like that a lot better than having you pull into yourself like a sea turtle."

He managed a smile and crooked a finger under her chin. "Sorry. I'm tired and irritable."

"You're forgiven." She picked up her shoulder bag and started for the door. "I'll talk to you later when you're not so grumpy."

In the doorway she turned to look at him, but he had his back to her. A shiver raced up her spine and her skin broke out in goose bumps. Maribelle hunched her shoulders and left Sebastian to his unpacking, but she couldn't help but think that somehow she had lost him. He wouldn't call her again. It was over, and Cabot Viverette's daughter had something to do with it.

When Sebastian heard the bell sing out that he was alone, he fell onto the sofa, stretching out full-length and draping an arm over his eyes. He crossed his ankles, settling more comfortably and letting the anxiety flow from his body. With its absence came scenes of yesterday when he and Everly hadn't circled each other like warring wildcats. It had been a good time, but a confusing one. He had been happy, yet terrified. She had been understanding, but she'd wanted too much from him.

He slid one foot up, bending his knee and moving it from side to side as his thoughts drifted back . . . back to the first time he could recall seeing her . . . *really* seeing her. It had been shortly after he'd arrived at the penthouse and had fallen into the big bed in Cabot's guest bedroom. He'd slept the sleep of exhaustion and had awakened hours later to peer wonderingly at an angel's face hovering above him. Her enormous eyes had pulled him to full wakefulness and her smile had warmed him through and through. He had reached up to touch her smooth cheek and make sure she was real, and she had laughed and grasped his fingers to confirm it.

"Back with us, Mr. Dark?" she'd asked in a voice that had soothed like church bells on Sunday morning. "We met earlier, if you'll recall. I'm Everly . . . Cabot's daughter."

"Everly . . ."

"Yes." Her light laughter had made him feel like a man again after months of deprivation. "Your new friend—Everly Viverette."

"My friend," he'd repeated dreamily, unsure of what she was talking about. It had been so long since he'd thought of people in terms of friendship. His fingers had closed around hers...tight, so tight that she had winced a little and laughed.

"Are you awake, Mr. Dark?"

"Are you a dream, Miss Viverette?"

"No."

"Then I'm awake, I guess..."

The memory dissolved and Sebastian wiped moisture from his eyes and sat up. He rubbed his face vigorously until his skin tingled and he found himself staring glumly at his meager surroundings. You've come a long way, he thought dourly. A long way to nowhere.

He sprang to his feet and paced the room, stopping at one box and then another, but finding no interest in unpacking their contents. Thoughts of Everly followed him, scraping his heels and tugging at his shirt-sleeves. He stood by the bay window with its view of his side yard where he had strung a hammock between two Spanish lime trees. The memories caught up with him again and held fast. He blinked, but the vision persisted of Everly sitting in a pear-shaped rattan chair that was suspended from the ceiling in Cabot's penthouse. She had looked elfinlike, engulfed as she had been by the chair, and he had dropped to his knees before her and pressed his face between her breasts. The silky material of her gown had added to his desire to possess her—to make the girl his woman.

"Bastian...oh, Bastian...I can hardly breathe," she had whispered yearningly.

"I want you," was all he could murmur as his hands had moved up to cover her straining breasts. She had arched into him, letting him feel the touch of her nipples against his palms.

And he had taken her there... there in the center of the living-room floor where dusk pooled. In the midst of it all, he had soared on the wings of an eagle and had felt the headiness of freedom for the first time in months, and he had thanked her for that, and she had looked at him with a mixture of happiness and confusion. She hadn't understood. She couldn't have known the depth of his gratitude. He had barely understood it himself.

Sebastian snapped back to the present and glanced down at the juncture of his legs where the material now stretched tight.

"Damn!" he swore viciously as he spun from the window and grabbed a leather jacket from the back of a chair. Shoving his long arms into its sleeves, he headed for the front door and locked it behind him.

He stood on the sidewalk in front of his office for a few moments as shadows lengthened at his feet. At the corner of Whitehead and Greene streets he headed east to Duval Street and his favorite hangout—Sloppy Joe's Bar, made famous by Ernest Hemingway. He dodged a few bicyclists and darted around a group of ogling tourists as he crossed the street. Bikes were parked in front of Sloppy Joe's and Sebastian entered the bar with trepidation, hoping that it wouldn't be full of tourists. It wasn't.

Sighing his relief at finding the bar relatively quiet and sparsely populated, Sebastian eased himself onto his favorite stool and beckoned the bartender.

"Afternoon, Sebastian. What'll it be?"

"Whiskey, neat," Sebastian answered, fishing in his jeans pocket for a folded bill that he placed on the shiny water-ringed bar. "How's it going, Bill?"

"Pretty good, thanks. The tourist trade's been brisk." The bartender placed the shot glass in front of Sebastian and chuckled when Sebastian tossed it back in one gulp. "Another?"

"Make it a double."

"Hit the spot, did it?"

"I needed it, that's for sure." Sebastian closed his fingers around the filled glass, but didn't bring it to his lips. He hooked his elbows on the edge of the bar and turned his head back to survey the dim interior. When he didn't recognize anyone, he swung back to face the bartender, but he found himself staring at his own reflection in the mirrored wall behind bottles and glasses.

He scowled at what he saw, but couldn't look away. What had she seen in him? he wondered. Why had she chosen him to love? Did she have a soft spot for wounded birds? That's how he thought of himself back then—a bird with broken wings who hopped around helplessly until he could heal and defy gravity again.

The fingers of his left hand lifted to grasp the gold eagle at his throat, while images of his past swarmed into his head like angry hornets. It might have been different if they *both* had been grounded—weak beings clutching at each other to keep from falling—but Everly had been vibrant and on the brink of success. Irrationally it had been her strength—the very thing he craved for himself—that had made him feel like a leech until he couldn't stand it any longer. The temptation to cling to her had been great, but he'd known that he would never get back to his old self if he continued to lean on her. It wasn't fair to her, either. She didn't need an emotional zombie in her life; not when her life was taking exciting directions.

Her first book with Blaire was being touted. She had everything to look forward to, and he had nothing. His life had been without direction, without purpose. Finally he had decided to break free of her sheltering love and strike out on his own.

Sebastian frowned at his mirror image. He could have been more tactful about it, he allowed, but he stood by his decision to leave her. It had been in her best interest and in his, although he had known that she hadn't understood his desperate need to escape.

How could he competently explain to her how he'd felt? He had become terrified thinking of a future with her when he'd learned not to count on things like "futures" and "plans" and "goals." He had recounted to Cabot his experiences in the Russian work camp, but he could never bring himself to talk about that time with Everly. With Everly he wanted only to live in the present and squelch the bitterness that filled him like poison.

Someone opened the door, letting a rectangle of sunlight fall onto the floor, and Sebastian heard his name sung out. He turned but could only see a shapely silhouette in the doorway. It wasn't until the woman had dropped a cool kiss on his brow and had closed a hand around his forearm that he recognized her.

"Oh, Anne. Hello." He leaned back to look at her shimmering golden hair and slanted blue eyes. "Long time, no see."

"And whose fault is that?" Anne Winters asked with a cool smile. "I believe you were supposed to call me about a dinner date? That was at least seven months ago."

"Sorry." He shrugged. What could he say? Sorry, Anne, but I met someone else and I forgot all about you. "Can I buy you a drink?"

"No, I'm meeting someone." She looked past him and waved to someone in the back of the room. "Good seeing you again. I'm still in the phone book and I still dine out from time to time."

"Right, I'll keep that in mind." He turned sideways to watch the seductive swing of her hips as she brushed past him. Tall, blond and beautiful, he mused, then reached for his drink and finished half of it. He'd dated Anne before he'd met Maribelle. Before Anne...ah, yes. Caroline Smithers. Before Caroline there'd been a brief dalliance with a long cool blonde named Lynette something-or-other.

His thoughts skidded to a halt and he sat straighter as the women merged in his mind. Tall...blond...pastel-eyed. All of them. Exact opposites of Everly.

He moaned deep in his throat and felt sick. What a silly game to play on himself. Did he think those blondes would keep his thoughts away from Everly?

A self-derisive laugh tumbled from him and he glanced at his reflection in the mirror and saw his wry smile.

"Sounds like you're in a good mood, Sebastian," the bartender said, eyeing him speculatively.

"Oh, yes." Sebastian raised the shot glass and winked. "I'm in a great mood."

The bartender moved to another customer and Sebastian faced himself in the mirror—glass raised, sad-eyed, hollow-cheeked. Just when he'd thought he was living in the present, his past had returned to haunt him. His elbow lifted from the bar as he saluted his image.

"Cheers," he said, then tossed the liquor to the back of his throat and ordered another.

Cabot picked his way across the strip of land that connected Cabot's Key and Little Bit. The tide was coming in, gradually covering the land and soaking his shoes. He leaped over a puddle and ducked under a low branch, then followed the footpath that led to the old house where he hoped to find his daughter.

Everly was there, sitting cross-legged on the ground and staring disconsolately at the pitiful structure before her. Cabot hung back in the shadows, rooted there by the woebegone expression on his daughter's face. Even in profile, he could see the pucker of her brows and the droop of her lower lip. She wrapped her arms around her bent knees and rocked back and forth, and sunlight moved in waves across her reddish-brown hair. She rarely let him glimpse her darker moods, preferring to keep the atmosphere light and amusing when she was with him. Therefore Cabot remained unnoticed for a few more minutes as he examined the petite bundle of loveliness.

With a father's pride, he decided she was the spitting image of her mother. Julianne, the French woman he had married after the war, had been small-boned and elfin-featured. His life with Julianne had been joyous but brief. She had been a loving wife and mother and Cabot had grieved for years after losing his young wife in a boating accident when Everly had been a toddler. He had grown used to people commenting that Everly didn't look anything like him. She was a genetic copy of his beloved Julianne.

What dark thoughts made his daughter look so lost and lonely? he wondered, then quickly chided himself for ignoring the obvious. Sebastian, he thought with a wincing smile. Why did this have to be so complicated? Why couldn't Everly and Sebastian shake hands and be friends? It was stupid to hold on to all these bad feelings.

Cabot combed his fingers through the sides of his graying hair and stepped forward. Hearing his footfalls, Everly jerked from her private world and her scowl became a beatific smile in the blink of an eye.

"Dad!" She jumped up and ran toward him, throwing her arms around his neck and letting him take her weight for a few moments before she set her feet back on the ground. She kissed one cheek, then the other. "I'm so glad to see you!"

"Not half as glad as I am to see you." He set her from him and smiled at what he saw. "You get lovelier each day."

"Oh, you old flirt." She laughed, grabbed his hands and swung them in the space between their bodies. "It's so good to be back here. I've missed it."

Cabot breathed in the crisp air and exhaled. "Ah, yes. There's nothing like the Keys, hmm?" He looked past her and his brows lifted and fell. "Your poor little house. It's seen better days."

Everly glanced at it, remembered her visit with Sebastian, and looked back at her father. "Yes, haven't we all? Know what? I was walking along the shore a few minutes ago and I saw a school of porpoises. It was beautiful! They broke the surface and arched in the air and water sparkled like diamonds on their skin."

"I remember one of the first stories you wrote...you must have been about eight or nine. It was about a girl who rode a porpoise named Imagine."

"Really?" She shook her head. "I don't recall that story." She lifted her face to the warmth of the sun, then tugged his hands. "Sit with me a while." Crossing her ankles, she lowered herself to the soft grass again, pulling her father with her. She glanced over his navy blue slacks and variegated blue-striped shirt and nodded her approval. "You look dashing. More dashing than usual. Life must be treating you pretty good."

"It is." His fingers closed around one of her hands and he brought it close to his heart, then to the ground between them. "Wish I could say the same for you. When I walked up on you, you looked as if you'd lost your only friend."

"Really?" Her dark brows rose. "Oh that! I was just feeling sorry for this old house and—"

"Everly Suzanne," he said in a singsong voice, "this is your old man. I know what's on your mind."

"You do?" She smiled and tipped up her chin in a challenge. "Tell me."

"Sebastian Jefferson Dark."

Her father's clairvoyance stole her breath and she looked away sharply, feeling as if she'd been violated. Was it a lucky guess or did he really know her so well? she wondered as her fingers plucked blades of grass. For the past hour she had been playing an exhaustive game of tug-of-war with herself. On one side was her belief that she should continue her cold war with Sebastian, and on the other side was her realization that she had kept her feelings for Sebastian under wraps and it might be a good idea to unwrap them and face the consequences.

Two years! a voice screamed in her head. It's been two whole years and you still can't look on him dispassionately. He comes near and your heart climbs into your throat. When are you going to get over him? *When?*

"Everly?" Her father's voice nudged her. "Honey, let's talk about it. We've never discussed what happened because I knew it wasn't any of my business, but I've changed my mind. I think you need to talk about it, and I'm more than willing to listen."

"Oh, Dad, I don't know..." She sighed, tore another patch of grass from the earth, then wiped her hands on her jeaned thighs. There were so many things she couldn't tell him—that she couldn't tell anybody except perhaps Sebastian. Intimacies couldn't be explored except between intimates.

"I'll make a deal with you," Cabot said, lacing his hands around one knee and leaning back. "You tell me what's on your mind and I'll let you in on why I'm so much more dashing than I used to be." He smiled and glanced sideways at her, catching the sudden interest in her eyes. "Any takers?"

"You wily old fox!" Everly shook a chiding finger at him and laughed. "You know that I can't resist a mystery. Okay, okay. You've got a deal." Once the pledge was spoken, she felt her courage shrivel. What could she say? Where should she begin?

"Did you hire him?" Cabot asked, giving her direction.

"Yes." She heaved a sigh and propped herself on stiffened arms. "And I'm already regretting it. I saw him this morning. He's coming by tomorrow." Her gaze met her father's for a moment. "Do you know a woman named Maribelle Aimsley?"

"Maribelle...oh, you mean Sebastian's friend, the beautician?"

"Yes, that's the one. I guess she and Sebastian are pretty...well, close."

"I wouldn't know. They're friends. Anything beyond that would be pure speculation. Why? Did you meet her?"

"Yes. She was with Sebastian when I barged in." She rounded her shoulders, feeling silly for having mentioned it. "It's nothing."

"You always say that when it's something." He tipped back his head to stare at a duck-shaped cloud that rapidly changed into a mushroom shape as he spoke. "When it happened...when I realized that you two were sleeping together, I was too shaken up to deal with it effectively. I couldn't help but think that you were too young, and that he was too unstable."

"You were right," Everly conceded. "But I don't regret it. I just wish I had understood up front that Sebastian wasn't offering anything permanent. I thought I was in the middle of a great, lasting love affair, but it was just one of those fleeting things. Ships passing in the night, so to speak."

"You're making less of it than it was," Cabot scolded.

"Oh I don't mean to. I'm trying to give you Sebastian's point of view, not mine."

"I want to hear yours," Cabot insisted. "From the heart, not the head."

"From the heart, eh?" she repeated, laughing a little to eliminate her sense of claustrophobia as the past closed in on her from all sides. "Dad, if I knew my own feelings I wouldn't be in such a fog."

"Do you still love him?"

His softly spoken question made the walls converge until she felt as if she couldn't breathe. Everly sprang to her feet and threw her arms wide, taking in great gulps of air.

"I don't know," she cried in anguish. "I shouldn't, I know that! But when I'm near him I...I get tongue-tied and confused. He scares me."

"Scares you?" Cabot propped his forearm on his bent knee and squinted up at her, but the sun blurred his vision. "Why does he scare you?"

"Oh, *he* doesn't scare me. Wh—what I feel for him scares me."

"What *do* you feel for him?" Cabot asked.

"A whole grab bag full of things." She hooked her thumbs in the back pockets of her jeans and stared up at the whispering palm fronds. "Anger, humiliation, regret, sadness and..." Her lower lip trembled. "And affection, damn it!"

Cabot bowed his head so that she wouldn't see his smile. It was clear to him, even though it wasn't to her. Everly still loved Sebastian. It was as simple as that, although he knew better than to tell her. She was in no mood to hear the truth or to believe it.

"How could I feel anything tender for that man after what...after he threw me over? It rankles me!"

"He might have had a very good reason for leaving you when he did," Cabot ventured, trying to settle her agitation.

"Are you going to take his side again?" she asked, whirling to face him with a belligerent stance, feet spread apart and hands on hips.

"Again?" Cabot asked with displeasure. "I've never taken his side against you."

"Yes you have! You think I've overreacted! Well, I disagree. I loved that man. I worshiped him, and he knew it. He didn't just end our affair, he defiled it!"

"How did he do that?" Cabot asked in a quiet voice, thinking that it was healthy that she was red-faced and shaking with rage. It's about time, he thought. Should have happened two years ago.

"He called me a crutch—*a crutch!*" Her voice lifted to a breaking point. "He said that, having been in prison for fourteen months, he would have taken *any* woman." Her lips twisted and tears filled her eyes before she turned away from Cabot. Lifting the tail of her shirt, she dabbed at her eyes and sniffed.

Cabot looked off to the side, feeling the bite of anger. How could Sebastian have said that to her? He could have been more kind. He didn't have to make Everly feel like a sex surrogate.

"I suppose you think that's okay?" Everly asked, her back still to him.

"No, I don't think it's okay. I think it's despicable."

"But?" She spun around, daring him to finish his thought.

"But he was under a lot of stress," Cabot added.

"Stress? And *I* wasn't?"

"Everly," he chided gently, "whatever stress you might have been under couldn't possibly compare to his, and you know it. The man's life had been cruelly interrupted through no fault of his own. He had spent more than a year being treated like an animal, and then was released and expected to continue with his life as if nothing had happened."

"He was so sweet back then," Everly said, slipping slowly into her own reverie. "So open with his feelings—like a child. He needed someone to love him and I was more than happy to oblige. The things he said to me...the way he touched me...it was incredible." She blinked slowly and emerged from her memories to find that her father's face had reddened and he was staring blindly at his gold watch. "He's changed. He's guarded, as if he trusts no one... nothing."

"When he came into your life he was vulnerable," Cabot explained, still staring at his watch's sweeping second hand. "Emotionally raw and grasping. The things he told me, Everly. The terrible things that happened to him while he was imprisoned. It's a wonder he wasn't a basket case. I imagine trust is something that comes hard for him these days."

"He trusted me once," Everly pointed out.

"But maybe he didn't trust himself," Cabot suggested. "Maybe he was the one who was really running scared."

"He was running, all right. Running away from me." She lifted her hair up from the back of her neck and sighed. "I guess I'll just roll with the punches for now. I've hired him. He wants to build the house. I'll take it from there and see what happens."

"Good plan." Cabot stretched his arms over his head and yawned. "Let's go back to the house."

"Hold on a minute, fella," Everly said, wagging a finger at him. "We had a deal, remember?"

"Ah, yes. So we did." He pushed himself to his feet and brushed grass from the seat of his trousers. "You've heard of Katra Kamenski?"

"Of course. She's known for her writings on the Holocaust."

"That's right." He shoved his hands into his pockets, feeling shy now that the confession was pressing against his lips. "Well, I've been seeing her—socially."

"Socially?" Everly repeated, finding his choice of words amusing. "Don't you mean 'privately'?"

"Yes, I guess I do. She makes me happy, Everly." He looked at her from beneath lowered brows and held his breath.

"Dad, are you smitten?" Everly teased, stepping up to him and placing a hand on his shoulder. "Is that why you're blushing?"

"Blushing?" He felt his skin warm and he laughed. "Yes, I suppose I am. She's a wonderful woman, Everly. Simply wonderful."

"Can I meet her?"

"Do you want to?"

"Of course! I want to see the woman who has finally captured my dad's heart. I was beginning to think that Mother would be the only woman to claim it."

"So was I." He offered a bent elbow and Everly linked her arm in his. "I think I can arrange a meeting," he said, grinning.

"You do that, Mr. Viverette."

"I love you, Little Bit."

Everly glanced up into his handsome face and love for him made her heart swell. She rested her cheek against his shoulder and sighed. "I know. Aren't I lucky?"

## Chapter Four

When did Cabot give you this place?'' Sebastian asked, lifting a low branch to let Everly pass under it.

"It was my present from him on my sixteenth birthday,'' Everly answered, ducking her head and shying away from him as she lead the way toward the clearing on Little Bit.

Sebastian dropped back a step or two to better enjoy the alluring fit of Everly's tan walking shorts and shocking pink, sleeveless T-shirt that exposed her midriff. She wore large, smoky sunglasses and a pink baseball cap. Sebastian decided she looked adorable.

"How do you get over here when the tide's in?''

"There's a boat moored on the west side,'' she flung back at him then murmured something he couldn't quite hear.

"What?'' Sebastian closed the distance and bumped into her when she stopped suddenly.

"My shoelace,'' she said, bending one knee and hopping on the other foot as she tried to tie the long dangling lace of her tennis shoe.

"Here. Wait a second." Sebastian stepped around her and captured her foot, then rested it on his thigh to tie the laces. "What size shoe do you wear—extra, extra petite?"

"Five-and-a-half," she said with a laugh. "What size do you wear—triple giant?" She hoped he would smile, but the movement of his lips couldn't be called that. More like a brief smirk, she decided, feeling cheated.

"Nine." He tightened the bow and his hands moved to the sides of the pink canvas shoe. The laces were white with pink sailboats and blue anchors. "Such tiny feet," he murmured as his fingers brushed across the damp canvas, and his gaze moved up her smooth, tanned calf.

Everly let her foot slip off his knee and away from his caressing fingers. "Thanks for your help." She walked past him and hurried toward the clearing. "The house is right up here." She flung out a hand, palm up, toward the house. "Ta-daaa! Welcome to a little bit of house on Little Bit Key." She was disappointed again when he didn't smile. On the contrary, he frowned.

"Are you sure you want to build a house here?"

"You don't like my Key?"

He shook his head. "No, I like the Key, but I don't think this is the best location. You wanted a view of the ocean, right?"

"Right."

"Then why not build closer to it?" He walked past the house and headed for the shore. "Come on. Let's have a look at the shoreline."

"It's sort of rocky," Everly cautioned, but he kept on walking. "This is the most level place on the Key."

"No problem. We can bulldoze if necessary."

She hung back a few moments, studying his long purposeful strides and erect spine. Had he lost the ability to smile? she wondered. Or had she lost her touch?

"Hey, wait up!" She hurried to his side and glanced up into his brooding expression. "You seem...well, out of sorts today."

"Do I?" He arched a dark brow, then shrugged. "Well, I have a slight headache. I spent too long in Sloppy Joe's yesterday."

"Ah-ha!" She pointed an accusing finger at him. "A hangover, is it?" Had she caused it, or had he taken Maribelle out for the evening? "I hope you don't do this sort of thing often."

"No, I don't. I should know better than to drink alone." He drew a short breath, glanced sharply at her, then lengthened his stride. Had he given away too much? He didn't want her to know that he'd tried to drown the memories of her in a glass of whiskey.

As he squeezed his broad shoulders between two coconut palm trees that leaned crazily toward the ocean, Sebastian slid in his boots on some crumbling rocks and he barely kept his balance as he trotted down an incline that ended at lapping waves. Everly wasn't so lucky. He felt her body slam into his, and he turned swiftly, his hands catching her elbows before her bare knees hit the jagged rocks. He took her weight and was surprised at how light she was—no more than a hundred pounds, if that. His fingers moved up taut soft skin to her upper arms and tightened.

Pulling her up to her feet again, her breasts flattened against his chest and her chin tipped up. Her full lips parted and her lashes threw shadows onto her cheeks. He felt her hands against his shoulders, not pushing him away, just resting there. Instinctively his hands found her bare midriff. Her skin was warm and well remembered. Sebastian exhaled a shaky breath, and his heart hammered with longing.

Everly felt the beat of his heart, strong and sure, while pulses came to life in odd places in her own body. A sea breeze combed through his sable-colored hair, lifting it off his forehead and throwing it back over his ears. It looked silky and she remembered the feel of it slipping through her fingers. Her fingers curled against his denim shirt and her palms pressed against the pearl snaps on his front pockets. One swift jerk would free the snaps down his shirt, she thought, and expose his tanned chest and flat stomach.

Her gaze lifted to the gold eagle at his throat, its wings spread wide, its claws extended and ready for attack. It brought back stinging memories of times when he had worn nothing but that eagle suspended on its rough strip of leather. She drew a deep breath to relieve the sexual tension that tightened in her breast, but the action was foiled. The scent of his after-shave, a woodsy musk, filled her head and she closed her eyes in momentary surrender.

The muscles beneath her fingers twitched and she realized that he was bending toward her. Her eyes flew open, but his were now hooded and somnolent. He was going to kiss her! Everly jerked back, her hands warding him off before she turned around and crossed her arms over her heaving breasts.

Sebastian's hands dropped to his sides and he stared at her rounded shoulders and imposing back. A breeze blew his hair into his eyes and, as he swept it back with one hand, he gritted his teeth to keep from shouting at her.

"Are you okay?" he asked, struggling to keep his voice level and not expose the depth of his disappointment.

"Yes, fine." Her cheerful tone was forced. Glancing around, she strove to keep her voice level. She pulled off her hat, leaving her hair to shine in the sunlight. "I don't think you could build a house here. Too rocky."

"Yes, you're right. Let's walk along the shore." He started to reach out and cup her elbow, but he checked the instinctive gesture, knowing that she wouldn't accept his touch. He set off, knowing that she'd follow at her own slower pace. He didn't know who he was more angry at— himself or her. His temples throbbed abominably and he pressed his fingertips to them. He decided he was mad at her. She was responsible for his hangover. She was responsible for that show of weakness a few minutes ago. She was responsible for the sick feeling of unfulfillment that writhed in his stomach like a nest of snakes. He whipped his head around to glare at her over his shoulder. She was lagging far behind. "Are you coming or not? What's the problem?"

Her gaze shot up to his, but the expression in her eyes was hidden by the smoky lenses of her glasses. "You don't have to wait for me. Go on!" She waved her hands at him in a shooing motion. "I'll be along." She folded the cap and stuck it in the back pocket of her shorts.

He stopped and turned sideways to wait for her, propping his hands at his waist as he stared out to sea where a triangle of white bobbed on the horizon. Great view, he mused to himself. Wish there was somewhere along here that was level enough for a foundation.

When she was a few steps from him, he started off again, his long-legged gait outdistancing her easily. Fifty yards up the shoreline, he slowed and came to a halt with a supreme sense of satisfaction. He'd found it. The perfect place for Everly's house.

The ground swelled up from the shore gradually then leveled to flat firm ground that was dotted with banyan and buttonwood trees. Baby-soft grass and patches of wild-flowers carpeted the area. Sebastian scrambled up the incline and strode to the largest banyan tree to stand in its shade.

"Everly!" he called when he saw the top of her head. "Up here."

"Oh, okay." She hiked up the incline and stopped to look around her. "This is nice."

"Come here and look at the view," he urged, holding out a hand that she ignored. He let his hand drop back to his side and wished he could swat her behind for being such a brat.

She stood beside him, one hand resting above her breasts as she took in the sight. The trees parted to frame a lovely seascape, and Everly smiled.

"Nice. Very nice." She turned around in a slow circle, nodding in agreement. "It's perfect, don't you think?"

"Yes. Perfect." Sebastian tore his gaze from her heart-shaped face and cleared his throat. "It will be a magnificent view."

"That's the ticket," she quipped, suddenly lowering herself to the ground as if she were out of wind. "It's cool here." Her ankles crossed and her knees came up to her chest as she linked her arms around her legs. "I'm going to rest before heading back to the estate." She angled a glance up at him. "Care to join me?"

He looked away from the temptation, sighed, and gave in to it. "Sure. Why not?" He sat down beside her, stretching out his legs and leaning back on stiffened arms. "A two-story house..."

"With those neat irregularly shaped windows," she added with a dreamy smile. "A red-gabled roof and...and..." She pursed her lips and turned her head to look at him. "You know those glass blocks? They're used in windows, and you can't see through them, but they let light in."

"Glass bricks," he said, nodding. "Yes, what about them?"

"I want those, too. Inside and outside. Of course, I want clear glass in some of the windows, but I like those glass bricks in things like bathroom windows."

"That's an interesting idea," he said, warming to the vision. "I'll keep it in mind. What else?"

"Sandstone walls, open spaces, skylights. Lots of light and timber."

"Okay. I'm getting the idea."

"And rounded edges."

He shook his head. "You lost me."

"I'm not fond of sharp corners. I like rounded ones. Smooth and flowing, you know?"

"The kind of thing that was big in the thirties and forties? Like Art Deco?"

"Yes, yes!" She whipped off her sunglasses, and her brown eyes shone with an inner light. "I wish I knew more about architecture. Remember those smooth walls that were painted pale blue or gray with thin horizontal stripes running across them? The stripes were usually silver."

He nodded. "Deco. It's making a comeback. You like that, do you?"

"I love it!" She smiled and dimples buried into her cheeks. "Can you design something like that?"

"It sounds like a hodgepodge, but I think I can create something pleasing to the eye."

"It will be beautiful, won't it, Bastian?"

Her exuberance, coupled with her nearness, sent a wave of longing through him that was so powerful he sprang to his feet to be rid of its grip. He turned aside and placed a hand at the back of his neck. The muscles were tense there, and he kneaded them.

Damn her! What was it about her that made him want to crush her mouth beneath his and feel the surge of her tongue? For a few moments his stomach quivered and he felt ill.

"Bastian?"

*Bastian!* Hearing her call him that made him feel worse. He sucked in air and exhaled slowly. Inner demons picked up hammers and whammed them against his temples.

"Are you all right?"

"Yes, damn it!" He squeezed his eyes shut and massaged his neck where muscles knotted.

"Okay!" She stood up, brushing her hands across the back of her shorts. What's with him? she wondered. "Let's go back to the estate before you bite my head off!"

"I told you . . . I've got a headache."

She shrugged. "So? I didn't give it to you."

"You didn't?"

Everly frowned at him. "What does that mean?"

"Nothing." His arm sliced through the air. "Forget it."

"Are you going to build the house?" she asked when he started striding back to the shore.

"Yes, but not right now."

She curled her upper lip at his sarcasm, then hurried after him.

When she reached the estate—Sebastian having arrived a good five minutes before her—Everly paused outside the front parlor and caught her breath before she went into the room where her father and Sebastian were conversing with the ease of close friends. For a few moments, she stood back and envied their relationship. Sebastian, lounging casually on the medallion-back sofa, seemed so accessible. It appeared that his headache was gone. Cabot stood near the sofa, a glass of tomato juice held in one hand. He smiled when he spotted Everly in the archway.

"There you are!" He held out his free hand to clasp hers. "We were wondering if you might have gotten lost!"

"No, I just wasn't in any hurry. Bastian, on the other hand, was out to set a new world's record in lifting them up and putting them down." She raised a foot and tapped one of Sebastian's boots. "Congratulations, champ."

"Thanks. I owe everything to my coach," he deadpanned, drawing a chuckle from Cabot. "And from years of running from unpleasant memories, persistent reporters and pretty-boy talk-show hosts."

Unpleasant memories? Was she one of them? Everly wondered, then forced out a laugh and added, "Not to mention all those women you've left in your wake." She wished she could kick herself.

Cabot lifted the glass quickly to his lips to disguise his smile while Sebastian applied three fingers to his right temple. His headache was back, Everly thought, and guess who's responsible.

"Sebastian is staying for lunch," Cabot said, tactfully changing the subject. "It'll be ready in a few minutes."

"In that case, you gentlemen will have to excuse me while I freshen up." Everly waved a hand in front of her face. "I'm all hot and sweaty from my romp over Little Bit." She placed a hand on her father's shoulder and kissed his cheek lightly before leaving the parlor and running up the stairs to the second floor and her lavender and deep-purple bedroom.

She showered quickly and dressed in a two-piece shorts set of cotton mesh lined with jersey knit. Aqua-colored palms decorated the white material and the blouse was fashioned like a man's undershirt except that it had a ribbed band at the waist. She ran a comb through her curly hair and tugged at the strands in the back, flipping some forward so that they curled toward her throat. Applying only a touch of makeup, she was more lavish with her favorite perfume, spraying it on several pulse points. She attached small gold anchors to her earlobes, stepped back from the mirror to study the result, then chided herself for trying to look pretty for Sebastian.

"Dumb," she muttered darkly to her image. "He's not interested in you." But she recalled that moment on the beach when he would have kissed her if she hadn't torn herself from his embrace. Maybe he did want her...just a little.

Wrinkling her nose playfully, she left the bedroom and went downstairs to the bright, sedate dining room where Cabot and Sebastian were already seated. They rose from their chairs when she walked in and waited until she was seated before they sat back down. Such gentlemen, Everly thought with an inner smile. All for little ole me! She draped the linen napkin across her lap and eyed the shrimp salad and conch fritters.

"Heavens, it's been ages since I've eaten conch fritters," she said, reaching for the platter and helping herself.

Sebastian told himself that he should quit staring at her, but he couldn't help it. Everly could throw on a pair of shorts and a shirt and look fabulous. She had an uncanny taste for fashion, knowing instinctively what would look great on her petite body, and this outfit proved it. The mesh top was alluring, teasing his eyes and imagination. But it didn't take much imagination. He remembered every detail. Small, high breasts. Light pink nipples. He lowered his gaze to his plate, and closed his eyes for a moment while he warded off the desire that blew through him like a fragrant Gulf breeze. Fragrant? He took a deep breath, and he could smell her perfume. White Linen. It was still her favorite. It seemed to him that the perfume was crooking a delicate finger, enticing him to come closer... closer...

"How's your headache, Bastian?" Everly asked, then added for Cabot's benefit, "Bastian indulged in a few too many drinks yesterday."

"Oh? That's not like you," Cabot said.

"I...I was celebrating." Sebastian speared a shrimp with his fork and brought it up to his lips. "The opening of my office, and my first client," he added, thinking that he sounded as if he were making excuses... which he was.

"Celebrating?" Everly's fork stopped just in front of her mouth. "I thought you said that you were alone."

"Did I?"

"Yes, you did," she answered, her eyes narrowing slightly.

"I was... at first." He shrugged. "You don't stay alone when you're in Sloppy Joe's."

"Sloppy Joe's," Cabot repeated with a long sigh. "It's been years since I've been in that place. You know, that was Hemingway's favorite bar."

"Or so the legend goes," Everly tacked on. "Someday the Key West residents will say—"

"Conchs," Sebastian interrupted. "That's what the natives call themselves."

"Oh, right. Anyway, someday the Conchs will be talking about Cabot Viverette's favorite haunts."

"They already are," Sebastian said. "I was talking to a vendor the other day and he swore to me that he and Cabot were fishing buddies." Sebastian paused to enjoy Cabot's surprised expression. "I didn't have the heart to call him a liar, but I know that you haven't been fishing since you were a kid."

"A legend in his own time," Everly said, turning adoring eyes on her father and fluttering her lashes comically. "Isn't it exciting to be famous?"

"Well..." Cabot hedged, looking at Sebastian, "it has its pitfalls, but I do like the attention."

"Not me!" Sebastian held up both hands and his eyes grew large. "Never again. I don't know how you two stand it."

"That's what I have a coauthor for," Everly admitted. "Of course, Blaire is a great writer, but she's also a born show-woman. She loves the spotlight, and I love the shadows. I didn't inherit Dad's penchant for adulation."

"I take issue with that," Cabot argued. "Adulation isn't my cup of tea, but I admit to enjoying occasional press tours and autograph parties."

"Admit it, Dad. You're a ham."

Cabot laughed, dabbing at the corners of his mouth with his napkin. "Guilty as charged. I guess you're relieved that you don't have to face another press conference," he added, directing his comment at Sebastian.

"I'm relieved that my life is my own again." Sebastian swallowed with difficulty and pointed his fork at the half-eaten fritter on his plate. "You actually like these things?" he asked Everly.

"Love 'em." Everly popped another piece of fritter into her mouth to prove it. "Um-umm!"

Sebastian shrugged, amazed that she liked the tough, tasteless fish. "The book was good for me financially, but I should have thought ahead and realized that it would mean reliving my experiences in the work camp over and over again. I guess I imagined it to be therapeutic, but it was . . . well—"

"Painful," Everly supplied, then looked at him with an expression of surprise as if she hadn't realized she'd spoken aloud. "I mean, I would think that it would be sort of difficult..." Her voice trailed off and she filled her mouth with shrimp salad.

"Yes, it was painful and extremely difficult." He kept his gaze on her face although he directed his comments to Cabot. "I wanted to escape that period in my life, but I found myself mired in it. I got so tired of being called 'Sebastian Dark, the innocent victim of the cold war between the United States and the USSR.' I wanted to be just 'Sebastian Dark, common man.'" Sebastian tried to catch Everly's gaze, but she seemed engrossed in picking bits of avocado out of her salad. He wanted to share a smile with her now that she'd revealed her understanding of his feelings about being placed on public inspection. He'd never known before that they shared an aversion to the spotlight. For some reason he felt closer to her, as if by finding this new common ground, the chances of them becoming good friends had improved measurably. But she kept her gaze averted, depriving him of the opportunity to smile into her eyes and share a moment of intimacy.

"You told me once that you felt like a carnival sideshow," Cabot said, pushing away his plate. "I tried to hog the spotlight and let you off the hook, but it seemed that every reporter wanted to hear from you, not me."

"Well, it's over now. Thank God." Sebastian placed his napkin beside his plate and folded his arms across his chest. "When is your next book coming out, Cabot?"

"In the spring. E. B. Herring has one coming out then, too."

Everly held up two fists in a boxer's pose. "Watch out, buddy. *Poplar Fiction* will knock you right off the best-seller list. Providing you make it there, of course."

"Ha!" Cabot's green eyes widened, then narrowed to teasing slits. "You upstart! I was making the best-seller list when you were writing about a porpoise called Imagine!"

Sebastian watched the tender, affectionate scene between father and daughter and felt like an outsider. Everly placed a hand on her father's forearm and leaned forward with a bout of giggles. Sebastian felt the corners of his mouth tip up at the sound of her musical laughter as it ran up and down the scale. Cabot kissed Everly's forehead through tendrils of reddish-brown hair. He ran his hand over the top of her head to the back of her neck.

Sebastian's heart constricted with envy. Ah! If only he could touch her like that; kiss her with loving certainty, run his fingers through her thick hair. There was a time—oh, what a time!—when her lips had welcomed him, and he had been free to caress every satiny inch of her. She had been his sunshine, his starlight, his savior.

He had taken, and she had given. When this unequal alliance had become apparent to her, and she had asked for restitution, he had shied away. Ultimately he'd lost her, and for a long, long time he had lived in shadow without her.

He blinked and dropped back into the present to find that Everly and Cabot were on their feet and looking at him expectantly. Sebastian stood up.

"How about having drinks on the veranda?" Cabot suggested. "It's a beautiful day and we should spend it in the sunshine."

"Yes," Sebastian agreed, looking at Everly. "The sunshine."

An uneasiness stole through Everly as she met Sebastian's sultry gaze. Something lurked in the depths of his aquamarine eyes; something she couldn't quite decipher. But while her conscious mind grasped at straws, her unconscious self tingled and set her pulses to throbbing. She looked away swiftly, feeling a tide of warmth creep up her neck to pool in her cheeks. Linking her arm in her father's, she walked with him through the house to the veranda, leaving Sebastian to follow.

Once they assembled on the porch, Everly sat on one of the high-backed woven-seat rockers and set the chair into a comfortable motion, her toes pressing against the cement floor. Sunlight played across the cement, picking out bright edges of shells. Shells were plentiful in the Keys and used for everything, including mortar. The paths on Cabot's Key and Little Bit Key were paved with shell slivers. The outside walls of the estate held shells and fossils amid the sandstone. Studying the many shapes at her feet, Everly toed one fan-shaped pink shell that was deeply embedded in the cement, and remembered her numerous shell-hunting trips with Blaire when they'd been teenagers. Between picking up conchs, sand dollars and tritons, she and her cousin had shared their ideas of a "dream man."

*"Quiet and strong."*

*"That makes sense, Blaire. You wouldn't let him get a word in edgeways anyway."*

*"Smart aleck! What kind of guy do you want, Everly?"*

*"Tall, dark and handsome, of course."*

*"What else?"*

*"Someone who really needs me in his life. I don't want to be an ornament, or someone who keeps house and tends children. I want to be essential, you know?"*

*"Yeah, I know. Cherished."*

*"Respected."*

*"Put up on a pedestal."*

*"No, Blaire. Equal. On the same level."*

*"That's not romantic!"*

*"Maybe not, but it's what I want...."*

Everly smiled at the memory, realizing that her standards hadn't changed. She still wanted to be on equal footing with the men in her life. Nothing else would do.

A brown scuffed boot stepped into her line of vision, and Everly looked up to find that Sebastian was offering her a rum and Coke. She took it from his long fingers and smiled her thanks.

"Not much rum and lots of Coke, right?" he asked.

Everly nodded before his offhanded remark made her aware of yet another thing he had remembered about her. "I'm surprised you still remember that," she admitted.

"So am I." He shrugged and turned to Cabot. "What's the title of this book that will be on the best-seller list in the spring?"

"I told you," Everly cut in with a mischievous smirk. *"Poplar Fiction."*

Cabot frowned good-naturedly. "That's the name of the number two best-seller. The number one best-seller will be *Under the Rose.* It's about a woman in the French underground during World War II."

"Oooo! That sounds interesting." Everly sat up, stopping the rocker's lazy motion. "Tell me more!"

"You'll have to wait and read the book," Cabot said, giving her a secretive smile. "It's the best thing I've done so far."

"You say that about every book you write."

Cabot shrugged. "What can I say? I just get better and better."

"And more modest with each breath you take," Everly added with a laugh.

"Excuse me?" Miss Martha said, stepping out onto the veranda and motioning to Cabot. "There's a phone call for you."

"Oh, thank you." Cabot started for the door, then turned back to Everly and Sebastian. "I won't be long. Enjoy your drinks."

Without Cabot to run interference, Everly fell silent and cautious. All too aware of Sebastian's proximity, she tucked her legs underneath her and sipped the rum and Coke.

Sebastian studied the crown of her head and the red highlights in her hair. His hands grew sweaty and his fingers slipped on the wet glass he held. He took a long drink, set the glass on a metal table, and wondered what to do with his hands. He wiped his palms on his shirtfront, and felt like a gangly adolescent.

"How's Blaire?" He rolled his eyes, thinking how stupid he sounded.

"Fine."

He waited for more. Silence screamed in his ear.

"What's she doing now that you've finished the book?"

"She's going to Canada for a vacation."

"Really?" He grabbed the tidbit as if it were a major revelation. "Where in Canada?"

"Quebec."

"That's great!" He looked away quickly when she raised her eyes to his in obvious speculation. "I mean, Quebec is beautiful. She'll have a good time."

"Right."

"Do you still have the same agent?"

"Yes."

He sighed, surrendering to her penchant for one-word answers. Stuffing his useless hands in his pockets, he faced her. "This is stupid. Surely we can talk to each other in a normal way. We used to talk for hours and hours and never run out of things to say."

"That was then and this is now." Her gaze lifted, met his, then lowered.

"Everly..."

"I tried to talk to you earlier, but you had a headache." She pulled her lower lip between her teeth and bit down hard. "Maybe *I've* got a headache now!"

"Oh, so that's the score?" He rocked back on his heels and glared at her. "You're going to be childish and vindictive?"

"Don't you think I have a right to be vindictive?" Her gaze finally flew to his and held. "After what you did to me? After telling me that I was nothing more than a...a sexual release for you? You're lucky I'm even speaking to you, Sebastian Dark!"

His brows lowered and his lips thinned into a straight, uncompromising line. "Will you make up your mind, please?"

"What do you mean?"

"When you came to my office I thought that you'd decided to be civil, if not friendly. Now you're telling me that you don't even want to speak to me unless it's absolutely necessary. How am I supposed to build a house for you when you feel this way?"

"I have to be your friend before you can work for me?"

"No, that's not what I meant."

"What *do* you mean?" She swung her legs off the chair seat and stood up. "Am I supposed to forget everything that's gone before? Do you think I have the ability to do that?"

"I think that you don't want to do it. I think you'd rather hold on to your bad feelings and bad memories instead of letting them go."

"That's not the problem." She turned sideways and shadows fell across her face as she bent her head. "The problem is that the memories—most of them—aren't bad. For me, that is."

His hands slipped from his pockets, and he felt his mouth drop open. He reached out and his fingertips brushed her arm. "Oh, Everly. They aren't bad for me, either. They're good. So damn good that I want to hold onto them even though I know it's useless to do so. Or, at least, I *think* it's useless." He held his breath, hoping she'd tell him to hold on ... to hold on for dear life.

Everly felt her lips tremble as words of love swam in her head. Tell him that you can't forget him. Tell him that you want to love him again. Tell him...tell him...tell him! His fingertips rested lightly on her forearm, and the touch of him made her hunger for his kisses and caresses. A shameful weakness stole through her as she lifted her gaze to his and saw the watchfulness there. He was waiting; waiting for her to say something ... anything.

"It would help if you'd apologize for being such a heel," she whispered, and his chest expanded as he drew a sharp breath. "You could have let me down easy. You didn't have to stomp all over my feelings."

"Everly, I tried to ... I didn't mean to hurt you."

"Are you apologizing? Are you sorry for leaving me?"

"I ... I don't know what to say." How could he tell her that he was sorry, when he knew—he *knew*—he'd done the right thing at the time. She didn't know what she was asking him to do. She still thought he'd been selfish, when all the time he was thinking of her.

"You could say something like 'I'm sorry, Everly. I was wrong and I know that now. You deserved better treatment.' " Her eyes were wide with hope and bright with unshed tears.

It sounded easy when she said it, but the words stuck in his throat. He couldn't say those things without prefacing them. He wanted her to understand that he'd been right. He'd tried to let her down easy, but she'd clung to him until he'd had to rip himself from her life. But it was difficult to talk of these things after the fact. It had always been difficult to admit his insecurities. No one understood the panic that billowed through him every time he was happy or contented. Bad things happened to good people. Happiness could be destroyed in the blink of an eye. He knew that from experience, but she didn't. She hadn't had her life shattered. She knew nothing about picking up the pieces of one's life and trying to get on with it again while battling bitterness and fear.

"You won't say it, will you?" she asked, her voice husky with emotion.

"Everly, I want to, but—"

"I'm back," Cabot said, his voice ringing merrily and grating on Everly's nerves. "That was the woman I've— Sorry. Did I miss something?"

Sebastian's fingers slipped off her arm and he shoved his hands in his pockets again and turned away from her. "No, nothing. Cabot, I have to get back to Key West. Thanks for lunch."

"Oh, well, it's good to see you again. Shall I see you to the door?"

"No, I know the way." Sebastian shook Cabot's hand. "Take care."

"You, too."

"Goodbye, Everly." He couldn't bring himself to look at her, so he headed for the doorway. "I'll be in touch once I've got some plans for you to look at."

Everly glanced up, her lips moved, but nothing came out. When Sebastian disappeared inside the house, she moved slowly back to the rocking chair and sat down in a heap of rejection.

Cabot smiled and turned to her. "That wasn't so bad, was it? I'm glad you two have decided to be friends again."

"Dad, don't shove Bastian down my throat!" Everly stood up as anger pumped through her. "It's enough to make me gag!"

"What?" The smile dropped from his lips. "Why are you in such a foul mood all of a sudden? All I said was—"

"Bastian is *not* my friend," she said slowly and deliberately. "He's just someone I've hired—nothing more. Is that clear?"

"Everly..." Her father took her hands in his, holding them lightly and moving his thumbs over her knuckles. "Don't be like this. Bitterness doesn't become you. Are you going to go through life hating every man who doesn't see eye-to-eye with you?"

"It's more than merely seeing eye-to-eye," she corrected firmly. "I held out the olive branch, Dad, and he turned his back on it."

"No," he whispered, his hands closing over hers tightly. "He didn't."

"He did!" She pulled her hands from his and brushed past him. "The man feels no remorse and he made that obvious. If you want to call him your friend, fine! But don't expect it from me. Friends like him, I don't need!"

Cabot sighed wearily as Everly stormed into the house. He rolled his green eyes heavenward and was glad he'd fathered just one child.

## Chapter Five

The brass bell above the door announced Everly's arrival with sharp sweet notes. She looked up at it, then across the room as Sebastian moved into view from the back of the building. His blue pin-striped shirt was open at the collar and its sleeves were rolled up to his elbows. She glanced over his navy blue trousers with their front tucks and sharp pleats, then forced her gaze away from him because he looked far too attractive—far too familiar.

Last week the office had been furnished sparsely, but Everly noticed that a few tasteful items had been added since then. A love seat covered in dark-gray corduroy, and a high-backed chair, upholstered in silver, looked good against the pale-blue walls and darker blue carpeting. A glass-topped, cherry wood table in front of the love seat held a charming antique dollhouse.

Everly went across the room to examine the dollhouse, which was furnished with detailed miniatures. "This is lovely. Where did you find it?"

"My parents gave it to me."

"You've seen them recently?" she asked, glancing at him from the corners of her eyes.

"I went back home a few months ago for my younger brother's wedding. When I told my parents that I was going to open my own business, they gave that to me. It was my grandmother's. My great-grandfather made it for her."

"How sweet," Everly crooned, touching a delicate crib in the nursery while she recalled how upset Sebastian's family had been when he'd decided to stay at Cabot's penthouse instead of at the Dark family home after he was released from the work camp. "So you're on better terms with them now?"

He lifted one shoulder in an offhanded shrug. "We always loved each other. We just didn't understand each other. It happens in the best of families." He motioned one hand toward his desk. "I have some preliminary plans I'd like you to look at."

"You work fast," Everly said, moving to sit in the chair in front of his desk. "It's only been a week!"

"Well, they're preliminary, as I said. Before I continue, I'd like to get your reaction to these sketches." He sat down behind his desk and opened a large folder, turning it around for her to see the contents. "There are three floor plans here, and I'd like to know which one you like best. Also, I've got a couple of exterior drawings in here."

Leaning back in the chair, he propped his elbows on its arms and tented his fingers in front of his face as he appreciated the woman before him. Her lemon-yellow sundress accentuated her tan, and the wide lime belt drew attention to her narrow waist. She was the only woman he knew who wore hats. This one was straw, wide-brimmed, and decorated with a yellow-and-lime printed hatband where two tiny black feathers were secured on one side.

She examined the first sketch then turned to the next one. She removed the perky hat, shook out her shiny hair, and placed the hat on the desk. He felt a smile tug at the corners of his mouth and, in an unconscious gesture, he pressed the sides of his fingers against his lips to stifle it.

"These are interesting," she murmured, leaning over the second drawing. "Is this a glass brick wall separating the office area from the library?"

Sebastian glanced at the place she indicated. "Yes, that's right, and the second floor bathroom has a shower enclosed by glass brick walls."

"Oh, yes." She nodded, smiled, and lifted her gaze to his. "I like this one."

"What about the exterior?"

"Well..." She wrinkled her nose. "I don't like either of them that much." A tiny smile touched her mouth. "No offense."

Sebastian spread out his hands. "That's business. What strikes your fancy? Contemporary, Victorian, Gothic, A-frame?"

"Gothic?"

He shook his head, realizing she was taking him seriously. "Everly, we've got to go with something that blends into the landscape. It has to be streamlined and understated. We don't want it to stick out like a sore thumb, do we?"

"No, but these just aren't..." She shrugged.

"Let me show one more to you. Those two have incorporated your suggestions. This one is of my own imagination." He pulled a tube of paper from the top drawer of the desk and flattened it out, securing the corners with small paperweights. "Take a few minutes to really look at it before you make up your mind."

She heeded his advice as she studied the interesting design. The first things that caught her discerning eye were the broad, sheltering roof and the louvered cypress doors. The house plan was compact and efficient, blending into the area without uprooting even one existing tree. She liked the airy openness of it, made possible by the louvered doors that could be closed up tight for complete shelter and privacy, slightly opened to let in light and air, or folded back to embrace the seascape and make the interior part of the exterior.

Sebastian leaned forward and tapped the paper. "The louvered doors are half-turned to scoop in coolness on the south and let out the warm air on the north," he explained. "The house is designed to take advantage of both the southern sun and the southeastern breeze."

A carport extended on one side of the house, and the terrace at the back of the house looked cozy and intimate. Upstairs a porch ran all around the house. A large triangular window in the master bedroom faced the ocean. Fine print indicated that the curtains on this window could be rolled up like a sail to open the second-floor bedroom to the view.

Everly shook her head, stunned by the beauty and simplicity.

"You don't like it?"

She looked up into Sebastian's scowling expression. "No. I mean, I like it! I love it!" She smiled when his scowl disappeared. "Oh, Bastian, you're so talented. I couldn't have imagined anything like this. I'm flabbergasted! How did you think of it?"

He leaned back in the chair again. "It just seemed appropriate," he said with great understatement.

"Appropriate," Everly repeated with a laugh. "Such modesty!" She tapped her fingers against the paper. "This is it. This is my dream."

He sat forward and removed a long strip of paper from the folder. "Okay. Now comes the hard part. Cost projections."

Everly concentrated on his detailed price list, and was relieved when the final figure was a third less than she'd expected. She should have known, she told herself, after giving Sebastian the go-ahead and writing him a retainer check. Sebastian Dark was conservative, so it only followed that he would be a cost-cutting architect.

When he'd accepted her check and had placed the folder in the desk drawer, Everly stood up and fit the hat back onto her head.

"Well, that was painless." She smiled and picked up her purse. "I'm excited. I can't wait to live in that fabulous place."

Sebastian rose stiffly to his feet, placed ten fingertips on the desktop, and drew a short breath. He seemed to be struggling with something before he finally blurted out, "Would you like to go someplace for a drink?"

Astonished by his invitation, Everly covered her reaction by glancing at her watch. "Oh, I...I can't. I'm in a hurry."

"I see." He let out his breath in a long sigh, lifted his chin at an imposing angle, and stared down at her. "I understand."

"I want to watch the sunset," she explained, wanting him to *really* understand. "It's been years since I've taken part in that Key West tradition, and I've missed it."

"Have you?" He gave her a measured stare that made her nerves tingle. "Mind if I tag along? I've never witnessed the event, but I've heard a lot about it."

"You've never seen the sunset?" Everly asked, amazed.

"Well, I've certainly seen the sunset, but I've never joined the crowd at Mallory Square. Would you mind my company?"

"No, of course not." She turned aside to fish her keys from her purse and to worry about the situation. Why did he want to go with her? she wondered. After their last meeting, she couldn't fathom why he'd want her company, or why she had accepted his. It was ridiculous!

"I'll lock up after us. Ready to go?"

"Yes," she murmured, pulling her key ring out of her purse as she headed for the front door that Sebastian was holding open for her. "We'll take my car."

"We could walk," he suggested.

"No, there's not enough time. I don't want to miss a moment of it." She went to the car while he locked the street door. Sitting behind the wheel she took a deep breath to steady her nerves, and chided herself for getting so worked up over such a trivial thing. He was going with her to Mallory Square. Big deal! So why was her heart hammering?

Sebastian folded himself in the front seat, and Everly laughed lightly at the way his knees bumped against the dashboard.

"Sorry it's cramped, but if I move the seat back I won't be able to reach the gas pedal and brake."

"No problem." He shifted sideways to give himself a little more leg room. "Let's go."

It took only a few minutes to go anywhere in Key West. The traffic increased as Everly drove the car toward Mallory Square. Natives and tourists alike flocked to the westernmost end of the Key to get a breathtaking view of the sunset. They passed the 0-mile post that marked the end of U.S. Highway One that reached all the way into Miami. Mallory Square was already drawing a crowd when Everly parked the car in a nearby lot.

Leaving her hat and purse inside the car, she handed her keys over to Sebastian after locking the car doors.

"You don't mind keeping those for me, do you?"

"Not at all." He tucked them into his trouser pocket, thinking that it was like old times. She used to leave her purse in the car often and give her keys to him. Wrapped in the memory, he unconsciously reached for her hand, holding it lightly in his as they started for the harbor. Realizing what he'd done he glanced at her, saw the surprise flit across her face, but stubbornly kept her hand in his.

Everly looked away to stare blindly at the milling crowd, although she was aware of only one thing—the comfortable warmth of Sebastian's hand holding hers. Just like old times, she thought with a wistful smile, recalling how they used to walk hand-in-hand everywhere in New York City; Central Park, the Village, the theater district, museums and restaurants. Her fingers moved almost imperceptibly, curving around the side of his hand. She glanced at him, but he seemed absorbed in his surroundings. His aquamarine eyes tracked the area, taking in everything at once. Everly smiled, thinking how handsome he looked, so tall and erect. Those startling eyes, that sultry mouth, that long brooding face and that hair, all soft and flyaway.

A flirtatious breeze lifted her skirt, and Everly let out a little cry of alarm as she fought down the billowing material with her free hand. Sebastian looked around to see what had made her cry out, and his eyes danced with mischief when he saw her fluttering hand and skirt. He released her other hand, giving her more ammunition against the sea breeze. The trade wind slacked off as suddenly as it had picked up, and Everly flattened down her full skirt and laughed with relief.

"Just like your father," Sebastian noted with a mocking tone. "You just love the attention, don't you?"

"Oh you!" She slapped his shoulder playfully, then spotted a good vantage point near the water. Linking her arm in his, she tugged him along with her. "Come on. I see a good place over here." Squeezing between two other couples, she grinned when Sebastian excused himself for crowding in.

"That's okay," an elderly man with a white walrus mustache told him. "The more, the merrier," he added cheerfully as he placed his arm around the stoop-shouldered woman at his side.

The sky was clear except for a bank of cumulus clouds hanging above the earth's rim. The red sun sat on top of the bank, but was sinking into it by the minute. A band provided tropical music with its steel drums and ukuleles, drawing more people to the docks in front of Mallory Square. Excitement began to feather along Everly's spine as the crowd became noisier and friendlier. A couple of hundred people had made the trek to see this spectacular show of nature.

She turned her back to the setting sun to scan the crowd. Three bongo players set up a pulsing rhythm, keeping time with the steel drum band that was playing its version of "Red Sails in the Sunset." There were few singles in the crowd, Everly noted. She spotted some families, but for the most part the sunset watchers were couples. Arms entwined, they stood all around her, oblivious to everything but the sunset and each other's adoring eyes.

Everly released a long whispery "Ahh" as she turned back to look at the glowing ball. The show was beginning, she noted, transfixed by the soft pastel colors that painted the sky. The sun was not so bright that it hurt her eyes. It undulated, slipping into the cottony bank of clouds and spilling violet, blue, yellow and pink colors as it went. Sebastian maneuvered around another couple to stand beside Everly. His hand sought hers, found it, and closed tightly around her fingers. She looked at him, but he was looking past her shoulder, an expression of disapproval pursing his mouth and pinching his brows together. Everly followed his gaze to a teenage couple a few feet away.

The boy, still bearing signs of adolescent blemishes, opened his mouth wide before meeting his girlfriend's eager lips. His hands moved down to cup her hips, and hers traveled restlessly up and down his back. Their hips ground against each other; their eyes were tightly shut; their cheeks flexed with the movement of their tongues.

Everly laughed and looked back at Sebastian. He was frowning; glaring balefully at the young lovers.

"Sebastian, what's wrong with you?" she asked, surprising herself with the question that had been buzzing through her head ever since she'd seen him in the estate's parlor. She shrugged, telling herself that it was out now so she might as well go for broke. "Don't you ever smile or laugh anymore? Why are you so *serious*? You used to laugh a lot."

He tore his glowering gaze from the panting young couple and shook his head. "Someone should throw water on those two."

"Oh, you sound like a crotchety old man!" Everly placed her hands in the crook of his arm. "Don't be so cross. Lighten up!"

Sebastian angled sideways and directed his moody gaze to the flaming ball of orange. "Sorry. I'm lousing up your sunset celebration."

"Don't fall on your sword over it," she teased, leaning her cheek against his shoulder for an instant before she realized what she'd done. She got a grip on herself, mindful that the old times weren't *these* times. "I just wish you'd smile! It wouldn't crack your face, you know." She let go of him and devoted her full attention to the setting sun. It had rid itself of the filtering clouds and was sinking into the ocean. She fully expected it to sizzle and spit when it hit the water, but it didn't.

The sun cut a golden pathway across the water and spread flaming wings across the horizon and up into the banked clouds, giving them silver linings just like in the song. The color of the world changed from autumn orange to summer gold. Gulls joined the show, soaring and diving in playful abandon. The crowd responded with cheers and wild applause, sending a rippling thrill through Everly. The hemisphere teetered on the edge of evening, throwing gold and amber across the heavens as it turned the waters of the Gulf of Mexico into an unbroken sheet of bronze.

Sensing the approach of nightfall, pelicans made for their favorite mangrove trees to settle comfortably until sunrise. Their big bodies looked like enormous fruit in the dwarf trees, limned by the sunset. Appreciative gasps and sighs of awe floated from the onlookers. The bands put away their instruments for the time being, letting nature's sounds provide the most appropriate music as crickets and frogs lifted their strange voices to serenade the last light of day.

The rim of the sun hovered for a suspense-filled moment before slipping under night's cover and then, in one giant stride, evening took the stage. Dressed in shades of indigo and silver, the dark emerged, and for a few bittersweet moments all was quiet.

Thundering applause washed over Mallory Square, jerking Everly from her sense of wonder. She clapped along with everyone else, laughing and loving this timeless tradition. Remembering Sebastian, she turned toward him. He was applauding, too, but his salute was not for the sunset or for the approach of evening. The expression on his face told her that he had been watching her, oblivious to nature's two-act play.

In that moment she was struck by the contrast between the Sebastian she used to know and the one who was touching her face with a gaze that was at once gentle and ravenous. This man was cautious, careful and never spoke without giving it plenty of thought first. The Sebastian she had fallen in love with two years ago had been spontaneous, joyful to be alive. He had been so open with his feelings that he made her feel self-conscious at times; she had been unable to believe he really meant the sweet, tender words he had lavished upon her. Those sweet words might still be within him, but this new Sebastian would never let them out. He was a man in a suit of armor—untouchable and cold.

So it came as a complete surprise to her when he gently touched her cheekbones where the first shadows of night had fallen, and his lips moved to release those words she had thought she would never hear from him again.

"You are the most beautiful woman I've ever seen. Do you know that? Do you know how exquisite you are, how the setting sun sets fire to your hair, how the dusk has made your eyes as dark as onyx?"

Everly glanced up and stars seemed to rush across the heavens. She lowered her lashes at the same moment that Sebastian's cool lips touched her mouth. His fingertips trembled against her cheeks as his mouth melted over hers to seal her fate. Everly raised her arms to wind them around his neck, his arms wrapped around her waist and he lifted her until her feet dangled inches from the ground. Her hands spread out across his shoulders and somewhere deep inside her she heard maniacal laughter—laughter at herself for being foolish enough to believe she could face Sebastian again without feeling even the smallest flicker of desire. Her body was making a liar out of her as it responded to his magnetic pull. Just as the tide feels the tug of a full moon, so did she feel the tug of him.

Unable to resist, she pushed her fingers up through the hair at the back of his head and felt it flow over her hands. His lips warmed against hers, and she felt them open to take her in. The tip of his tongue traced along the seam of her lips until she relaxed, and then his tongue scraped across the edges of her teeth and surged wantonly into her mouth.

Determined to keep something of herself from him, she didn't meet the thrust of his tongue, but curled hers back. Seeking, but not finding, the invader withdrew, and the pressure of his mouth diminished. Everly opened her eyes and saw that his were still closed. She turned her head, and his mouth brushed across her cheek. He set her back on her feet, but he kept her body arched against his. The curtain of his lashes lifted. His eyes questioned hers, then his arms fell away.

Everly smoothed back her wind-tossed hair and looked around her in a moment of confusion. The crowd was dispersing into couples who wandered arm-in-arm toward the parking lot, which held as many bikes as it did cars.

"How about that drink now?" he asked, angling a glance at her.

"Uh . . . sure, why not?" She wet her lips and tasted him there. "Where do you want to go?"

"How about the Pigeon House Patio?" he suggested, his voice light but his eyes still smoldering with passion.

"Fine. Haven't been there in a long time. I could go for a strawberry daiquiri." She was more than happy to pretend the kiss they'd shared hadn't happened.

"I haven't had one of those in a long time, but for some strange reason it sounds good."

"It'll be good for you," she said, trying on a smile. "No hangover."

"Yes, you're right." He ducked his head, staring at the asphalt parking lot, wondering what had made him so bold a few moments ago. Had he really said those things to her? Where had those words come from? She must think he was crazy! No wonder she was ignoring the whole episode!

When they reached the car he handed over the keys, then settled in the passenger seat while she climbed into the driver's side. Looking in the rearview mirror, she applied a cinnamon-colored lipstick to her full lips, blotted them on a tissue, then snapped her purse shut and started the engine. Sebastian felt a wild urge to smudge the carefully applied lipstick with his mouth and tongue, but he stayed rigidly on his side of the car. His heart was still tapping furiously against his ribs from that last kiss on the dock; his mouth was still tender from the encounter. He looked at her, trying to read her expression, but failed to do so.

Down boy, he cautioned himself. You're lucky you got away with that kiss. The way she feels about you it's a wonder she didn't knock your block off.

The Pigeon House Patio Restaurant was located on Whitehead Street, not far from Hemingway's house. Its claim to fame, other than its quiet atmosphere and friendly bartenders, was that Pan-American Airlines had been founded on that very spot. A plaque in front of the place proclaimed this, drawing curious tourists inside.

A Patsy Cline record was playing when Everly and Sebastian entered the bar. With a sob in her voice Patsy sang about falling to pieces, and Everly could sympathize with her dilemma. She had fallen to pieces after Sebastian Dark had blown through her life like a typhoon, and she didn't want to repeat the experience. But she couldn't deny the attraction he still held for her.

Choosing a corner table near a street window, she and Sebastian ordered daiquiris and fell into an edgy silence until the drinks arrived. The tangy refreshment revived Everly, and she sat back in the chair with a long sigh of contentment, determined to enjoy this time spent in Sebastian's company. Looking at him, she saw that he was gazing out the window in moody contemplation.

"A penny for your thoughts, Mr. Dark," she said, pulling his gaze around to hers.

"Oh, I was just thinking how odd people are around here. I mean, to actually applaud a sunset!" He scoffed and shook his head. "Weird."

"Weird?" Everly sat up straight, stung by his assessment. "What's weird about it? Can you think of anything that deserves applause more than a beautiful sunset? We're so fortunate that we got to see it!"

Sebastian shrugged, pulled the plastic straw from the glass, and swallowed some of the daiquiri. It was sweet yet tart, and much better than he remembered. "I didn't mean to offend you. I just think it's a strange tradition, that's all."

"I think it's delightful." She fell back in the chair, regarding him with a mixture of irritation and regret. "Once again, I'm stunned by the changes in you. The man I used to know celebrated life instead of ridiculing it."

"I'm not—" He pressed his lips together and frowned. "Things are different now."

"They sure are—more's the pity." She lifted the tall glass and sipped the fruity drink through the straw. Glancing around, she recognized some of the people that had been at Mallory Square. The bartenders were asking the stock question of the customers—"Where are you folks from?"— and Everly heard answers ranging from "San Antonio, Texas" to "Ontario, Canada."

"I wonder why the people around here celebrate the sunset instead of the sunrise?" Sebastian asked, looking around the bar. "It seems more fitting to celebrate the beginning instead of the ending."

Everly smiled into his questioning eyes. "I imagine because the sun rises in the east and sets in the west, and this place isn't called Key West for nothing."

His brows shot up. "Ah," he murmured, conceding her logical point, and smiling at his own lack of it. "Makes sense." He looked across at her and saw that she was staring at him in open-mouthed shock. "What? What's wrong?"

"Nothing!" Her dark eyes widened in disbelief. "Don't stop! I like it!"

"Like it? What do you like?"

"Your smile." She graced him with one of her own. "I was convinced that you'd forgotten how it's done. You have such a disarming smile, Bastian, you should use it more often."

"Disarming?" He felt his lips stretch into another one. "Maybe I should at that." Feeling a tide of warm color wash over his face, he ducked his head. "Quit looking at me like that. You're embarrassing me."

Everly laughed, pleased that she had found a chink in his armor. "He smiles! He blushes! He admits that he has feelings! Is there no end to the wonders of this man?"

His head snapped up. "I have feelings," he said defensively. "Did you really doubt that?"

"Well..." She shrugged and ran her fingers up and down the sides of the wet glass. "You hide them so well, that I *did* have my doubts."

"You haven't given me much chance to show my feelings," he pointed out sharply. "Up until now, you've taken every opportunity to cut me off at the knees."

She started to argue, but a reasonable voice inside her stayed her tongue. He was right, of course, she conceded. She hadn't made it easy for him. Because she was filled with bitterness, she had repeatedly lashed out at him, wanting him to pay over and over for his mistakes. He *should* pay, another inner voice argued, but Everly was tired of listening to it. What good could come from it? She wasn't the type to hold on to bad feelings. It was better to let go—to be free, unencumbered by the past and its disappointments.

"I'm sorry," she said, and smiled when shock tensed his features. "I've behaved badly. Dad said that bitterness doesn't become me, and I agree with him. I'll never forget the pain I suffered because of you, but that's over and done with." She gave a little shrug and laughed self-consciously. "I'll make a concerted effort to be my usual charming self when I'm with you."

His hand moved across the table to rest on top of hers, and his thumb nudged the garnet and diamond setting on her ring. "Thanks, I needed that."

She smiled, although disappointment wafted through her. She would have liked to hear him apologize, but he was still withholding that. She extracted her hand from his and closed it around the frosty glass.

"These are delicious, aren't they?" She took another long sip, pretending not to notice his sigh of frustration at being headed off at the pass.

"Yes. Just the right drink after watching the sunset." He held up the glass and studied it. "It's the same color as the sun when it was hanging above the horizon."

Looking out the window at the gathering darkness, Everly recalled the event and the way Sebastian had looked at her and spoken to her. "Have you been happy here?"

"The Keys have been good for me," he answered after a few moments. "The life-style is slow-paced and the people are friendly."

"What made you decide to leave Cabot's Key and open your own business?"

"Time. I realized that it was speeding past me and I had nothing to show for it except the writers' colony. Cabot's Key was a...a refuge I needed, but it was high time that I struck out on my own."

"A refuge," Everly repeated. "From me?"

"No, no." He shook his head in a stern denial. "Nothing like that. It was a refuge from the publicity about the book. When the interviews became too much for me, I could always come back to Cabot's Key for a few days of solitude."

"You left before the book was published, Bastian," she noted crisply. "You weren't running from publicity, and we both know it."

He fell silent for a few moments, shifting in his chair and leaning forward as he lowered his voice, "Everly, I wasn't running away from you. I was running away from me."

"What?" Everly narrowed her eyes in suspicion. "I don't buy that."

"It's true. It's...it's hard for me to explain or to talk about that period in my life, but I felt closed in. I was suffocating."

"Suffo—" Everly's teeth clicked together. Her love suffocated him? Was that supposed to make her feel better?

Sebastian raked his fingers through his hair in frustration. "I wish I could make you understand..."

"I wish you could, too."

He sighed, started to speak, stopped himself, then tried again. "You see, I wasn't fully recovered back then. I was happy to be free again, but there was more to it. I was an emotional cripple in a way, and I couldn't handle a love affair."

"Oh? I seem to remember that you handled it very well." Her words were clipped and frosty.

"Maybe for a while, but you have to admit that it was one-sided. I couldn't give you what you wanted."

Her eyes bored into his. "And what did I want?"

"Marriage." The word fell from his lips like a stone.

Everly glanced down at her hands and realized that she had shredded a cocktail napkin. Brushing aside the confetti, she closed her fingers into tight fists. "Marriage? I don't recall proposing to you."

"Everly, you know as well as I do that marriage was on your mind. A man knows when—"

"A man *thinks* he knows a woman's heart, but he's usually listening to his own ego. I wanted to make you happy and that's it."

He shook his head, not believing her for a minute. "Let's drop it. We're getting nowhere fast." Reaching into his trouser pocket, he withdrew his wallet, flipped it open, took out a bill, and tossed the money on the table. "Let's go," he said curtly as he stuffed the wallet back into his pocket.

They left the bar and Everly dropped Sebastian at his office. He thanked her for the afternoon and waited at the curb until she'd driven away.

Sebastian unlocked the door and flipped on the overhead light. As he blinked against the sudden brightness he locked the door and crossed the office to his living quarters. He switched on a table lamp, and turned off the light in the office. Hunger gnawed at his stomach; he opened some cereal and, eating from the box, sat by the bay window. Crunching noisily on the crispy toasted rice, he stared moodily out the window at the shadow-draped yard. His grinding jaws stilled as a memory dropped into his mind.

"You're my first lover, Bastian."

"That's not important. I want to be your best lover."

"You will be. You'll be my only lover."

"Relax, Everly. I won't hurt you. It'll be wonderful, I promise."

"It's already wonderful. I love the feel of your skin against mine. Hold me tight, Bastian, and never let me go."

"I won't... I won't... I promise, I won't."

A moan escaped his throat and the cereal box fell from his hands, its contents spilling across the carpet. Sebastian covered his face with his hands in shame. He'd lied to her, but it had been the truth when he'd said it. Didn't that count for anything?

His hands slipped down his face. Should he keep her at arm's length to avoid hurting her again? The recollection of her soft mouth and the sweet taste of it filled his senses and robbed him of his noble intentions. Hell, he could no more keep away from her than he could hold back the dawn. He had to make her understand that there was no such thing as "forever" or "living happily ever after." He thought those things had existed once, but now he knew better.

Everly finished reading the last paragraph of *Wrong Place, Wrong Time* and the book fell across her thighs. She let her head drop back to the cushion on the chaise lounge and stared up through a mist of tears at the whispering palms above her.

Emotional cripple... suffocated... Sebastian's words came back to her with a better understanding. She shuddered as the overall impact of the book shot through her like a bolt of lightning. She removed her sunglasses and wiped away her tears, then relaxed on the chaise lounge again. Her admiration for Sebastian had been rekindled as she had read about the horror he'd undergone in the work camp. What kind of person would she be if she had survived that sort of ordeal? she wondered. Could she hope to be as well adjusted as Sebastian seemed to be? The torture, the defiance, the fear, the belief that you had been abandoned and forgotten—

"Ah, there you are," Cabot said as he stepped out onto the veranda. "Sunbathing, are you?"

"Y-yes," Everly said, pulling up the back of the lounge so she could sit up in it. When her father's gaze fell to the book in her lap, Everly's hands closed over the thick volume and a sheepish smile curved her mouth. "I can see why it was a best-seller."

"You've never read it before now, have you?" Cabot asked, easing himself into the rocker near her.

"No. I—I couldn't bring myself to read it when it first came out. Bastian and I had broken up and...and..." She shrugged and turned her face from his. "You know, I've discovered something rather interesting."

"Oh, what's that?"

"That it's easy to hate someone when you never see him. After Sebastian left, I whipped myself into a rage and cursed his name and everything about him. In my mind I made him a monster. But now that I'm forced to see him from time to time, I find that he's not a monster after all."

"Disappointed?" Cabot asked, a smile in his voice.

"Terribly," Everly said, facing him with a grin that was there and gone in the blink of an eye. "Dad, why did he choose to stay with you after his release instead of going to his parents' home?"

Cabot ran his fingers through the sides of his iron-streaked hair and sighed. "Well, Sebastian wasn't the only one who felt that the government and the military had deserted him in his time of need. The Dark family has a long tradition of patriotism. They're first class flag-wavers and proud of it." He locked his fingers behind his head, and his cotton knit shirt stretched tightly across his chest.

Everly smiled, thinking that her father was a dashing sixty-year-old with his salt-and-pepper hair, olive-green eyes, and a well-toned body. He wore white shorts and a blue-and-yellow striped shirt, which accentuated his bronze-colored skin.

"How did you get into the picture?" she asked. "I don't recall much about your involvement in the situation. All I remember is that you told me that you were bringing home a guest, and then Sebastian showed up at the penthouse looking like death."

"I knew Sebastian's father; I served in the air force with him. He called me to see if I could do anything to get Sebastian out of the work camp. I made some inquiries and, well, one thing led to another and I was caught up in the whole thing. It was a mess!"

"How so?" Everly asked. She glanced down at her scantily clad body encased in a black-and-white wet-look swimsuit of spandex. It left her back exposed and dipped into a revealing oval neckline in front. A butterfly lighted on her knee, and Everly shooed it away with a gentle hand.

"Oh, it was a case of too many chiefs and not enough Indians. Everyone was stepping on everyone else's toes, and nothing was being done for Sebastian. I used my limited leverage and got a top Pentagon official to look into the situation. He contacted a Russian diplomat he knew. The diplomat made a formal inquiry into the situation. Two months after that, Sebastian was released."

"Right, but I still don't understand why Sebastian came to live with you."

Cabot shrugged in a helpless gesture. "He couldn't face his family, and they were uncomfortable around him."

"Why?" Everly asked, swinging her feet to the cement floor.

"Sebastian no longer believed in the high ideals of patriotism his family had preached ever since he was a kid. He lost his belief while he'd been in the work camp. His father, who is about as far Right as you can get, couldn't understand why Sebastian had signed a confession of guilt. It was the first and only blemish on the Dark family's military history."

"Oh, for heaven sakes!" Everly shot up from the lounge, crossed her arms tightly against her breasts, and began pacing. "What a bunch of drivel! He didn't know what he was signing! It states that in your book!"

"There's more to it than that," Cabot said softly. "Sebastian's father felt as if he'd let his son down. He prided himself on his contacts with the military, but he couldn't get anything done through those contacts. It took me, an outsider, to get the ball rolling." Cabot gripped the chair arms and a sad expression covered his tanned face. "Everyone was dealing with a lot of guilt, and Sebastian wasn't in any condition to sort through it all with his family."

"He told me that he's seen them since then."

"Yes, I think they've ironed most of it out, but I don't think Sebastian will ever be completely at peace around his family again. In fact, I don't think he's ever really discussed his feelings with them. They've all just shoved it under the rug and they pretend that nothing happened. It's so tragic, don't you think?"

She nodded, unable to speak at the moment because her throat had tightened with misery.

Cabot glanced at the book, then back to her. "Why did you decide to read it now?"

"Because I have no intention of shoving it all under the rug and pretending it didn't happen. I've done that for two years and it's made me bitter and narrow-minded. I want to *know* what makes Sebastian Dark run from any sign of emotional attachment.''

"You're still in love with him, aren't you?''

Her father's soft question shot through her like an arrow. She drew in a sharp breath, then exhaled it in a long sigh as she threw up her hands in utter confusion.

"I don't know," she almost wailed. "I *did* love him, but I don't know what I feel anymore. He's so hard to reach...so difficult to understand. I thought I knew him inside out back in New York, but there are times now when I wonder if I made him up." She paused and a smile trembled on her lips. "Like I made up that porpoise called Imagine.''

Cabot nodded and started the chair rocking back and forth. "When you met Sebastian, he had his guard down. Since that time, I get the feeling that he's built a damned fortress around himself.''

"So do I!" Everly admitted, relieved to know that her father felt the same sense of being shut out. "It's exasperating.''

"I suppose you'll just have to decide whether or not you're up to climbing those walls..." His voice trailed off and he glanced at her slyly.

"Have you forgotten who you're talking to?" Everly asked, adopting a boasting attitude. "When I was younger, I was the best tree climber in the neighborhood! Fortress walls won't keep me out, buster.''

Cabot laughed, then sobered suddenly. "Do you think it's worth the trouble, Everly?''

"Ah, now *that's* a question I don't have an answer to," she admitted. "Guess I'll have to wait and see.''

Cabot stood up and gathered her against his chest. "I know how he hurt you last time, honey. I don't want to see that happen again.''

"You think I do?" She gave a little laugh, leaned back in his arms and kissed his smooth-shaven chin. "I wish you'd make up your mind, Viverette. First you tell me to bury the hatchet, and now you're cautioning me not to bury it too far underground."

Cabot made a weary face. "I'm a father. I don't have to make sense."

"Oh, I see." She laughed and gave him a fierce hug. "I won't hold you responsible if I can't get over those fortress walls." Rubbing her cheek against his cotton shirt, she added in a whisper, "There's still something there between us, you know. When I'm around Bastian, I can feel the slightest thread of connection. At first it made me furious to think that I could still have feelings for a man who called me a 'crutch,' but there's no use in denying it. It's there. Invisible, but so strong and binding. I often wonder if he feels it, too."

"Leave it to you to fall for a mysterious man," Cabot said, trying to add some levity. "Couldn't you have fallen for a simple man with simple tastes and simple goals? No!" He smiled and pushed her back so that he could look into her shining eyes. "You had to get tangled up with a man right out of one of your books!"

"Pardon me, Mr. Viverette, but I believe you're mistaken. He happens to be right out of one of *your* books." She glanced over her shoulder at the book beside the chaise lounge. "*That* book, to be exact."

Cabot joined her in a burst of laughter and ruffled her hair playfully as Sebastian stepped from the house onto the veranda.

He stood stock still for a few moments, appreciating the lure of Everly's swimsuit, then his gaze drifted down to the book on the floor near her feet and at the sight of it anger rose in him.

Sebastian's jaw hardened as he stared at the book, and his lips thinned into a brittle line. Why had she chosen to read it *now*? He cleared his throat, and Cabot spun around to face him.

"Sebastian!" Cabot held out one hand and pumped Sebastian's. "Good to see you."

Everly sat down, saw the book, and kicked it into the shadows under the lounge. She looked up, started to smile, but saw from Sebastian's narrowed eyes that she had been too late in concealing the evidence. "Hello, Bastian," she murmured, grabbing a tube of suntan lotion. She squirted some of the lotion into her palm and busied herself with smearing it on her arms and legs.

"Can I get you a drink?" Cabot asked, always the charming host.

"No, thanks. I stopped by to ask Everly to come over to Little Bit when she has a chance. They're laying the foundation and I'd like her to see the perimeters of the house."

"Laying the foundation?" Cabot echoed. "You're not wasting any time, are you?"

"It's been a few weeks since Everly approved the blueprints, and I didn't have any trouble finding a crew." Sebastian leaned around Cabot to stare pointedly at Everly. "Well?"

Everly snapped to attention. "What? Oh, sure. I—I'll be right over. I've got to change into something else..." She glanced down at her revealing swimsuit, then back to Sebastian. "Be there in half an hour."

"Fine." Sebastian gave a short choppy wave, did a crisp military about-face, and marched back into the house.

Cabot turned slowly to face his daughter, one brow cocked in an unspoken question.

Everly managed a weak smile as she bent over and pulled the book out from under the lounge. "So much for covert actions," she said, and Cabot laughed.

## Chapter Six

As she approached the clearing, which the old house dominated, Everly stumbled to a halt and looked around to get her bearings. The Key was too small to get lost on, but she experienced a moment of utter confusion as she stared at the place where the house had been—had always been ever since she could remember. It was gone now as if it had been blown away by a hurricane.

She blinked as she turned in a circle and tried to adjust herself to its absence. The clearing looked forlorn and naked without the ramshackle structure. It needed something, she told herself. Anything to fill the void.

Moving on, she made her way to the building site, mentally preparing herself for what awaited her. Sebastian was miffed, she thought as she recalled his livid expression when he spotted the copy of *Wrong Place, Wrong Time*. She wasn't sure *why* he'd been so aggravated, but she was sure he'd enlighten her. He was probably itching to yell at her, and she was itching to hear his reasons for being so upset that she'd read Cabot's book.

She'd changed from the revealing swimsuit into a modest pair of culottes and matching blouse of navy blue with a nautical collar and tie. A sailor cap went with it, but she hadn't taken time to find it among her many hats.

Hats. They were her passion, her fashion trademark, and while she took a lot of ribbing about them, she knew that her acquaintances had come to expect her to wear one.

Before she reached the building site, she could hear the grind and hum of heavy machinery that turned out to be a cement truck and bulldozer. Sebastian stood near the cement truck, watching as a river of gray poured into a large frame. Khaki shorts revealed his long tanned legs, and his T-shirt was the same color as his eyes. Everly remembered that he favored shades of blue, and it amazed her that she knew so much about him. Their time together had spanned only three short months, but she knew him better than any other man in her life—with the possible exception of her father.

He looked up, saw her, and waved her to his side. He was still scowling.

"It's bigger than I thought it would be," Everly shouted above the noise and pointed to the foundation. She received a curt nod. "The place where the old house stood looks naked. Maybe we should build something there."

"Maybe. Like what?"

"I don't know." She shrugged. "What do you think?"

"A greenhouse...gazebo, maybe?"

"A gazebo," she said, smiling. "That would be great."

"What do you think of it?" he shouted as he waved a hand at the foundation being poured.

Everly was at a loss for words. What was there to think about a foundation? What was she supposed to say? She looked at him and laughed. "It's fine, I guess. Let's put our handprints in it when they've finished."

His scowl increased and he walked away from her to speak with the man who was controlling the bulldozer. Everly made a face at his back, then whirled around and started for the main house on Cabot's Key. Let him stew in his juices, she thought. If he wanted to act like a stubborn mule, fine!

Fingers closed like a vise around her upper arm and she gasped as she was spun around roughly to face Sebastian.

"Where are you going?" he demanded.

"Back to the house." She wrenched her arm from his hold. "I've been dismissed."

He glanced ahead at the path that snaked across the Key. "Let's take a look at the clearing."

She fell into step beside him, glancing at him from time to time and wondering if she should open the can of worms or give him the honor. When they reached the clearing, he stopped after he had put a few yards between the two of them.

"Why were you reading that book?"

"Ah-ha!" she jeered before she could stop herself. He threw her a curious look, and she stared at the tassels on her leather shoes. "I mean, I was wondering when you'd get around to that."

"I couldn't help but notice, especially when you took such pains to hide it from me."

"I didn't . . ." She glanced up, shrugged in self-defense, and returned to the study of her shoes. "I'd never read it before, and since my father wrote it, I felt I should."

"Am I supposed to buy this?"

His droll sarcasm sent her gaze to his. "Are you calling me a liar?" she asked in a challenging tone.

"Yes."

"Then *you* tell me why I was reading it, since you don't accept my explanation."

He folded his arms across his chest and adopted a cocky stance. "You were reading it to find out more about me— which, I might add, is a total waste of time."

"What an ego!" Everly tipped back her head to stare at the blue sky. "Will you listen to that? The man thinks I've got nothing better to do than to make a study of him!" Her gaze dropped back to his and her eyes were ablaze with indignation. "Give me a break!"

"Do you think you're the first woman who's read that book in order to know me better?"

A bitter smile tipped up one corner of her mouth. "I'm sure there've been a number of them, but I'm not in their pathetic league. I already know all I care to know about you." She turned her back to him and wrestled with the truth he'd thrown in her face. She might have admitted that she *had* read that book to better understand his complex nature, but she'd cut out her tongue before she'd tell him that now. How dare he equate her with the other women in his life!

"I'll tell you what I've told all the others," he said, and his voice seemed nearer as if he were moving toward her. "The man in that book isn't me. It *was* me, but not any—"

"Don't!" She pressed her hands against her ears and squeezed her eyes shut. "Don't treat me as if I were one of your...your Key West groupies! I deserve better than that!"

Sebastian stood behind her and slightly to one side so that he could see her tightly closed eyes and gritted teeth as her lips pulled back in a grimace. His anger disappeared and he stepped in front of her and pried her hands away from her ears.

"You're right," he said when she opened her eyes. "You *do* deserve better. I'm sorry." He forced her hands down to her sides. "And I deserve the truth, don't I?"

She seemed to crumble against him, and his arms went around her in a protective gesture. They stood like that for a few minutes while graceful birds swooped overhead and called down to them. Finally, Everly straightened from his arms and moved away from him.

"I'd never read the book before," she said so softly that he strained to catch her words. "When it was published I hated you so much that I couldn't even bear to see your name in print."

"Why now?"

"Oh, I've been thinking about . . . about us. I was curious, like everyone else who read it. You never talked to me about the work camp, and I wanted to know what had made you look like you did when I first saw you."

"How did I look?"

Her lashes lifted slowly until her gaze came to bear on him. "Like a wounded animal." He averted his eyes quickly, but she pressed on. "Kicked, whipped, starved, dazed. You don't even remember arriving at the penthouse, do you?"

He couldn't look at her, so he stared up at the swaying treetops. "No. The first thing I remember is being in bed and you came in to introduce yourself. I thought you were a vision at first . . . an angel."

She smiled, recalling that day when he'd finally emerged from his odd sleepwalking state. "While I was reading the book I kept wondering what sort of person I'd be if I'd endured what you went through. I think—no, I *know* that I'd be seeing a psychiatrist. You never did, did you?"

"No. Helping with the book was therapeutic, and I worked out the rest by myself."

"You have a strong will. Stronger than mine."

One corner of his mouth lifted in a half smile. "Don't sell yourself short."

"Do you really think you can forget Siberia?"

"I can try."

Everly shook her head. "You can't forget something like that, Bastian. No matter what you say, the man in that book *is* you. He's you in a horrific situation, but he's still you." She could tell by the way the muscles in his jawline flexed that he didn't like her assertion. "What you went through back then has shaped your personality, your ideals, your beliefs, and the way you relate to people. Whether you like it or not, I learned a lot about you from reading that book."

"I wish it had never been published," he said, jamming his hands into the pockets of his shorts.

"It's been beneficial," Everly argued. "It made money, most of which went to you, and it made it possible for you to get your life back together."

"Get my life back together?" he repeated dubiously. "I think I could have gotten myself together a hell of a lot quicker if I hadn't had to repeat my work camp experiences over and over again for the media. I kept telling myself that I was helping by shedding light on the Russian prison system. You know, I wasn't the only innocent person in that work camp. The place is full of them, and they're still there!" A shudder coursed through him, shaking him to the core. "They're still in that hellhole with no chance of getting out."

"Do they ever try to escape?"

"Escape?" His glance was sharp. "Escape to where? We're talking Siberia here, Everly. It's nothing but mile after mile of frozen wasteland. A man could freeze to death within twenty-four hours and not be anywhere near civilization. It's a perfect place for the undesirables, let me tell you. The prisoners used to chant, 'No hope, no faith, no chance.' That was our camp song."

"You gave up hope, didn't you?" she asked, knowing the answer from reading the book.

"After about six months, yes. Reality finally set in and I stopped thinking in terms of 'when I get out of here.' I was there for life, and I just prayed that my life would be short. I mean, as far as I knew, no one had any idea where I'd been taken. One of the guards told me that my parents had been sent an official verification from the Kremlin that I had been killed in a bar fight and that my body had been cremated."

"But that was a lie!"

"I know that now, but at the time it sounded just like what those bastards would do." His eyes became red-rimmed and he rubbed his hands up and down his face as if washing away the memories. "My dad will never understand...never forgive me..."

"What?" Everly went to him and held his hands in hers. "What won't he forgive?"

"My signing that damned Russian document; my confession that I was a spy for the U.S." He jerked his hands from hers and paced back and forth, his shoes flattening the carpet of grass. "I knew better! I mean, I was trained! I'd gone through countless briefings before I went over there. The first thing you're taught is never—*never!*—sign anything." He clenched his teeth together and kicked viciously at a patch of wildflowers. "But I was so tired and confused. They beat the living daylights out of me, and all I wanted was to get the hell out of there."

He leaned against a coconut tree, crossed his arms, and looked over to her. "None of it would have happened if I hadn't given that guy a carton of cigarettes."

Everly nodded, remembering that crucial part of the book. "But what were you doing with cigarettes? You don't smoke."

"I did then. I found a great way to give up cigarettes. Fourteen months in a Siberian work camp is a sure cure." He laughed, but it was forced and without humor. "I was in one of Moscow's watering holes and I met this guy who spoke English."

Everly sat down a few feet from him, and looked up into his face. She knew the story, but she let him go on because he seemed to want to tell her about it.

"I was so damned happy to meet someone who spoke English that I became friends with him in the space of a minute or so. He even knew where Connecticut was!" He tipped back his head and sighed. "I didn't ask him what he did for a living. I didn't care. We played a few games of darts. He sang some Russian folk songs. We bought each other rounds of drinks. Stuff like that. Innocent stuff." He squinted against the sun and Everly could tell that he was thinking back to that night in a Moscow bar. "I remember noticing how he kept looking at my cigarette pack with greed, and I finally asked him if he wanted one. He grabbed it. So I thought, 'what the hell?' I had three cartons of Marlboros in my duffel bag, and I gave him one of them. He was overjoyed!"

"And you were being observed?" Everly asked, hugging her knees to her chest and waiting for the inevitable.

"Yes, I guess so. All of a sudden, out of nowhere, we were surrounded by uniformed soldiers. One of them grabbed me by the scruff of the neck, and the next thing I knew, I was handcuffed, my ankles were shackled, and I was in the back of an armored truck."

"They thought you'd passed a message to that guy?"

"Yes, in the cigarette carton. My drinking buddy was a filing clerk in the top secret division of space weapons. I didn't find that out until after I'd been released and was back in the States."

"They interrogated you?" Everly asked, getting him back on track.

"Well, I wouldn't exactly call it that. They asked me a question. I answered. They hit me. Then they'd ask another question. I'd answer. They'd hit me."

"What questions?"

He shook his head in complete bafflement. "Military stuff." His eyes met hers briefly. "Classified information, my dear. I went through a grueling debriefing when I finally got back to the States, and I really don't recall much of anything about those questions they asked. Suffice to say, my interrogators thought I was a spy."

"Did you try to explain that they had the wrong guy?"

"I gave them my name, rank, and serial number. I was trying to be a good little soldier." The last was said with a twist of bitterness. "They weren't impressed."

His touch of irony made her smile. He slid down the tree trunk to his haunches, his elbows resting on his knees and his arms outstretched in front of him. The sun peeked through the branches and fronds, bathing the clearing in buttery light that attracted butterflies and bees to the dandelions and sweet clover. His gaze followed the bouncing flight of one particularly fat bumble bee, then he sighed and examined his woven fingers.

"By the time they stuck that paper in my face and told me to sign it, I was willing to believe anything. I figured that they'd had time to examine the cigarette carton and talk to the Russian I'd given it to, and that everything had been sorted out." He made a disparaging sound and grimaced. "I knew better than to sign, but I wanted to believe them. I wanted to believe that I'd be free as soon as I signed my name. The officer who handed it to me was smiling, and I remember that he patted me on the shoulder. He told me that it was a standard release form. It was in Russian, and I was too tired to translate it. I signed my name, looked up and saw the smile dissolve into a wicked smirk, and I knew I'd been duped. *Damn!* How could I have been so stupid?"

"You didn't do anything wrong," Everly argued, desperate to ease his conscience. "They lied to you!"

"Right, but I'd been briefed by air force intelligence. I knew better than to believe them. I was just so...so tired and scared. One of my ribs had been broken, and every time I took a breath, I felt as if I were going to pass out."

Everly closed her eyes against the pain his words contained. She remembered how he'd looked the first time she'd met him: wan, hollow-eyed, his lips chapped and cracked, a bruise riding his left cheekbone, his hair shaved off until only dark stubble remained on his head. She swallowed hard and forced her thoughts away from that day.

"What happened after you signed the document?"

"They put me on a train headed for the work camp. It was full of men—old, young, sick. A couple of them spoke English, and they told me where I was headed and what was in store for me, but nothing could prepare me for that place." His hands gathered into tight fists. "We made shirts."

"What?" she asked, confused for a moment, then nodding when she realized he was talking about the work he had done while in the camp.

"I sewed on buttons at first, then I was moved to cuffs." He smiled, shook his head and relaxed his tense fingers. "The shirts were made out of a heavy wool material, and we all wished we could have one of those shirts. It was so cold! I was always chilled to the bone, and I had a cold the whole time I was there . . . sneezing my head off. Lots of men died of pneumonia. Everything was wet and muddy. In the spring we chopped wood, but most of the time I sat in front of an old foot-pedal sewing machine." He leaned his head back and laughed, but again the sound was mournful. "I can't look at a sewing machine without wanting to scream and smash it to bits."

She was silent, sensing his need to talk in this rambling way.

"I was in the 'foreigner' side of the prison, and the Russians were on the other side of this huge wall that you couldn't see over. They'd shout to us every once in a while. The men on my side were Canadian, British, French, and one other American. He said he was with the army intelligence."

"A spy?"

"Yes, a real one. He called me the 'resident bogus spy.' He tried to be my friend, but I . . . well, I stayed off by myself. I didn't want to make friends there. His name was Archie Summerfield. He died a few weeks before I was released. One of the guards shot him for stealing a shirt from the sewing room."

Everly closed her eyes, warding off the moan that was tightening her throat.

"The guards were always poking us with the butts of their rifles. If you looked at them, they slapped you to the ground. If you spoke to them, they spit in your face. One of the guards—we called him Ivan the Terrible—was a psychopath. He was dying to open fire on us. One night we were playing poker, and Ivan came in. One of the prisoners offered to deal him in, and Ivan took him outside and beat him to death."

Everly sucked in her breath and turned her head in a sharp movement of denial. It was too barbaric...too horrible. Reading about it had been bad enough, but it was worse to hear it from Sebastian.

"We were helpless. All we could do was sit inside and listen to the man's screams and Ivan's laughter. We were cowards, concerned only with saving our own skins." His voice lifted from its deep monotone. "I'm sorry, I shouldn't be going on and on about this."

"No, I'm...it's okay." She stared at him, again recalling how sick and cowed he'd looked when she first saw him in New York. It was difficult to imagine that the healthy tanned man before her was one and the same. "I have such admiration for you, Bastian."

"Admiration?" He shot up to his feet. "I don't deserve admiration. If I'd done what I'd been trained to do...if I hadn't signed that damned admission of guilt, I wouldn't have ended up in that work camp. If I hadn't been such a coward, I would have tried to prevent some of the things I witnessed in there."

"And you'd probably be dead." She stood up and faced him. "You have nothing to be ashamed of, Bastian."

"My father says—"

"I don't care what he says," she interrupted, placing her hands on his forearms. "No one has the right to judge you, not unless they've been in the same predicament. None of us know what we'd do in that situation. You got through it, and that's all that matters. There's no right and there's no wrong in it."

She felt the muscles in his arms relax under her fingertips, and his mouth softened into a smile.

"Thanks." He leaned down and dropped a kiss on her forehead as his hands spanned her waist. "This is nice, isn't it?"

"What?"

"Talking quietly, instead of arguing and verbally circling each other. I like it when we're like this."

She felt that strong, almost irresistible tug of attraction, and she wiggled from his loose embrace. "I guess you'd better get back to your crew."

"Yes, I guess so." He looked in that direction, then swung back to her. "Have you been enjoying your holiday? I haven't seen much of you lately."

"Oh, I've been swimming, sailing, sunning." She smiled and shrugged. "I love being lazy. I wish someone would pay me to do it." She enjoyed his rare smile for a few moments; it seemed to make her bold. "Bastian, I'm going into Key West Saturday for some good old-fashioned sight-seeing. I was wondering...how would you like to be my guide?" Seeing his startled expression, she added, "I mean, if you already have plans, I understand."

"No, no. I don't have any plans." He tipped his head at a curious angle and grinned. "I'd be happy to play tour guide. Come by around ten o'clock and I'll treat you to coffee and croissants. After breakfast we'll embark on my very own super-duper tour of Key West."

"Great. I'll be there."

He reached for her hand and pulled her a step closer to him. "Truce?"

Her fingers closed around his. "Truce."

His gaze moved over her shiny hair. "Wear a hat Saturday."

She laughed and squeezed his hand. "You like my hats?"

"Yes, and I like what's under them" He swooped down to kiss her, and she was an easy prey to his passion. Still holding her hand he pulled her close to him and spoke against her lips, "I suppose you know by now I'd like to make love to you again."

Her head jerked back, breaking contact with his marauding mouth. She felt her eyes widen. "We can't. I mean, we're not good for each other. We proved that two years ago."

"Correction. We made love together as if we'd invented it."

"The lovemaking was...was good," she conceded, "but the relationship was destructive. I don't want to repeat it. I think we should keep this strictly platonic."

"Platonic?" He let go of her hand and looked at her as if she'd suggested that he sprout wings and fly to the moon. "That's impossible. It's unnatural."

"Are you telling me that you've never had a platonic relationship with a woman?"

"No, I'm telling you that I can't have that kind of relationship with you."

"Bastian, we couldn't make it work the first time and—"

"And that was then and this is now," he cut in, throwing her own earlier assessment back into her face.

"No!" She backed up a few steps. "If we can't be friends, then forget it."

"Okay, okay!" He held up his hands in surrender. "I'll give it a whirl." He pointed a finger at her and grinned. "I'll expect you at ten on Saturday."

She eyed him warily for a few moments before agreeing. "Yes, at ten."

He gave a wink, then strode from the clearing, leaving her to ponder his credibility.

It doesn't matter, she thought with a shrug as she started toward Cabot's Key. She would set the pace. First she would be his friend and then she'd decide whether or not she wanted to be his lover again. She wouldn't jump into anything this time around, she vowed to herself. She was all too aware of how vulnerable she was to Sebastian Dark's considerable charm, but she was determined to take it one step at a time.

A silly childhood chant flitted through her mind, and she laughed at the innocent traditional implications of it.

Everly and Sebastian, sitting in a tree.
K-I-S-S-I-N-G.
First comes love, then comes marriage,
Then comes Everly with a baby carriage!

It didn't work out that way, she thought with a slight frown. With Sebastian it was:

First comes love right from the start,
And then comes Everly with a broken heart.

Not this time. This time it would be different. If love made another appearance it would be mutual, not one-sided. She wouldn't take Bastian's love for granted. No assumptions. No imaginings. This time she would be sure of his feelings.

He said that he wanted to make love to her again, she mused as she crossed from Little Bit to Cabot's Key. Well, as far as she was concerned, Bastian had *never* made love to her. She'd made love to him, but for Bastian, love had never entered into it. He'd made that painfully clear before he'd run off to the Keys.

He was wondering why he had dredged up all that stuff about the work camp in front of Everly when he heard the bell ring above the door. Sebastian glanced at his watch—ten o'clock on the nose—and called out, "Back here!" Stepping around the table, he held out one of the chairs at the table set for two.

"Ah," he sighed when Everly came into view, "I knew you wouldn't disappoint me." He reached out, grasping her hand, and pulled her toward the chair. Before she could sit down, he hooked a finger under the wide brim of her hat and peeked at her big brown eyes and shy smile. "Now *that's* a hat."

She rewarded him with a melodious laugh. "You like it?"

"Love it." He leaned back an inch to examine the milliner's creation. The brim was broad and flexible, dipping gracefully at the center of her forehead. It was made of white straw, and had a narrow black ribbon around the band that was tied in a bow at the back. It went perfectly with her white romper and black strapped sandals. She pirouetted for him, giving him a glimpse of the back, which exposed a triangle of skin. Sebastian smiled. She wasn't wearing a bra.

"Now that you've seen the total look, I'll remove this," she said, whipping off the hat and hanging it on a ladder-back chair.

"I like the total...look," he murmured, letting his gaze slip down to her firm tanned legs. He cleared his throat of its huskiness and held out the chair for her again. "Madam, your breakfast is ready."

"Thank you, sir." She sat down, smiled at him over her shoulder, then flipped the linen napkin across her lap. "Did you bake these croissants yourself?"

"Surely you jest," he said, sitting across from her. "Do you see an oven in this place? I bought them at the bakery down the street. The coffee, however, is home-brewed." He poured the coffee, then gestured to his white knit shirt and black shorts. "We're color coordinated."

"So we are," she noted, her gaze moving across his broad shoulders. "What's on the agenda?"

"I thought we'd do some shopping at Mallory Square, then hop on the Conch Train for the traditional tour of Key West."

"I hope that Hemingway's house is on the itinerary."

"It is," he assured her. "And the old lighthouse, the naval station, the southernmost house and the railroad museum."

"Wow!" She took a huge bite of the flaky croissant. "We'd better hurry if we want to get all of that in!"

He smiled, realizing how much he enjoyed her company. He'd looked forward to this day, going over it time and again in his mind. He wanted it to be perfect. That day in the clearing held promise, and he wanted to make good on it. He wondered if she'd spent most of the morning selecting just the right outfit. He'd discarded one shirt after another, then tried on jeans, trousers, shorts—even a suit! It had taken him a full fifteen minutes to make a decision on which pair of tennis shoes to wear!

"These are good," she said, brushing croissant crumbs from her fingertips. *And you smell delicious,* she tacked on mentally, breathing in the aroma of his after-shave. His shoulders and chest seemed broader in the white knit shirt that was open at the collar. His Adam's apple moved up and down as he swallowed, and for some reason she felt a current of sexuality sizzle through her. "Are we going to shop for anything in particular?"

"Shells and sponges, of course," he answered, his eyes sparkling like the Gulf waters. "You can't have too many of those in Key West." He regarded her for a few lingering moments, then added, "Tell you what, you buy me something, and I'll buy you something."

"Really?"

"We'll surprise each other . . ."

"Like we used to," she finished, completing his unspoken thought.

"Yes, like we used to." He could tell by her rapt expression that she, like him, was thinking back to those shopping excursions in New York when they'd always bought little surprises for each other. He still had those impromptu gifts—a brass letter opener that had an anchor on one end, a pair of gold cuff links with his initials engraved on them, an ebony collar bar and an ivory comb. "Do you still have the things I bought for you?"

Her lashes lowered, shutting him out. "No. I—I got rid of them."

"Oh. I have mine."

"You do?" Startled brown eyes met his.

"Yes." He shrugged indifferently, but it pained him that she had thrown away his gifts. He remembered them, too: a teddy bear, three lacy, embroidered handkerchiefs, a crystal perfume bottle and a Yankees baseball cap. "You even got rid of the Yankees cap?" he asked before he could stop himself.

She nodded and bit her lower lip. "I didn't want any reminders at the time."

"Oh, I see." He shook off the disappointment. "Well, let's get going. Key West awaits you, dear lady." He stood up and waved one arm toward the door in a sweeping gesture. "I hope those shoes are comfortable, because we're walking."

"They're comfortable," she assured him, picking up her hat and fitting it over her cap of shining hair. She looked at him with a hint of trepidation, gave a swift shrug, and linked her arm in his. "Let's go, pal."

His head turned slowly, and his gaze was burning and full of wrath. "Don't call me that!"

She flinched, alarmed by his mercurial mood change. "What?"

"Pal," he said, almost spitting out the word. "I'm not your pal."

"I thought we were friends."

"I'll tolerate that, but I won't be your 'pal.'"

"Okay, okay," she said in a soothing voice. "Let's not split hairs."

He gritted his teeth, resisting the urge to give her a good shaking and inform her that this palsy-walsy stuff rankled his manhood. He wanted to make love to her until she was moaning beneath him and willing to forgive all his past transgressions. *Pals* didn't make love to each other, so he wanted no part of that kind of relationship. However, he tamped down his temper and guided her outside into the Florida sun.

They strolled to Mallory Square with Sebastian setting a slow pace that gave Everly the opportunity to window-shop and reacquaint herself with the business district. Once at the square, Everly left Sebastian's side, warning him not to follow her, and set off to find something special for him. She went through the shell shop, but failed to discover anything that Sebastian would find delightful. She did, however, purchase a shell necklace and some purple-hued barnacles that she planned to use as a planter. That was the problem with shopping, she thought with a little smile. Every time she went shopping for someone else, she ended up buying things for herself.

She squeezed by a crowd of tourists, who were looking through racks of T-shirts, and came upon a display of wind chimes. One in particular caught her eye. Made of wood and cane, it was a small house on stilts with tubular chimes hanging from its center. She set it swaying and it sang sweetly, giving out a tinkling tropical sound. Thinking of the side yard attached to Sebastian's office building, she removed the wind chime from its peg and went to pay for it. She tucked the white-wrapped gift into the larger sack that contained her own purchases, then went in search of Sebastian.

He was in the shop next door, leaning over to peer into an aquarium that contained a society of sea horses, crabs and a baby octopus. A sack was tucked under one arm, and Everly wondered what he'd found for her. She tapped him on the shoulder, and he glanced sideways and smiled.

"That didn't take long," he said, straightening from his view of the watery world. "Let's walk to Hemingway's house and then we'll take the Conch Train."

She nodded, linked her arm in his, and let him guide her through the crowded shop to the street. Halfway to Hemingway's house, Everly couldn't stand a moment more of suspense.

"What did you get me?" she asked, swinging a hip against his.

He laughed, pretending to be knocked off balance by her unorthodox nudge for attention. "All in good time. All in good time," he chanted as if to a precocious child.

"Bastian! Let's exchange gifts now!"

"No, not now. We're almost to Hemingway's. Let's go through the house, catch the train, and find a secluded little spot to exchange our gifts."

"Oh, you're no fun," she grumbled, clutching her sack and itching to give him the wind chime. "I think you'll like your gift. It's musical."

"Shh!" He gave her a stern look. "No clues."

"Give me just one. I gave you a hint."

"W-e-l-l," he said, drawing out the word. "Just one hint? Okay. Not to worry."

She threw him a perplexed glance. "So, what's the clue?"

"That *is* the clue," he said with a mysterious smile. "Not to worry."

"That's it? It doesn't make sense."

"It does if you know what I've bought for you."

"What a lousy clue!" She felt like stamping her foot.

"Spoken like a true mystery writer," he noted with a touch of sarcasm.

"I don't really write mysteries," she corrected. "They're more like suspense stories."

"Then you should love the suspense." He laughed lightly at her murderous glare. "Go over there and stand in front of the house. I want to take your picture."

"You've brought a camera?"

"Sure!" He motioned for her to cross the street to Hemingway's house. "Go on," he said, pulling a small camera from his pocket.

"No, wait." She approached a couple who were snapping pictures. They looked in their mid-twenties. "Excuse me, but I was wondering if you'd mind taking our picture."

"Don't mind at all," the young man said with a big smile.

Everly turned and motioned for Sebastian. "Bastian, come here. I've found a willing photographer."

Sebastian held out his hand to the other man. "Hello. I'm Sebastian Dark."

"I'm John Preston, and this is my wife Barbara." John took the camera from Sebastian. "Oh, yes. I know how to work this." He smiled at them again. "Are you two married?"

"No," Sebastian said, glancing sideways at Everly. "We're just friends."

*Just friends.* The bland depiction of their relationship took the wind from her sails. Everly looked at him, knowing that the sadness she felt was reflected in her eyes.

Sebastian and Everly took their places in front of the brick wall that surrounded the property, and stood just to the right of the iron gates that gave entrance to visitors. There was an awkward moment when they didn't know what to do with their hands and arms. Everly edged closer to Sebastian, then moved away, remembering his "just friends" description. Sebastian threaded the fingers of one hand through hers, frowned when John called for them to "get closer together," and finally released her hand and slipped his arm around her shoulders.

"A little closer," John urged from across the street.

"Oh, hell!" Sebastian muttered darkly, then pulled Everly against his side. "This is stupid," he added, glancing down at her stiff smile before plastering on one of his own.

As soon as the picture was taken, Everly and Sebastian separated. Everly remained where she was while Sebastian crossed the street and retrieved his camera. John and Barbara waved and called, "Nice to meet you!" They moved off, arm in arm.

Everly turned away from the tenderness of the couple as envy swamped her. She found herself staring blindly at the admission gate, and at the woman who sat behind a card table.

"How many?" the woman asked.

"Uh...two." Everly let Sebastian pay their way, then moved forward through the gates. The two-story house loomed before her, its front porch bracketed by gigantic palms. From her previous visits, she knew that the house had been built of coral rock quarried from the grounds in 1851 by Asa Tift. Hemingway took ownership in 1931 and lived in the house off and on until his death in 1961. It was in this house, during his Key West years—roughly from 1928 until 1940—that he wrote several of his now famous novels: *For Whom the Bell Tolls*, *Death in the Afternoon*, and *To Have and Have Not*.

The colonial house, with its wide porches, was set in a lush tropical setting.

Everly stopped beside a circular fountain. Red hibiscus floated in the water, circling lazily.

"This way, please!" A woman waved Sebastian and Everly forward. "We're getting ready for a tour!"

They joined the others and began the tour in the front of the house. Everly barely listened to the tour guide, recalling the information from her previous visits. She glanced at Sebastian from time to time, noticing that he was giving most of his attention to the architecture and furnishings.

"This is the dining room," the tour guide said. "Please notice the Spanish walnut table and chairs, the Venetian glass chandelier and the Italian black marble fireplace. This wildebeest," she added, pointing up to the mounted trophy, "was shot by Mr. Hemingway. He was a respected game hunter and loved to go on safaris in Africa."

Sebastian sidled up behind Everly and said close to her ear, "Disgusting hobby, isn't it?"

She nodded. "Take note of all of this," she whispered. "Some day people will be touring the house you're building for me."

"Maybe you should go out and shoot something so that I can hang its head on one of the walls."

"Shoot something?" She gave a mock shudder. "Like what?"

"A particularly vicious book reviewer?"

She pressed her lips together to keep from laughing aloud, then followed the others to the next room. It was warm in the house, and she removed her hat. Fanning herself with it, she glanced back to see Sebastian dawdling by the fireplace, running his lean fingers across the black marble.

The tour progressed upstairs, and Everly was grateful when they stepped out onto the second-floor porch for a breath of cool air. Sebastian seemingly had dropped out of the tour, and Everly didn't have the energy to go to find him. It was the hottest part of the day, just after two o'clock, and Everly noticed that everyone in the tour was dripping with perspiration.

Sebastian rejoined them in the backyard, looking cooler and more energetic than anyone else. Everly motioned him over to a pen that held a dozen or more kittens.

"Hemingway cats," she explained. "They're all over the place. Some of them have—"

"Six toes," Sebastian cut in. "I know. I've been here before."

"Aren't they cute?" She slipped a finger through the chicken wire and touched the velvety nose of a white kitten.

"Our group is going up to Hemingway's office," Sebastian noted, taking her arm and leading her away from the playful kittens. "We don't want to miss that."

"I vaguely remember his office," Everly said, mounting the outside stairs up to the loft room.

"An elevated walkway used to connect this building with the main house," the guide called back to them.

The line of tourists came to a halt as small groups stood outside the open door to Hemingway's office and peered inside. Everly and Sebastian were in the last group, and Sebastian stood back to let Everly lean over the threshold and survey the white room with its gleaming tiled floor. Most of the furnishings were rattan, and, again, animal trophies adorned the walls.

"This is a very macho room," Sebastian said over her shoulder.

"He was a macho man," Everly added, glancing at him. "A man's man."

"Yes, he prided himself on that. You can see that aspect of him coming through in most of his books. He was big on strong male characters and weak women characters."

"Well, there's something to be said for the macho man."

"Do you admire Hemingway?" Sebastian asked.

"Of course."

"Then chew on this," he said, lowering his voice to a hoarse whisper and leaning into her face. "I doubt if Mr. Macho Hemingway would ever have agreed to a platonic relationship with a woman." He drew back, and one dark brow lifted in a haughty salute. "Admirable, wouldn't you agree?"

She stared at him, speechless, and he grinned and started down the stairs. After a moment she followed him, feeling the sting of his biting observation.

The tour ended, and as Everly looked around she was suddenly astonished by the philodendron that grew everywhere—on the ground, from the trees, on the porches, over the sidewalks.

"I'd love to have some of this," she said, dropping to her haunches to stroke one of the variegated, waxy leaves. "Look at how big these leaves are! This one is as large as my hand!"

"You can plant some of that stuff on Little Bit, and in a few years, it will be growing just like this."

"Yes, but *this* is Hemingway philodendron," she explained as she stood up. "It's not just any old plant."

Sebastian threw her a comical look. "Oh, right. How foolish of me!"

Everly wrinkled her nose at him, then moved off in the direction of the side porch. "I'm going to buy a few of his books and some postcards."

Sebastian waited until she'd disappeared from view, then he squatted beside a mass of philodendron, looked around surreptitiously, and chose a thick, healthy vine.

## Chapter Seven

Everly finished the last succulent bite of lobster, then leaned back in the chair and rolled her eyes heavenward.

"I'm positively stuffed," she admitted, smiling across the table at Sebastian. "It was delicious."

"What about dessert?"

"No thanks. Couldn't eat another bite."

"More wine?"

"Yes, thanks."

Sebastian refilled her glass, then topped off his own. "For a little spot in the ocean, there's a lot to see on Key West."

"I'll say!" Everly sipped the dry white wine, then asked, "What time is it?"

He checked his gold watch. "Six-thirty. We've certainly made a day of it."

"You know what I'd like for dessert?"

"I thought you didn't—" He saw her wicked grin, and smiled. "What?"

"My present."

"When it comes to presents, you're like a little kid," he admonished gently. "You really want it now? Shouldn't we wait until—"

"I want it—now!" She held out her hands, palms up, and wiggled her fingers with greedy impatience. "Gimme!"

"Well, there's more than one. During the afternoon, I picked up a couple of other things for you." He leaned sideways and picked up the sack resting beside his chair. Glancing around the restaurant, he paused dramatically, then dipped one hand into the sack and removed a leafy stalk. His eyebrows lifted and fell as a villainous smirk claimed his mouth. "I swiped this for you."

"What is—!" Everly sucked in her breath and grabbed the long vine. "It's philodendron!"

"From Hemingway's yard," Sebastian added.

"When did you get this?"

"While you were buying your postcards."

"Oh, Bastian!" She dunked the rooted end into her water glass, then delivered a tender smile. "You couldn't have gotten me anything I would have wanted more."

"That's only the beginning!" He reached inside the sack again and pulled out a yellow bumper sticker. "I saw this in the post office and couldn't resist. It'll look great on your new car."

She read the black-and-red letters aloud, "Key West. I Went All the Way." A wistful smile floated across her lips, and she whispered as if to herself, "Yes, I sure did." Her gaze lifted to his, boring into the deepest part of him, and he shifted uneasily in the chair.

The waiter came to clear the table, providing a welcome diversion. Everly smiled and held on to the water glass that had become a temporary home for her philodendron.

"Would you like a plastic cup for your...your plant?" the waiter asked.

"Yes, that would be nice."

"I'll get one for you."

Everly laughed, sharing the joke with Sebastian. "I wonder if he knows that he's now an accomplice to your crime?"

"Shh!" Sebastian glanced around cautiously. "You never know who might be in earshot."

"Oh, right." She nodded gravely, then grinned. "The place is probably swarming with Feds."

He reached into the white sack. "Remember the clue I gave you?"

"Yes," she said with a frown. "Not to worry. Some clue."

He removed a small woven straw box and placed it in front of him, then crumpled the sack. Everly leaned closer, examining the red, yellow and green straw box. It had a lid and was no more than four inches wide and two inches high.

"What is *that*?"

Sebastian pushed it closer to her. "Open it."

"I hope there isn't anything crawly in here," she said, prying the lid off. "What's this?" She dumped the contents onto the table, then picked up one of the five tiny figures. Each stick figure was dressed differently. Their clothes were made of cotton yarn.

"Worry pals," Sebastian said, placing emphasis on "pals." "You seemed to want a pal, so here are five of them for you."

Everly gave him a measured glare, then examined each doll in turn. "Where does the worry part come in?"

"When you're worried or troubled about something, you take out these dolls. One worry for each doll. You tell them your troubles, talk it out, then put them back into their box and your worries along with them."

"Not to worry," she repeated, understanding the clue. "This is a great idea. Everyone needs a sympathetic ear from time to time. Now I have five of them." She put the figures back into their straw box, pushed on the lid, then reached one hand across the table to grasp Sebastian's.

"Thanks for the surprises," she said, smiling into his shining eyes. "I won't get rid of these. I'll keep them forever."

"That's a long time." His hand moved on top of hers, curling protectively around it.

"Would you like your gift now? I only have one for you."

"One's enough." He let go of her hand so that she could remove the sack from her purse and hand it to him. He peeked inside, glanced at her, and grinned. "A wind chime!"

"You like?"

"I like." He pulled it out of the sack to look it over. "This looks like something I'd design," he said, referring to the house. "Minus the chimes of course."

"I was thinking that it would be nice if you hung it in one of the trees in that side yard."

"Yes, you're right." He tapped the chimes and listened to their music. "Pretty. When the wind makes them sing, I'll think of you." He put it back into the sack and laughed under his breath. "Of course, I don't need anything to make me think of you. I've been doing it a lot lately."

Her heart stilled for a moment, then beat wildly, sending a tide of color into her face. She gathered up the bumper sticker and straw box, and tucked them into her purse.

"I wonder where the waiter is with my plastic cup," she murmured.

"No comment, huh?" Sebastian asked, backing her into a corner. "I take it that discussion about us is forbidden?"

"I don't see any reason to discuss us." When he was silent, she looked up into his brooding gaze. She breathed deeply, trying to relieve her bout of nerves. "Oh, here he comes." She smiled in relief when she spotted the waiter. He handed her a plastic cup, and Everly transferred the philodendron from the water glass to the cup. "There! Thanks," she said, giving the glass back to the waiter. When he'd left them alone again, she forced herself to look at Sebastian. He was still studying her intently, and she knew he was waiting for her to elaborate on her earlier statement. "Bastian, it's been such a lovely day, let's not spoil it by dredging up the past."

"I have no interest in the past, only in the present."

"And I can't be satisfied with the present until I understand the past," she said, lifting her chin and presenting him with a level no-nonsense stare. If he insisted on this conversation, fine, she thought. But it would take place on her terms. She wouldn't let him shove everything under the rug.

He laid a credit card on top of the bill, and the waiter whisked it away. "What about the past—specifically?"

"I'm still waiting for an apology." She arched a brow at his look of surprise. "That's right. An apology. You said some terrible things to me, and I expect an apology unless, of course, you meant what you said back then."

"You have a memory like an elephant," he said, frowning as he signed his name to the credit card slip. "I don't even remember what I said."

Everly waited for the waiter to move away before she leaned closer to Sebastian and stated succinctly, "You're a liar. You remember what you said, verbatim!"

A wounded expression tensed his face before he looked away from her all-too-knowing eyes. "Yes, I remember."

"And?"

"And I'm sorry for hurting you."

"But you're not sorry for saying them?" Her hands curled into tight fists as she waited for the other shoe to fall.

"In a way." He gritted his teeth and stared at a spot just past her shoulder. "Everly, I wasn't being self-serving. I just didn't think you deserved being hampered by me."

"Hampered? How was I being hampered?"

"Your career was just taking off, and I was going nowhere. You had everything going your way, but I was a shambles."

"Not true." She shook her head in a firm rejection. "You were making progress. Given a little time—"

"Two years. Is that what you call a 'little time?'" He folded the receipt and tucked it into his pocket. "It's only recently that I've got back on my feet and started a new life." He pushed back his chair. "Let's continue this outside where there aren't so many witnesses."

She gathered her belongings and walked outside with him. Night was falling in soft shades of lavender blue and deep purple. Stars sailed into view amid wisps of clouds. They walked along Front Street for several minutes before he finally spoke.

"I was in no condition to take on a permanent relationship."

"What about now?"

"Now?" He stopped, caught her arm, and turned her to face him. "Are you considering that possibility?"

"It's crossed my mind, but it can't be like it was before. I've learned from my mistakes."

"Oh, I see." He looked toward the harbor where a half-moon was cutting a path across the water. "Well, I guess you're determined to drag all of this out in the open, so let's get it over with." Keeping a grip on her arm, he steered her across the street to the harbor and the benches that provided a stunning view of the Gulf waters.

Everly sat down on one of the benches, but Sebastian propped one foot on the seat and crossed his arms on his thigh. The wind ruffled through his hair, lifting it and letting it fall across his forehead. Shadows fell beneath his high cheekbones. A worry line appeared between his eyes, and Everly knew that he was searching for a way to begin. For a while the only sound was the lapping of waves and the sigh of the breeze.

"Okay, let's talk." He looked down into her face with an intensity that was unnerving. "I know what you want me to say, but I want to be honest with you."

"Good, that's what I want, too." She set her purse and the plastic cup to one side, and tried to prepare herself for what was to come, but it was impossible. She had no idea what he was planning to say or what her reaction would be. She stared at his crossed arms, unable to look him straight in the eyes.

"It's true that I was trying to end it—our affair, that is. I told you I felt suffocated, but it was more than that. I felt you wanted something from me that I wasn't able to give."

"Are we back to that?" she interrupted, her eyes lifting to his. "Marriage? That's what you're getting at, isn't it? I don't know what put that notion in your head, but—"

"*You* put that notion in my head!"

"Me?" Her head snapped back and her eyes widened.

"Everly, be sensible. Use that elephant's memory. Don't you recall talking about going out and finding an apartment for us? How many times did you ask me to go furniture shopping with you?"

"Oh, *that*. Well, that's not the same as a marriage proposal. I just thought it would be more comfortable if we found a place of our own. You could simply have said no. You didn't have to overreact! Dad was upset when he found out that we were…were lovers. I was just trying to make you see reason. I wanted us to find a place of our own and—"

"And phrases such as 'find a place of our own' translate into marriage plans, as far as I'm concerned. I tried to be gentle. I tried to make you understand that I wasn't ready for that kind of thing. I didn't know what I was or where I was going. I sure as hell didn't want to drag someone into that limbo with me!"

"But, Bastian, I loved you!" She felt tears well in her eyes as she stared up into his impassive face. "You made me feel as if I were an object! You said that you would have had an affair with anyone at the time and that I just happened to be handy!"

"I know." He ran a hand through his hair in a weary gesture and his voice reflected his inner strain. "I said some terrible things, okay? I'm sorry, but I didn't know any other way to get through to you! It was so—so perfect the way it was, but you wanted to change things. You wanted me to set up housekeeping and you wanted to talk about a future, and I couldn't think about those things! I was recovering slowly, but you didn't understand that. You thought that I *had* recovered, but I hadn't and I knew it." The words tumbled out as if he'd been keeping them bottled up for a long time. "Everly, you were good medicine for me, but I was poison for you."

"I guess I did pressure you," she said, staring at her clenched hands. "I didn't realize it until now. I was so much in love that I . . . I wasn't seeing things clearly. I was taking too much for granted." She glanced up quickly. "But things are different, aren't they? You've got it together. You've got your own business, your own life."

"Yes, but . . ." His foot slipped off the bench and he turned and sat down beside her. Turning sideways, he slipped an arm across the back of the bench, and Everly shifted to face him. He touched her back, tracing the triangle cutout in her blouse. His gaze moved over her face and her hat. "My bewitching Mad Hatter," he murmured softly. "That's how I've always thought of you. You were a fantasy come true; a wonderful character who made me almost believe in . . . in . . ."

"In what?" she asked breathlessly. He was so close that she could feel his breath on her face.

"In things that a grown man shouldn't believe in," he finished and his brows lowered in a stern expression. "Everly, it's difficult to have a lasting relationship without trust."

"You don't trust me?" She moved back, and his hand slipped inside the back opening of her blouse. His hand was warm, but his eyes were cold and fathomless. "When have I ever deceived you? I've always been totally honest with you."

"Yes, you have," he agreed, then abruptly stood up and stepped closer to the edge of the dock. "This is hard for me to say, but it must be said." He paused, looked out at the moving ocean, then continued in the same hushed tone. "I used to believe in faith, trust, honor—all those pie-in-the-sky, all-American dreams, but I don't anymore. After existing fourteen months in that hell, I learned that the only thing I can depend on is me. I can't let myself be vulnerable if I want to survive."

Everly rose from the bench and went to stand beside him. Leaning forward a little, she peered up into his face and stared at this...this stranger before her. Where had he come from? she wondered. There was a haunted, hunted look in his eyes and an uncompromising jut to his chin. He looked as cold as if he'd been born of marble instead of flesh and blood. For a few moments she could think of nothing to say to him, but his last statement smoldered in her mind and brought a question with it.

"Survive? Survive what?" she asked, wondering if he really viewed life as something akin to a war zone.

His gaze shifted to her and it was as frosty as an Arctic blast. "I won't be hurt anymore. I won't be victimized."

"Bastian!" She grabbed his forearms, forced him around, and shook him in a fit of desperation. "Listen to yourself! You're talking like a jungle fighter!"

"If you'd been through what I went through—"

"Oh, stop it! You said that you want to put the past behind you, but you're wearing it like a hair shirt!"

"You don't understand. You haven't survived—"

"Don't preach to me about survival!" She shook with an inner rage that mounted with each word she spoke. "I survived you! After you left me, I was devastated. I felt like a fad that had gone out of style. You put my love for you right up there with pet rocks and poodle skirts!"

"It's not the same, Everly."

"Oh, I see." She folded her arms across her heaving breasts and glared at him. "My pain isn't as real as your pain. My feelings aren't as important as your feelings." She narrowed her eyes and felt hatred knot in her heart like a fist. "Selfish," she hissed right into his face. "I pity you, Bastian. They broke your spirit, didn't they? They beat you into submission. You never escaped their prison. You're living in it right this moment!"

"Shut up!" The tight grip of his hands bit into her upper arms, and his eyes blazed with a wild rage. "They didn't! They didn't touch me! I'm free. As free as this—" His fingers closed around the eagle suspended at his neck. "As free as this eagle!"

Everly stared at the gold eagle and shook her head. "No you're not." She looked into his angry blue-green eyes and her heart constricted with pity. "You're confined to your own, small, empty world."

His lashes fell and a shuttered expression commanded his rigid features. "I think we should go back to the office so you can drive home." His voice was rock-hard. "I knew you wouldn't understand."

"You're right. I don't."

Without waiting for him, she whirled and began walking briskly toward Whitehead Street. Sebastian followed a few paces behind her, and Everly never looked back. She would never look back again, she vowed to herself. The past was full of broken promises that could never be mended. She had been foolish to think differently; so foolish to think that Sebastian could love her if given another chance.

At her car, she unlocked the door and started to get in, but Sebastian placed a hand on her shoulder and spun her around. She pressed back against the car, giving him a wary look.

"I can't help what I am, any more than you can help what you are. Neither of us is perfect."

"So?" She tipped up her chin to see past the brim of her hat.

"So why don't we quit trying to change each other? If I could change the past, I would. I can't, so let's deal with the here and now. I'm glad that you're moving to the Keys. I've missed you." He lifted one hand and let his fingertips trail down the side of her face. "I didn't know how much until I saw you that day at Cabot's Key. It was as if . . . as if the sun had suddenly lifted itself above the horizon. That's the effect you have on me, Everly. You're like a sunbeam in an otherwise gloomy world."

"If your world is gloomy, that's your fault," she snapped, unable to put aside her hurt feelings. He had said that he didn't trust her, so how could she mean anything to him?

"Everly," he almost crooned. "We could be so good for each other. Can't you put down your sword?" His fingers brushed across her lips, and her head snapped back.

"How can we be good for each other when you don't trust me?"

"And how can I be expected to trust you when you won't let me get close to you?" he countered.

"Wait a minute." She propped one fist on her hip and narrowed her eyes in a cagey squint. "Let me get this straight. Are you saying that you'll learn to trust me if I jump into bed with you? I think I've heard this line before back when I was a teenager, but it was different then. It was something like, 'If you *really* love me, you'll sleep with me.' I didn't fall for it then, and I'm not falling for it now. I *have* been your lover, and look where it got me!"

"We're different now."

"I'm different; you're not!" She wedged herself behind the steering wheel and started the car. "You're still saying pretty things with no feeling behind them."

He reached inside the car and grasped the steering wheel, then bent over and thrust his face close to hers. She stared straight ahead, refusing to look at him.

"Listen to me, and look at me when I'm talking to you!" He gripped her chin and forced her head around. "Everything I've told you is true. I didn't want to hurt you back then. I don't want to hurt you now. You mean so much to me, Everly!"

She stared into his eyes and tried to believe him, but all she could believe was that he'd changed. He didn't trust anyone. He didn't *want* to trust anyone. She jerked back her head and his hand fell away.

"Pretty words," she said, spearing him with a cutting glance.

"Go on!" he roared, motioning for her to drive away. "I'm sick and tired of trying to patch things up with you!" He stepped back and his upper lip curled in a snarl. "I'm beginning to think you're not worth the effort!"

She pressed down on the accelerator and the car shot forward. *Don't look back,* she cautioned herself, but she glanced in the rearview mirror and tears for what might have been blurred her vision.

"How does it look?" Cabot Viverette asked, waving an arm to indicate the festive ballroom.

"Fit for a queen," Everly said, stepping onto the highly polished hardwood floor. Her gaze swept over the room that hadn't been used for ten years. Murals graced the walls, each one depicting dancers of bygone eras; some in powdered wigs, others in waistcoats and petticoats. "I always thought it was a shame to keep this room closed off and unused."

"When the house was built, I fully intended to have lots of parties here, but I never found the time." Cabot shrugged and examined a tall vase full of orchids and hibiscus. "This party is a special occasion."

"Is it an engagement party?" Everly asked, whirling to face her father. She smiled at his shocked expression. "Does Katra know?"

"Yes. I proposed over the telephone and she accepted."

"Oh, Dad." Everly went to him and hugged him close to her. "I'm happy for you. I'm sure she's a lovely woman."

"You'll find out for yourself in a few minutes. Lewis went to pick her up at the Miami airport and..." He let go of Everly to glance at his watch. "They should be here by noon and it's eleven-thirty now."

"Nervous?" Everly asked as she straightened Cabot's shirt collar.

"Excited," he corrected. "I'm a little old for an engagement party."

"Dad, don't be silly. Age has nothing to do with love. I'm dying to meet the woman who won your heart."

"She's..." He struggled for the correct word. "Uncommon."

"Uncommon?" Everly laughed lightly. "As in one of a kind?"

"Yes, like you." He kissed the tip of her nose, then stiffened when he heard the sound of a car's engine. "That's her!"

"Calm yourself." Everly grasped one of his hands and led him toward the front foyer. "Your voice is cracking like a teenager going through puberty!"

Katra Kamenski stepped into the foyer and her gentle smile embraced both Everly and Cabot. She held out her hands, and Cabot almost tripped over himself as he hurried to grasp them.

"Katra!" He kissed her left temple, slipped an arm around her shoulders, and looked at Everly. "Katra, this is my daughter. Everly, this is Katra Kamenski."

"Hello. Welcome to Cabot's Key." Everly squeezed the woman's strong hand. "I hope you'll be happy here. By the way, congratulations. I know that etiquette dictates that I should be congratulating Dad, but I think you've caught quite a guy."

Katra's laugh was robust, yet completely feminine. "You're right." She looked at Cabot, then back to Everly. "He's a wonderful man."

"Thanks." Everly laughed, and ran a forefinger down Cabot's cheek. "I raised him myself."

Cabot chuckled, enjoying the joke that was partly true. "We raised each other, I suppose. Everly and I have been inspecting the ballroom. It hasn't been used in years."

"Thanks for giving us a good reason to throw a huge party," Everly said, moving to Katra's other side and linking arms with her. "Come and see for yourself."

When they reached the ballroom, Everly let Katra and Cabot move ahead of her. She stood back to view the couple and decided that they were meant for each other. They were almost the same height, and both had silvery-gray hair and faces that reflected full lives. Katra was dressed in a tailored white suit that, no doubt, bore a designer's label. Her long silvery hair had been gathered into a French twist. Katra turned to face Everly; her gray eyes were alert and her smile radiant.

"All for me?" she asked, laughing gaily. "Are you inviting the entire population of the Keys?"

"Almost," Everly said. "Dad wants everyone to have the pleasure of meeting you. I hope you're not overwhelmed."

"Not at all. People are my passion." She laughed again, throwing back her head. "I've never met anyone that I didn't find absolutely fascinating."

"She's right," Cabot said. "Everyone loves Katra, and Katra loves everyone."

Hearing the click of heels behind her, Everly turned and motioned Miss Martha into the room.

"Katra, I want you to meet an indispensable person here at Cabot's Key. Miss Martha, this is Katra Kamenski." Everly smiled at Miss Martha and added, "Dad's intended."

Miss Martha curtsied, then seemed surprised when Katra stepped forward for a cheek-to-cheek greeting.

"Cabot has told me about you," Katra said, holding Miss Martha's shoulders and leaning back to examine her sloe eyes. "But he didn't tell me how lovely you are! I know many men who would be delighted to meet you."

Miss Martha's lips parted and her skin flushed a deep crimson. "I—I'm pleased to meet you, ma'am."

"Katra," the other woman insisted. "We must use first names because we're going to be good friends."

Miss Martha recovered from her momentary shock and a smile played at the corners of her stern mouth. "That would be nice. May I show you to your room?"

"How kind of you!" Katra slipped an arm around Miss Martha's waist. "I'll settle in and see the two of you later," she said to Everly and Cabot, then left with Miss Martha.

Everly covered her mouth with her hand to keep from laughing aloud. Cabot's eyes shone with amusement and a grin overtook him.

"Poor Miss Martha," he said, chuckling. "She was all prepared to be the courteous servant. Katra doesn't believe in social levels. Everyone is on equal footing as far as she's concerned."

"I like her, Dad," Everly said, kissing his cheek. "I really like her. You're absolutely right. She's uncommon. Delightfully uncommon." She turned slowly, viewing the stunning room. "This party is going to be fabulous! I can hardly wait for Saturday night to arrive."

"Everly..." Cabot's voice contained an edge of uneasiness.

"Yes?" Everly asked, catching her father's worried frown. "What's wrong, Dad?"

"About the guest list..."

"You need help with it?"

"No, I've already sent out the invitations."

"And?" Everly asked, crossing her arms and waiting for him to get to the point.

"And I invited Sebastian. He's already accepted."

Everly held her breath for a moment, warding off a sense of foreboding. "I see." She gave a little shrug. "That's nice. I'm glad he's coming. He's been a good friend to you."

"You . . . don't mind?"

"No." She forced a bright smile to her lips. "It's your party, isn't it? You can invite whoever you like."

"I don't want you to be uncomfortable. I want you to enjoy the party."

"I will." She wrinkled her nose playfully. "Bastian won't spoil anything for me. Don't worry."

"You two aren't speaking, are you?"

"It's not that severe," she assured him. "We just don't have anything to say to each other. We said it all a couple of weeks ago." She turned away, feeling uncomfortable under her father's intense scrutiny. "Have you been over to Little Bit? The house is taking shape. It's going to be beautiful."

"You know, I thought that when you went to meet Sebastian the other weekend, it meant that you two had come to some kind of terms."

"We did." She smiled, but her lips trembled. "We decided to stay out of each other's way. It's best, Dad. Really, it is."

Cabot sighed and stared at the toes of his shoes. "Well, at least you tried."

"Yes . . . we tried." Everly walked briskly to the French doors at the far end of the room, opened them, and escaped into the bright sunshine outdoors. She looked in the direction of Little Bit where Sebastian was working with the crew. So close, but so far away, she thought. Untouchable, and he likes it that way.

One story above Everly, Katra looked out the window of her bedroom and noticed the slump of the young woman's shoulders. Sunlight fell over Everly's face, giving Katra a clear view of her sad expression. She was looking off into the distance, and Katra tracked her gaze, but could see nothing.

"What is over there?" Katra asked, pointing to the south.

"Little Bit Key," Miss Martha answered behind her. "It belongs to Everly."

"Ah, yes. And she is having a house built there?" Katra asked, looking over her shoulder at Miss Martha.

"Yes. Sebastian Dark is the architect."

Katra's dark brows rose as realization dawned. She turned back to the window and looked down at the sad young woman. "Would Sebastian Dark be working with his crew on Little Bit?"

"Yes, he's there almost every day. He supervises and lends a hand when it's needed."

"I see. It is clear now."

"Pardon me?" Miss Martha asked. "I don't understand."

"No," Katra said, turning from the window and smiling at the thin woman dressed in dark somber colors. "But I do."

## Chapter Eight

Everly found a secluded corner of the ballroom behind the orchestra and took a few minutes to view the festivities. Her father had spared no expense, she thought as she looked past the twenty-piece orchestra at the gilded ballroom.

The four crystal chandeliers had been dismantled and cleaned by Miss Martha and the staff. Lewis had gathered bouquets from the grounds, and Miss Martha had arranged them in tall vases and streaming garlands. The hardwood floor had been polished to a glossy finish, and the air was redolent with expensive perfume and spicy aftershave. Three portable bars had been set up in the foyer outside the ballroom, and the parlor had been transformed into a quiet place where the guests could retire from the formal dancing for informal tête-à-têtes.

It was like a fairy tale, Everly mused as she took in the tuxedoed men and elegantly-gowned women. The guest list included fifty friends and associates of Cabot's, and all of them had come. The announcement of Cabot Viverette's impending marriage had caused a stir in literary circles, and everyone wanted to meet the woman who had captured Cabot's devoted attention.

The object of his affection held court across the room from Everly. Resplendent in a rosy creation of silk organza, Katra Kamenski had never looked lovelier. Her silvery hair had been gathered into a French knot, and the minimal cosmetics she'd applied enhanced her natural high color and emphasized her large gray eyes. Everly recognized Cabot's agent, business manager and editor among those who were hanging on to Katra's every word.

How does she do it? Everly wondered. How does a woman make herself enchanting? Maybe it's inbred, she thought. Not something learned, but something ingrained.

Everly sipped her champagne, and shifted her attention from Katra to Cabot. He was dancing with a fellow writer who had made a name for herself by creating page-turning sagas. Everly suspected that this woman and Cabot had been lovers a few years ago, but nothing much had come of it. Until recently, Cabot Viverette had been a hard man to pin down.

Her father looked younger tonight, Everly thought. His tuxedo was a perfect fit, lending him even more sophistication. Everly couldn't remember when he'd smiled so much! He's really enjoying this, Everly thought with a smile of her own. She looked at Katra again, wondering what it would feel like to make a man *that* happy.

A movement at her side drew her from her reverie, and she looked sideways to find that Sebastian was easing around the orchestra platform.

"What are you doing hiding back here?" he asked, sidling up next to her.

"I decided that this is a good vantage point to take it all in."

"Quite a party." Sebastian reached up to check the black bow at his throat. "Can't remember the last time I was at a bash this big."

"I don't think I've ever been to anything quite like this. I keep thinking of Cinderella and Snow White and all those other fantastic stories."

Sebastian grinned and located Cabot on the dance floor. "Cabot is a charming prince tonight. Who's that he's dancing with?"

"Damselle Donner," Everly replied, glancing at Sebastian from the corner of her eye while his attention was still arrested by the other woman. Sebastian was positively mouth-watering, she thought as warmth stole through her. A Prince Charming in the flesh! She looked away quickly when he glanced at her. "She's pretty, isn't she?"

"Who?"

"Damselle."

"Damselle who?"

Everly poked him with her elbow. "Stop that."

"Can I help it if I only have eyes for you?"

She angled a disapproving glance at him. "Remember the story of Pinocchio? His nose grew every time he told a lie?" She touched a fingertip to his patrician nose and his nostrils flared. "Yours just grew an inch."

He took the champagne glass from her, setting it on the edge of the orchestra platform, then he captured her hands and stepped back to examine her orchid, watered-silk gown. She felt self-conscious under his intense scrutiny and she glanced down at the scooped bodice and layered skirt. Sebastian winked and made a clicking sound of approval.

"Smashing." His gaze moved up to the pillbox hat and the veil that stopped at the tip of her nose. "And you're the only woman in the room who was chic enough to wear a hat."

"Chic? How about daring?" She smiled, enjoying his emollient mood. After their last fiasco, she'd half expected him to steer clear of her during the party just as she'd avoided him since that day in Key West.

"Enough of your hiding," he said, pulling her around the platform. "Dance with me."

Her skin tingled when his hand splayed against her back that was exposed by the cut of her gown. His other hand held hers, bringing it against the front of his shirt near his heart. She was at a disadvantage since he was so tall she couldn't see over his shoulder, and there was nowhere to look except at his shirt or his face. She stared at one black button for a minute before chiding herself and lifting her eyes to his. He was smiling as if he knew exactly what she was feeling.

"Do you realize that we've never danced together before now?" he asked sotto voce.

She shuffled through her memory. "You're right! Well, what do you think? Can I cut the rug or can I cut the rug?"

His laughter rumbled in his chest and vibrated against her hand. "I've been on your trail all evening."

"You have?"

"Yes. I thought I'd pass out when that man..." He paused and looked from one side to the other. "That guy over there. The one with the bushy red mustache."

"Gerald Attilier," she said, not bothering to look for him. He was the only one with a red mustache. "He's an old friend of my father's. What about him?"

"I overheard when he asked you your sign and you said—" He chuckled before he could continue. "You said, 'Do not fold, bend or mutilate!'"

Everly tensed her lips to keep from laughing. "That was mean of me."

"It was delightful," Sebastian corrected her. "And then!" He snickered again. "Then he said that he was born in Buffalo, and you said—"

"That's good news for Albany," Everly finished, feeling guilty for being such a smart-mouth. "I shouldn't have given him such a hard time, but I can't tolerate that man. He's been married to a lovely woman for twenty-five years and he plays around on her every chance he gets. Hey!'' She narrowed her eyes and scowled playfully at him. ''Why have you been eavesdropping on my conversations?''

''Just testing the waters,'' he said, adopting an air of mystery.

''Come again?'' She squeezed his hand to get his attention.

''I thought it would be better to observe for a while before I approached you.''

Her gaze dropped to the black button on his shirt. ''Bastian, about that day in Key West. I said some things that—''

''We both said things we shouldn't have,'' he interrupted, drawing her closer to him. ''I'll forgive you if you'll forgive me.''

''I don't understand your outlook on life, but I learned a long time ago not to try to change a leopard's spots.''

The orchestra struck the last chord of the song, but Sebastian kept Everly in his embrace until the next song began.

''One more, shall we?''

''Why not?'' she said, following his lead. ''Have you met our guest of honor?''

''Briefly. Cabot asked me to be his best man at the wedding.''

''He did?'' She felt her eyes widen at the implications. ''I'm Katra's maid of honor.''

''I assumed you would be. Do you like Katra?''

''What's not to like? She's beautiful, intelligent, compassionate. Everything a woman is supposed to be.''

''But do you like her?''

''Of course.'' She leaned back to look up into his face. ''Don't you?''

"Well, I don't know her yet, but I admire her. I've read her work. She's the epitome of courage."

"You should talk with her."

"Why?" he asked too sharply.

Everly's lips parted in surprise. What had put that ring of defensiveness in his voice? "Because she's fascinating," she answered after a moment's hesitation. "She has a dramatic flair that's riveting. When she talks, I find myself spellbound by every word."

He visibly relaxed. "Yes, I'm sure she's quite a conversationalist." He felt her wobble and saw her frown. "What's wrong?"

"My heel." She stopped and looked down at her orchid heels. "One of them is loose and I'm going to break my neck if I don't watch out." She tested the heel. "Excuse me, will you? I'm going upstairs to change into a different pair."

"Okay. I'll wait right here."

She laughed, resting a hand lightly on his chest. "Enjoy yourself. This might take a while. I'm not sure I've got a pair that will match this gown."

Sebastian watched her until she disappeared around the corner, then he turned and found himself staring into Katra Kamenski's unwavering gray eyes.

"Mr. Dark," she said, smiling and taking one of his hands in hers. "I've wanted to speak with you. Do you mind?"

"No, I—"

"Let's step out onto the terrace." She waved her other hand in her face. "I'm wilted!" She turned and pulled him after her. They headed for the open French doors. A few other guests were on the terrace, but they went back inside and left Katra and Sebastian alone.

Katra sat on the low wall that circled the terrace and pulled Sebastian down beside her.

"Ah, this is much better." She shifted sideways to face him. "We're kindred spirits, yes?"

"We are?" He cleared his throat and glanced around for an escape route. He'd avoided Katra all evening, although he'd caught her looking at him several times. Once she had motioned for him to join her, but he'd pretended not to see her. For some reason he didn't want to talk to her. Something in her eyes told him that she saw right through to his soul. There was no hiding from her, no shield strong enough to keep her out.

"Of course. We have wrestled with the Beast and lived to tell about it."

He felt the wound inside him gape open and he stood up and would have moved away if Katra hadn't grabbed his sleeve.

"Please, don't run from me." She turned imploring eyes up to his. "I want to be your friend. Won't you let me?"

"I don't want to talk about that," he said, knowing she grasped his meaning by the sadness of her expression. "Anything but that. I came here to enjoy myself, not to discuss my nightmares."

"So you still have them?" she asked, gripping his hand as if she'd seized a telling clue. "You still battle them?"

He turned his face from her and stared longingly at the French doors. "Please, Miss Kamenski. I don't want to be rude but—"

"Katra," she interrupted. "Call me Katra, Sebastian. I feel as if we know so much about each other. Don't you?"

"No."

"Don't do this," she coaxed. "When a fellow sufferer holds out her hand, don't bat it away!"

Against his will, he moved his gaze slowly to hers, and was caught like a pin to a magnet. He felt his resistance ebb away because she seemed to understand all the pain and fear inside himself. His knees buckled and he collapsed on the wall beside her. He ran his free hand through his hair and wondered what she wanted of him. What did she need to hear? What would satisfy her?

"I look into your sea-green eyes and I see unhappiness," she said, her voice seeming to vibrate around him. "What do you see when you look into mine?"

He didn't want to look, but he did. Her eyes absorbed him. "Peace," he said with a rush of breath.

"It can be yours," she assured him. "All you have to do is accept your past and then it can't hurt you."

"But it does hurt. It changed me. It haunts me."

"That's because you try to submerge it. Don't you know by now that fear thrives in dark places? That it can only be vanquished by exposing it to sunlight?"

He shook his head, confounded by her logic. "I was so naive back then, but I'm wiser now."

"And alone," she added softly. "So alone."

"I have friends," he objected.

"Distant friends," she said, smiling in a knowing way. "You keep them at a safe distance. Do you think they won't understand your anguish?"

"They don't."

"I do."

He listened to the sincerity of her tone, and saw it mirrored in her face. Sebastian covered her hand with both of his and held on to the comradeship she offered.

"What is it you fear most?" she asked. "That all will be taken from you again?" She smiled when he drew a sharp breath. "Do you think you're alone with that feeling? That's why it's taken you two years to finally strike out on your own. You've wanted to, but were afraid to embark on your career for fear it would all be for naught. Lightning can strike twice, yes?"

"Yes, it can. Nothing's forever."

"So you have chosen to live apart from others?"

"I don't."

"You *do*," she insisted. "I've observed you this evening. You stand back and watch others. You've danced with only one person tonight—Everly Viverette."

"She's an old friend of mine."

"Yes, a close friend." Her eyes flashed amusement. "Cabot told me. But my point is this: you observe life instead of living it. Why is that, Sebastian?"

"Because I don't want to be disappointed again . . . hurt again."

"What a defeatist attitude," she chided. "That's like saying that you won't drive a car because you don't want to have a wreck, or that you won't marry because you don't want to be divorced!"

"Look, I can't help what I am." He pulled his hand from hers and stood up, keeping his back to her.

"But you *can* help it. You *must* help it." She stepped in front of him, making him meet her challenging gaze. "Don't think that I haven't gone through the stage you're in now."

"Stage? Is that what I'm about?" he asked flippantly.

"Yes. I was in this stage of recovery for several years, but I finally grew tired of my own company, sick of my own self-pity, and weary of my endless melancholy. I'd like to see you move to the next and final stage of your recovery."

"You talk as if I've gone through major surgery," he scoffed, but inside he was churning with self-reproach. The image she was painting resembled him too closely.

"You have in a way," she acknowledged. "You had a chunk of your life carved out. It can't be replaced, but it can be filled with something else, Sebastian."

He fumbled with his wing-tipped collar, feeling a clammy sweat break out on his skin. "What's the final stage?"

"Acceptance. Accept the past and carry on."

"So easy," he said sarcastically.

"Not so easy, but *necessary*."

"Look here, this is silly." He sighed and looked past her to the dancing couples. "I appreciate what you're trying to do, but—"

"Sebastian, what good is tomorrow if you are unhappy today?"

Her question unnerved him and he realized he had no answer for it.

"Tomorrow, tomorrow, tomorrow," she whispered, standing on tiptoe to command his elusive gaze. "They stretch before you like empty promises. The only thing you can be sure of is today." Her hands gripped his arms above the elbows, forcing him to pay attention. "Embrace it while you can and tomorrow be damned!"

He regarded her for a few tense moments before the words began spilling out, unbidden and frightfully revealing. "Sometimes I want to scream at the top of my lungs for no earthly reason. When I'm happy, I get scared. I think that it could end so suddenly like it did before. I had my whole life planned. I got my degree, I joined the service, I served my country, and the next step was to begin my career and find a woman to love. Then everything went haywire. I had no control. It could happen again, Katra. Don't you see? I couldn't go through it again. I barely survived it. To have everything that means anything to me taken away again...I couldn't bear it." He sucked in his breath and swallowed hard. "How can you trust anything after what you've been through? I admire you, but I don't think I can emulate you. It's not in me. I'm not that strong."

"So now that you've survived, you're going to surrender?" She brought her hands up to frame his face. "Open your heart, Sebastian. Start with me and let me be your friend. You can trust me, can't you?"

Her kindness overwhelmed him, bringing a smile of relief to his face.

"I can try." He wrapped his arms around her waist and gave her a fierce hug. "I'll try," he promised against her silvery hair. "The next stage can't be any worse than this one. You're right. I have been lonely. I suppose when you get right down to it, we're a clannish race and not meant to be alone.''

''That's true,'' she said, laughing lightly as she pressed her cheek against his shirtfront. ''You've lived in your single cell too long. It's time to break out of it.'' Katra was silent a few moments then she said, ''No wonder she frets so over you.''

''She? Who?''

Katra leaned back in the circle of his arms and smiled cunningly. ''Mr. Dark,'' she scolded gently, ''don't be obtuse.''

He laughed with her, realizing that he couldn't hide anything from this woman. She had an uncanny sort of x-ray vision.

Inside the ballroom Everly moved through the crowd in search of Sebastian. She stepped around a couple who were dancing cheek-to-cheek, and saw Sebastian and Katra on the terrace. Everly stood frozen to the spot, baffled by the sight of them embracing each other like lifelong friends. She turned aside, feeling as if she'd eavesdropped on a private moment.

''There you are,'' Cabot said, touching her elbow and frowning when she jumped. ''What's wrong?''

''Nothing. I—I broke a heel and had to change into another pair.'' She lifted her skirt to show off her silver heels. ''See?''

''Yes. Why did you jump out of your skin just now when I touched you?''

''No reason.'' She glanced over her shoulder. Katra and Sebastian were laughing, their arms still around each other. ''Someone has stolen your intended, Dad.''

Cabot looked past her shoulder. ''Hmm. I'd better check this out.'' He smiled, and returned his attention to Everly. ''I was hoping they'd become friends.''

''Well, it looks as if they've hit it off.''

''Jealous?''

Her gaze snapped to Cabot as his gentle teasing struck home. "Of course not!"

"I'm joking!" Cabot held up his hands in mock terror. "Calm down, Little Bit." He looked past her, and smiled as Katra approached them. "Hello, dear. Where's Sebastian? I saw you two out there and I was beginning to get jealous."

"Oh, really Cabot!" Katra linked her arm in his. "Sebastian went home."

"Home?" Everly echoed with dismay. She whirled around to find that Sebastian was nowhere in sight. "Just like that?" She had hoped he would dance with her again. There were still bridges to mend.

"Everly?" Katra placed a hand on her shoulder and turned her around. "I gave him food for thought." She smiled when Everly shook her head in confusion. "We'll discuss it later. For now, let's enjoy the rest of the evening."

"Right!" Cabot slipped his arms around Katra. "This is my dance. All mine."

As they merged with the other dancers, Everly turned away and went to her corner behind the orchestra. Enjoy the rest of the evening? she thought, repeating Katra's words. What was there to enjoy about it now that Prince Charming was gone? This wasn't the way it was supposed to go, she thought with a frown. *She* was supposed to leave before the stroke of midnight, not Sebastian!

Everly could hear the thwack-thwack of hammers where she stood on the terrace. Behind her, the ballroom was silent with not an echo of the festive party that had been here two nights ago. No telling when it would be used again, Everly mused as she sat on the low wall and wondered if she should go over to Little Bit and "accidentally" bump into Sebastian. He was probably over there, she thought with a smile of anticipation. During the party he had been friendly, but it bothered her that he had left so abruptly.

"Am I intruding on deep thoughts?"

Everly turned and lifted a hand in greeting to Katra. "Not really. I was wondering when the ballroom would be used again."

"During my wedding to your father," Katra said, sitting next to her. "You *are* going to be my maid of honor, aren't you?"

"Yes, of course. I'm glad we're using the ballroom again. It's such a beautiful room."

"Were you really thinking of the ballroom or were your thoughts somewhere else? Perhaps on Little Bit?"

"Well, I *was* wondering how the house was coming along," Everly admitted with a sheepish grin. "I was thinking of going over there in a few minutes." She glanced at the other woman. "Would you like to come with me?"

"No, I think you should have some time alone with Sebastian."

Everly tensed and glanced nervously at Katra. "Sebastian? I'm sure he's too busy to chitchat."

"Never too busy for you," Katra said, laughing a little. "I think you've stayed away from each other long enough. What has it accomplished? You need to talk to him."

"What did you say to him the other evening? He left so suddenly. Was he upset or angry?"

"No, nothing like that," Katra assured her. "We talked about our common bond. We've both been prisoners of the times."

Everly slid off the wall and moved to the side of the terrace, her gaze focused on the treetops over Little Bit. "He doesn't like to talk about that, does he?"

"No, but we talked, nevertheless."

Everly smiled, but kept her back to Katra. "You have a way of drawing things out of people. Was that why Bastian was so eager to leave the party? Did he say things to you that he didn't mean to say?"

"I think he wanted to be alone with his thoughts. He's at a crossroads, and I believe he's trying to decide which path to take next."

Everly was intrigued, and she turned to face Katra. The woman wore an enigmatic smile. "What kind of crossroads?"

Katra rose to her feet and her brightly colored caftan swirled around her slim body as she moved to stand near Everly. "He can embrace life or he can shove it away. It sounds silly, doesn't it? What sane person would choose the latter? But it's a dilemma when you've had your life disheveled and have finally rebuilt it. There is a nagging fear that your happiness is only temporary."

"I think Bastian has already decided to live alone," Everly said, then sighed with longing. "I wish I could reach him. I wish he would trust me. He told me that he couldn't trust anyone except himself. He said that his survival depended on keeping to himself." Everly was taken by surprise when Katra slipped an arm about her waist and gave her an affectionate hug.

"There's still hope that he'll realize he needs people. Be patient. Be there for him when he decides to open himself to love and trust again."

"Why is he being so hardheaded about it?"

"He's frightened."

"Of what? Of being happy?" Everly asked, shaking her head in confusion. "That doesn't make sense."

"But it does. The more you have, the worse it is when you lose it."

"What should I do? Should I keep pestering him? Sometimes I think he wishes I'd drop dead."

"No, he doesn't," Katra scolded gently, giving Everly's shoulder another squeeze. "Don't open the wounds, Everly.

Just be yourself and let him see how wonderful it is to be with you.''

"Hah!" Everly frowned. "So far being with me hasn't been so great for him. We always get into a fight.''

"Quit fighting and start loving," Katra said with a teasing smile. "Make yourself easy to fall in love with. You did it once, you can do it again.''

Everly smiled and her thoughts rushed back to New York. "Sometimes I wonder why he fell in love with me, and other times I wonder if he fell in love with me at all. When he left, he said that I was merely convenient.''

"He didn't mean it," Katra said. "You know that in your heart, don't you?''

"Yes, but I wish he'd tell me so! He avoids an out-and-out apology. It's infuriating.''

"Listen to me," Katra said, turning Everly around and giving her a stern look. "You want him to forget his past and start living in the present, yes?''

"More than anything, I want that.''

"Well, follow your own advice! Forget the past and what was said back then. Begin again with a clean slate.'' Her stern expression dissolved into a tender smile. "How many people are given the chance to fall in love all over again? You're so lucky, Everly!''

Tears burned her eyes, and she leaned forward and pressed a kiss to Katra's cheek. "I can see why Dad has fallen in love with you. You're a wonderful human being.'' Everly wiped the tears from her eyes and raised her chin. "Thanks for the advice. I'm going to follow it.''

"Good. Now go over there and find him. Talk to him. Laugh with him. Woo him!''

"Right!" She wilted a little as her self-confidence waned. "I haven't wooed anyone in a long time. Not since Jimmy Smith in sixth grade! I hope I remember how.''

"You'll do fine. It comes naturally when you're with a man who makes your heart sing.''

"Do I look okay?" Everly asked, stepping back so that Katra could examine her blue coveralls and white shirt. "I look like a carpenter, don't I? I should change into something else."

"You look wonderful. Go on!" Katra gave her a little push, making Everly laugh.

"I'm going." Everly stepped over the wall and started for the other Key. She waved over her shoulder at Katra, then concentrated on being lovable. How did one go about that? she wondered. How did she manage it before?

Her fretful thoughts came to an abrupt halt when she came to the clearing and saw that it was no longer bare. A gazebo structure stood in the center of it. Sebastian stood on a ladder that leaned against the wood frame. He wore tight blue jeans, work shoes, and nothing else. Everly started to call a greeting, but the words stuck in her throat as her gaze moved longingly over his darkly tanned chest and muscled arms. He finished hammering in a nail, then reached down into the carpenter's belt strapped around his waist. He must have seen her in his peripheral vision because his hand froze halfway to the belt and his head snapped up.

"Everly! How long have you been standing there?"

"Just a second," she said, having no idea how long she'd been admiring him. "I thought you supervised the crew."

"I do." He reached into a pocket on the belt and withdrew a long nail. "But I'm a carpenter at heart. I thought I'd throw together this gazebo while the crew worked on the house. What do you think?"

"I like it." She moved closer to examine the eight-sided structure. "Will there be glass panels?"

"Yes. Smoked glass so that you can see out, but others can't see in. A bench will run all around it inside." He positioned the nail, gave it a light tap, then a few hard whacks.

Everly drank in the sight of his body, slick with perspiration. He perspires like that when he makes love, she thought, then felt her face flame with embarrassment. Her eyes widened, focused; she noticed Sebastian's bemused expression while he watched her.

"What's wrong?"

"Wrong?" She backed up a step. "Nothing. Nothing's wrong. What could be wrong?"

"Well, I don't know," he said, laughing under his breath. "But you sure look guilty. What have you done?"

"Nothing!" She swallowed and brought her voice down to a civilized level. "I just came over to see how things are going."

"Everything's great." He grinned, shook his head, and withdrew another nail from the pouch. "Are you going to be around later this evening?"

"Why?" She grimaced, hearing her sharp, shrill tone.

"I thought I'd come by after I've finished work. Think you could part with a glass of lemonade for a hot, weary man?"

"Hot?" She felt her skin heat up again. "Yes, sure. I'll be at the house. See you later."

"Hey!"

"What?" she asked as she spun around to face him again.

"Aren't you going to look at your house?"

"House?" she asked vacantly, then sucked in her breath in a sharp gasp. "Oh, my house! Yes, that's why I came over here."

"Well, it's that way," he said, pointing his hammer in the right direction.

"I know," she said, ducking her head and making fast tracks toward the noisy construction crew.

From his high vantage point, Sebastian watched her for a couple of minutes before he turned back to his work. He laughed softly as he replayed the weird exchange. She seems rattled today, he thought, then wondered what was bothering her.

"Women," he muttered. "Go figure!"

Then he hit his thumb with the hammer and blamed Everly for his poor aim.

"Look what you made me do," Sebastian said, holding out his black thumbnail for Everly to see.

She grasped his hand, and looked at it with dismay. "Ouch! That looks painful." Her eyes met his. "How did I make you do that?"

His fingers closed around hers before she could withdraw her hand. "I was wondering what had made you act like a scared rabbit and I hit my thumb with a hammer. See? It's all your fault."

Everly gave him a dubious scowl then looked up at the overcast sky. It was dark on the patio, but light from the windows provided enough illumination for her to see Sebastian's face. He sat next to her on the glider that he had set into a lazy back-and-forth motion.

"No, I don't see. It's not my fault that you didn't have your mind on your work. And I *wasn't* acting like a scared rabbit." Her heart raced as she denied his accusation. Just the touch of his hand made her breathless.

"You weren't being yourself," he insisted. "You acted— in fact, you're acting the same way right now! Are you nervous around me for some reason?"

"No," she said with exaggeration. "Don't be silly. This afternoon I wasn't sure if you might be mad at me. You left the party the other night in such a hurry that I thought I might have offended you in some way."

"Now who's being silly?"

She shrugged. "One minute you were there and the next minute you were gone."

"I'd had enough of the party, that's all. It had nothing to do with you."

She listened to the creak of the glider for a few minutes as she enjoyed the simple act of holding his hand. "Bastian, do you think we could start over with a clean slate, so to speak?"

"Don't see why not," he answered lazily.

She turned sideways to look at him. "I'm willing to forget our past. I mean, I don't want to entirely forget it because most of it was...well, wonderful. But I want to forget the bad stuff. Do you?"

"Yes." He leaned his head back against the cushion then lolled it sideways to see her eager expression. "Yes, I'd like to forget all the bad stuff. There are some things you can't apologize for, Everly. Some things are so unjust or so painful that an apology adds insult to injury. I think it's best if we quit trying to make amends."

"So do I," she said, relieved to have that said and over with. "We can't go back, and I don't want to. I wasn't the epitome of maturity back then. I'm older and wiser now."

"And more beautiful."

Her heart raced again and she wondered if he could hear it pounding away in her chest. "This is my best light." She glanced at the cloudy sky that obliterated the moon and stars. "Total darkness."

"Oh, hush!" He sat up, pulled her closer, and his lips brushed across hers. "Can't you accept a compliment? You never have learned to do that, have you? Let me start again. I'll say, 'You're beautiful,' and you say, 'Thank you.' Got it?"

She nodded, smiling at his stern instructions.

"You're beautiful."

"Thank you, but I've heard that over and over again until I'm simply bored with it." She rolled her eyes and heaved a weary sigh. "Beauty is the cross I must bear."

He chuckled and propped an elbow on the back of the gilder. His fingers moved through the side of her hair, and tenderness softened the planes of his face. "I've missed that, you know. I've missed your sense of humor, your modesty, your wisecracks. Oh, hell! I've missed you."

She started to issue one of her beloved wisecracks, but his lips stopped her. His openmouthed kiss wasn't teasing or tender. This kiss meant business! Everly's eyes closed, and a whimper of relief swept through her. The Sebastian she remembered and had loved was in her arms again, she thought as she wound her arms around his neck and pressed her body against his. Her nipples hardened the moment they made contact with his chest, and she wished he was shirtless as he had been this afternoon. Why did he have to put his shirt back on? she moaned inwardly. She wanted to feel his flesh instead of cotton.

His tongue swept into her mouth, found hers, and parried with it for a few moments before his lips lifted away. His hands moved down her back, slipped under the hem of her shirt, then moved up along her spine.

"Oh, Bastian, that feels good," she murmured, pressing her face in the curve of his neck. His distinctive scent mingled with the smell of wood shavings. She smiled against him. "You smell like lumber."

"You smell sexy," he whispered. His mouth left moist circles on the side of her neck. "Let's go up to your room."

She drew back from him. "We can't."

"Why not?"

"Dad's in there," she said, nodding toward the doors that led into the house.

"Cabot's in your room?"

"No," she said, frowning at his literal translation.

"So, let's go to your room."

"This is Dad's home," she insisted, holding him away.

"So? We made love in his home before."

"We're not going to make a habit of it." She faced front, needing some breathing room.

"Then come back to my place with me." He lifted one of her hands and placed a kiss in her palm.

"No."

"Why not?"

"We just decided to start all over again," she reminded him. "I'm not going to jump into anything."

"I don't get you." He stood up, paced a few steps from her, then whirled around. "What's your game?"

She rolled her shoulders and gave him a cagey grin. "I'm courting you."

*"Courting me?"* he repeated, his eyes wide with disbelief. "Everly, we've already done that. Let's cut through the games and go for broke. What do you say?"

"Oh, no. We agreed to a clean slate. All that stuff before didn't happen. Remember?"

He ran a hand through his hair and cursed softly under his breath. "You led me right into that, didn't you?"

She laughed and stood up. Placing her hands against his chest, she raised herself on tiptoes and kissed his rough cheek. "It'll be fun. The chase is the most exciting time in a relationship."

"Says you." He looked into her dark eyes for a few moments before gathering her in his arms. His mouth molded over hers, and his hands curved around the back of her neck. His thumbs moved under her jaw and found her fluttering pulse. "I suppose I should be grateful that you don't just want me as a friend any longer."

"No, I want more than that from you."

"I'm ready and willing," he said, rubbing his mouth against hers in a grinding, urgent way. "Just say the word and I'm yours."

She felt her resolve waver. She wanted him, she acknowledged, but not now. The time wasn't right. She needed more reassurance that it was her he wanted and not just a sexual encounter.

"I should go back inside," she said, leaning back to avoid his eager lips. "I told Katra that I'd help her with the wedding plans this evening."

"That's just an excuse," he said.

His mouth fastened on hers again and his hands moved up under her shirt to her unfettered breasts. His tortured moan filled her head as he filled his hands with her soft breasts. To her complete surprise, he lifted her shirt and took one of her firm nipples into his mouth. Everly was about to protest loudly, but the tug of his mouth on her breast drove the words from her mind. Her knees quivered and she threw back her head in mindless ecstasy.

"Bastian, we shouldn't." She heard the huskiness in her voice, and it snapped her back to what she was doing and where it was leading. "Bastian, please stop. Please!"

His lips surrendered her tight, throbbing nipple. His face was set in grave lines as he pulled down her shirt and stepped back from her. "You mean it, don't you?"

"Yes, I mean it." She crossed her arms over her breasts. "There's so much we need to talk about before this gets completely out of hand."

"I guess you're right." He puffed out a short breath. "I *know* you're right. Making love was never a problem for us, was it?"

"No, but making sense of everything *was* a problem. It happened too fast before. Let's take it slower this time around." She held her breath, hoping that he'd see it her way.

He picked up the glass of lemonade she'd given him and finished it, then set the glass back down.

"Thanks for the lemonade." His blue-green gaze captured hers. "And thanks for offering me a second chance. Hope it works out this time."

"So do I." She released her breath slowly. "Would you like to stop by tomorrow evening?"

"I'd like to, but I can't. Shipments are coming in and I'm going to be busy the next few days. I've got another job or two I'm working on besides your house."

"That's great! Other houses?"

"One other house. The other job is renovation of a business office on Truman Avenue." He tucked in the hem of his shirt and started edging away from her. "Sorry I got carried away, Everly. I guess you could say that you go to my head."

"Don't apologize for that!" She smiled and lifted a hand to wave at him. "I'll see you around. Don't be a stranger."

"I'll call you. I guess you'll be busy with getting the wedding planned."

"Yes, and we don't have much time. Ten days to plan a wedding for sixty guests!"

He stopped in the shadows, and she couldn't see his face. She squinted, trying to see something besides the glitter of his eyes.

"I never really courted you before, did I?"

"Well, not really," she admitted. "We sort of fell into each other's arms. I suppose it was because we were in such close proximity. We were living together in a way." She waited and when he didn't say anything she wondered if her eyes were playing tricks on her. "Are you still there?"

"Yes, I'm here. Good night, Everly."

"'Night."

She heard him move away, deep into the shadows. He was so like his name, she thought. So mysterious and hard to see through.

## Chapter Nine

Don't you think it's an odd custom to rehearse a wedding?'' Everly asked as she wedged herself beside Sebastian on the love seat in the front parlor. Bursts of laughter and friendly banter filled the room, and Everly leaned closer to Sebastian to make herself heard over the joviality. "I think it's just an excuse for the wedding party to get a free meal and drinks.''

"We should get something for our efforts,'' Sebastian rejoined with a haughty lift of his brows. "Do you know all of these people?''

"Yes, but not well. I know Dad's agent and editor, but the others are just speaking acquaintances to me.'' Her attention was arrested by the revealing cut of Damselle Donner's after-five. "Damselle is in fine form,'' Everly noted with more than a little sarcasm. "She and Dad were an item a few years ago. Did you know that?''

"No, but I suspected it.''

"Why?" Everly asked, glancing at him. "What tipped you off?"

Sebastian's eyes moved to encompass the woman's perfect figure encased in a flame-red dress that left little to the imagination. "She's *too* happy about Cabot getting married. When she smiles, I can hear her teeth gnashing."

Everly laughed, covering her lips with one hand. "Good observation."

"That dress is really something," Sebastian said, then gave a low whistle. "I've heard of backless dresses, but that one comes close to being frontless."

Everly lifted her glass in a toast to Damselle. "When you've bought 'em, flaunt 'em."

"Really?" Sebastian turned, astonished, to Everly. "They're cosmetic, are they?"

"That's what I've heard," Everly said, shrugging it off.

"You don't like her, do you?"

Everly considered her answer for a few moments. "Let's say that I respect her in the way a skin diver respects a shark." She straightened and gave a long sigh. "As much as I'd love to sit here and dish the dirt with you, I should be a good daughter and mingle with Dad's guests."

"I understand. Go ahead. Mingle."

She made a face of regret, then stood up and crossed the room to speak with the minister who would perform the ceremony tomorrow.

Telling himself that he should be congenial as well, Sebastian pushed himself up from the comfortable love seat and was heading for Katra when he was intercepted by Damselle Donner. She parted the sea of guests and headed right for him, and Sebastian thought of a shark gliding silently through deep water.

"Did you know that, with the possible exception of Cabot, you're the most handsome man in the room?" Damselle asked, placing a hand on the sleeve of his white dinner jacket.

"I hadn't noticed," he replied, making a concerted effort not to stare down at her shadowy cleavage. His male sensors picked up her female signals and he couldn't help but feel pleased that she had winnowed out the other men. "Is this your first time as an attendant?"

"Yes, but I bet you're used to being the best man." Her smile sizzled with sex appeal. "I thought I'd met all of Cabot's friends, but he's kept you from me."

"I don't think it was intentional on his part."

"I wouldn't be so sure," she said, almost purring. "I hear that you're an architect."

"That's right." He looked past her and saw that Everly was watching them from the corner of her eye. Uneasiness doused his pleasure at being propositioned.

"And a man with a past," Damselle continued, twirling a long strand of her black hair around her index finger. "An exciting past, I might add. When I read *Wrong Place, Wrong Time* I was burning with curiosity. I saw you on a few talk shows and I said to myself, 'Now there's a man to be reckoned with.'" She let go of the ebony strand of hair and ran the tip of her finger across her full lips. "You designed the writers' colony, didn't you?"

"Yes, that's right." He was trapped, with Damselle on one side and Everly on the other, tugging at him as if he were a length of rope. He knew who would be the victor. Deep inside, he knew that Everly had claimed him long ago. He looked down at Damselle's classic features, and adopted an aloof attitude. "You'll have to stay at the colony sometime. Writers love it." He removed his arm from her loose grasp. "Excuse me, Miss Donner."

He turned away from her openmouthed look of surprise and left the parlor, admitting to himself that he was more surprised than Damselle. When was the last time he'd spurned a beautiful woman's advances? He couldn't remember. Sebastian went to the back of the house to the kitchen area. It wasn't until he swung open the door and saw Miss Martha that he realized his intentions.

"Hello, sweetheart," he said with a warm smile. He went to the center island where Miss Martha was adding finishing touches to a meat and vegetable tray. Dropping a respectful kiss on her cheek, he ignored the furtive glances of the other kitchen help. "Getting ready for the big bash?"

"Weddings," Miss Martha said with a long sigh. "They're wonderful and draining! I won't be sorry when the happy couple head off for their honeymoon. These past two weeks have been murder." Her dark eyes lifted to his. "Don't tell him that I said that. I wouldn't want Cabot to think that I'm not happy for him."

"Your bellyaching is safe with me," Sebastian assured her. "It's been a long time since I talked with my favorite gal. I thought I'd come in here, have a cup of coffee, and enjoy your company, but if you're too busy—"

"I'll take a break for you." She looked at the swinging door. "Shouldn't you be out there with the others?"

"They won't miss me."

"In that case, have a seat and I'll get you that cup of coffee."

He sat at a small table in the corner while Miss Martha poured fresh coffee into two cups. Fatigue was evident in the slump of her shoulders and the deep lines at the sides of her mouth. Poor thing must be running her legs off, he thought. The pace was usually slow and sedate on Cabot's Key, but the impending wedding had supercharged the atmosphere. She sat down across from him, and swept some stray tendrils of hair from her lined forehead.

"After tomorrow things will return to normal," he assured her. "Think you can last that long?"

"I believe so." She glanced at the five others in the kitchen. "I have a wonderful staff. Why have you been making yourself so scarce?"

"I've been swamped with work. Isn't that great?"

"I'm happy for you." She took a sip of the coffee, and pressed one hand to the small of her back in a weary gesture. "I haven't had a chance to look at the house you're building for Everly, but she tells me it's stunning."

"It is. You'll have to come over and have a look at it after the wedding."

She looked at him over the rim of her cup and the corners of her eyes crinkled. "Have you enjoyed those picnic lunches I've prepared for you and Everly during the past few days?"

Sebastian wagged a finger at her. "What are you *really* asking, Miss Martha?"

Her lips pursed to keep a smile at bay. "It's become a daily ritual, hasn't it? Lunching with Everly, that is."

He unbuttoned his jacket, letting it fall open. "To answer your hidden question: yes, I'm enjoying Everly's company. The past few days have been constructive for both of us."

"Will there be another wedding for me to oversee soon?"

He turned his head away sharply, feeling like that damned piece of rope again.

"Sebastian?" Miss Martha strained forward. "I'm sorry. I'm too nosy. I overstepped my bounds and—"

"Don't be silly," he said, facing her again. "We have no boundaries between us." Looking at her sweet lovely face, he felt petty for making her feel apologetic. "I haven't ever told you how much you've meant to me, have I? Well, it's high time that I do." He curved his hands around the cup and let its warmth seep into him. Old habits are hard to break, he mused as his stomach tightened and the need to protect himself surged through him. He made a concerted effort to beat down the feeling and open himself to Miss Martha. Her friendship had been constant when he'd needed it the most. She deserved to know how much she meant to him.

"These past two years have been difficult for me," he said, keeping his voice low so that the others couldn't hear him. "I've had to sort through a lot of things. What I'm trying to say is that you've been a good friend. You encouraged me, listened to me and counseled me in your own quiet way, and I appreciate it."

"Why, Sebastian!" Miss Martha set her cup down in its saucer and fell back in the chair. "I never thought I'd hear you say that. What's happened recently? You've changed."

"I'm trying to change," he admitted. "I guess I've always been comfortable around you because you don't ask much from people. You're reserved and so am I, but I've been *too* reserved, too distant."

"You had a right to be."

"No, not really." He glanced at the others in the room, making sure they were busy with their work and not listening to his heartfelt confession. "When I think of all the people who tried to be my friends, it makes me sad. I turned them all away, but you stuck by me. No matter how remote or self-centered I was, you were there for me. I can't thank you enough, Miss Martha. You're one of the finest women I've ever known."

Her slanted eyes filled with tears and, for the first time since Sebastian had known her, she smiled. It was a genuine warm grin, and it took years off her face.

"I don't know what to say," she whispered, then cleared her throat and removed the smile from her lips. "I'd like to take credit for this change in you, but I think those picnics must have had something to do with it."

"Yes, you're right." He rocked his head to one side in a helpless gesture. "What can I say? Everly Viverette is a persistent young woman. I'd like to think that she's bringing out the best in me."

"She is, and I'm glad."

"Katra Kamenski has been a catalyst for me, too," he admitted. "We share a lot of the same experiences, but she's progressed further than I have. She's so happy. So carefree. I want to be like her. I'm tired of watching my back." He laughed self-consciously and held out his arms from his sides. "So, what do you think of the new me?"

"I like him, but I believe that he's the 'old' you. I always wondered what Sebastian Dark was like before he visited Russia. Now I know."

He held up a cautionary finger. "Not entirely. I'll never be the same man I was back then. I was younger, for one thing, and more idealistic. I'm still a little jaded, and I can't change that." He dropped his gaze and frowned into his coffee cup. "There are some things that I'll always carry with me," he said in a low whisper. "Those things have made me a cautious man. I suppose I'll never be impulsive again."

Miss Martha touched the high collar of her black dress in a furtive motion, then rested her hand on top of his. "Has Everly noticed the difference in you?"

"I think so. It's hard to tell." He looked serious as he thought of the afternoons on Little Bit when they'd shared picnic lunches and discussed her house and how she would furnish it. Although their conversations had centered on things like picking out tile, carpet and wall coverings, he had been aware of the bond growing stronger between them, and he wondered if she had felt it, too. This connection had never been as apparent to him as it was a few minutes ago when he'd rejected Damselle Donner because he felt as if he were cheating on Everly. He combed his fingers through his hair in a moment of confusion, and saw that Miss Martha was observing his silent quandary.

"Something troubling you?"

"It's nothing. I'm just champing at the bit." He smiled when she shook her head. "You remember Maribelle Aimsley?"

"Of course. One of your lady friends."

He chuckled. "One of my 'Key West groupies,' to quote the acid-tongued Miss Viverette. Maribelle called on me the other evening and she was in her usual sex-starved state." He paused when Miss Martha uttered a protest. "Now, come on, Miss Martha. Am I really saying something you don't already know?"

"Go on," she said, swallowing hard and glancing around at the others.

"Well, to make a long story short, I ended up sending her away. Unsatiated, I might add. That's not like me." He hooked his elbow over the back of the chair, scowling at this strange turn of events. "And just now the one and only Damselle Donner threw a pass at me and I let it sail right over my shoulder. *That's* not like me, either. When it comes to women's passes, I've always been a great receiver."

"You've no idea why you're dropping these passes?" Miss Martha asked, readily joining in with the allegory. "Are you missing all the passes, or does it depend on who's throwing them?"

He grinned, delighted that Miss Martha was loosening up and teasing him back. "You might have hit on something." He lifted his lapel to sniff the fragrance of the pink rose pinned there, then he unpinned it and handed it to Miss Martha. She took it and held it to her nose. "Changes can be wonderful or scary. This particular change is a little frightening for me."

"I fell in love once," she said so softly that Sebastian had to strain to hear her. "I was frightened, too."

He was stunned into silence. He'd known this woman for more than two years, and she'd never revealed anything personal to him. Miss Martha in love? Who? When? The questions crowded his mind, but he kept quiet and let the silence draw the answers from her.

"I was twenty-one and I was working at an insurance company. He was my boss and he was married, but he was unhappy." She pressed the rose closer to her nose, letting it obscure the lower half of her face. "He never made any sweeping advances toward me. He was subtle, but I felt his affection for me. One day he told me that he would divorce his wife if he knew I would wait for him."

Sebastian was barely breathing. He realized he was leaning far over the table; he sat back and tried not to appear too eager for the rest of her story.

"I couldn't make myself encourage him. I was so frightened that I could only stare at him. Finally, I turned and left his office. I resigned my position two weeks later." The rose lowered slowly to reveal full lips that trembled ever so slightly. "I've never come close to loving like that again. I can look back now and know that I was on the very brink of a love that would last a lifetime, but it's too late for me. Because I was afraid of what might have happened, nothing happened." She pressed the rose against her heart. "You and I became friends because we had both lost a chance at abiding love. That's what bound us to each other. I understood how you felt. It had nothing to do with the prison you were in, but with the woman you had left behind."

He nodded, suddenly realizing how astute she was. Why hadn't he figured that out for himself? Why was it that women like Miss Martha and Katra could see things so clearly while he groped in the darkness like a blind man? It seemed that he'd been running for a very long time but hadn't made any progress. Running from his grim prison life. Running from the happiness that Everly had offered so freely. Running, running, running on a treadmill that kept him in place.

"No one had to tell me that you were running from love," she continued in that hushed riveting voice. "I could see it. I recognized it from my own experience. I hope you don't run this time."

"I'm not going to," he said with a certainty that surprised him. "Things would have been different back in New

York if I'd been more confident of my feelings. I was about as stable as a puff of smoke."

"Tell Everly that."

"I have!" He looked around, realizing that his sudden outburst had drawn the attention of the others. "She's only beginning to listen to my lame excuses," he said in a more quiet tone. "Lately she's been wonderful. Everything's been better between us. I guess she had a good idea about taking it slow and—"

"Hello, Everly!" Miss Martha stood up so suddenly that she almost tipped her chair over.

Sebastian stiffened, whirled around in the chair and knew that he looked as guilty as sin. "Everly!"

"Sebastian!" Everly mimicked, widening her eyes to mirror his expression. "Miss Martha!" she said in the same startled tone, then propped her hands at her waist and sized them up with alert brown eyes. "So what's going on here? Should my ears be burning? From the look on your faces, I'd say that my ears should be aflame!"

"Now why would we be talking about you?" Sebastian asked, standing up and buttoning his jacket.

"Because I'm a fascinating subject," Everly said without a hint of modesty.

Sebastian grinned and touched a fingertip to her nose. "That, you are."

Everly glanced from Sebastian to Miss Martha, then shrugged. "Well, the party's over."

"It is?" Sebastian asked, then laughed when he realized that Miss Martha had said the same thing.

"It is," Everly assured them. "Damselle Donner asked me where you'd disappeared to, so I thought I'd find out."

"Is Damselle still out there?"

"No, she left a few minutes ago. She asked for your phone number and I gave it to her." Everly threw back her head and laughed when Sebastian delivered a murderous glare. "I'm kidding! She *did* ask, but I told her that there was a handy volume called a telephone directory nowadays, and that your name was probably in it.''

"Sounds as if you were a charming hostess," Sebastian noted dryly, but he was inwardly pleased. "I hope you didn't offend her."

"Offend Damselle Donner?" Everly asked. "Impossible. She laughed in perfectly pitched dulcet tones and congratulated me on one-upping her. She's really a grand *old* gal." She gave a resigned shrug when Miss Martha issued a sound of displeasure. "Well, she's not that old, but she's too old for you, Bastian."

"Is that so?"

"Yes, unless you're into relics."

"If your father could hear you!" Miss Martha said, feigning horror. "He'd be appalled."

"He'd be delighted that I'm such a good student," Everly said, linking her arm through Sebastian's and leading him from the kitchen. "Who do you think sharpened my tongue, Miss Martha? Cabot Viverette is the king of wicked wit."

Sebastian looked down at her as she strong-armed him through the swinging door. "Where are we going?"

"I want you to help me with a little midnight vandalism," she whispered. "Shh. Dad and Katra are in the parlor and I don't want them to hear us leave."

"Leave? What are you up to?" he whispered back, then found himself tiptoeing along the tiled floor with her. She led him to the front door and outside, then took one of his hands and pulled him with her toward the garages. "What are we going to vandalize?"

The night was black, making it hard to see a foot or more in either direction. Sebastian looked up at the cloudy sky, then at the woman who was running ahead of him.

"Dad's Mercedes," Everly whispered over her shoulder. "Lewis is supposed to have put the streamers, tin cans, spray paint and poster boards in the garage this evening. Everything should be all set for us."

"I haven't decorated a wedding car since I was a teenager," he said, opening the side door to the garage then flipping on the overhead light. Cabot's silver Mercedes glinted expensively under the fluorescent lights. Beside it were three sacks. Sebastian looked into one of them and pulled out a roll of white crepe paper. "I don't believe we're going to do this."

"Of course we are! What's a wedding without a decorated car with all kinds of stupid signs taped to it? Here are the tin cans. Oh, good. Lewis has already strung them together. Why don't you attach them to the rear bumper while I sort through this other stuff."

"This is crazy," Sebastian said, but he took the cans from her and tied them to the bumper. When he'd finished, he stayed crouched behind the car and watched Everly tie streamers to the mirrors and door handles. She was still dressed in the flouncy yellow cocktail dress, and she made him think of buttercups and sunshine. He couldn't count the number of times he'd wanted to kiss her in the past few days. Making love to her had been a persistent fantasy that followed him like a shadow. It was playing with him now, making him tense and overheated. He wiped perspiration from his brow and stretched up from his crouched position.

"What now?" he asked.

"Here," she said, shoving a can of spray paint into his hands. "Spray some messages on these poster boards. Be creative."

"Should they be G-, R- or X-rated?"

She considered the choices, then shrugged. "Whatever you feel like."

He bit his lower lip to keep from telling her that he felt X-rated, and had felt that way ever since that evening on the patio when he'd wanted to seduce her. He took off his jacket, folded it, and placed it on the front seat of the car, then he removed his cuff links, and started to put them in his pocket when remembrance stayed him. He held the cuff links under her nose.

"Remember these?"

She stared at the gold cuff links she'd bought him, from one lover to another. "Yes, I remember." She cleared her throat nervously and fidgeted with the ruffles on her skirt. "I bought them at Tiffany's."

He smiled and tucked them into his pocket, then began rolling up his sleeves. "Do you ever wish you'd kept the things I bought for you?"

"I have lately," she admitted, then turned away and said in a bright, almost forced voice, "Let's hurry and get this car decorated. I don't want Dad to suspect anything."

Sebastian picked up a poster board and a spray can and tried to recall the silly phrases he'd seen on honeymooner cars. Hot Springs Tonight? No, he thought with a shake of his head. That wasn't classy enough for Cabot and Katra. He aimed the spray can and wrote in black block letters JUST MARRIED.

"How's this?" he asked, showing it to Everly.

She winced, crinkling her nose in distaste. "Boring and traditional."

"You think of something better," he challenged, handing her the can and another poster.

"Let's see," she said, looking up for inspiration. "How about this?" She wielded the spray can with expertise, then showed him her creation. "'Better Late Than Never,'" Sebastian read aloud. "How true. Give me that can. You've inspired me." He took the spray can from her and grabbed another piece of poster board.

Everly stood next to him, laughing when she saw what he was writing. "'The Wait Was Worth It.'" She nodded appreciatively, and curved one hand in the crook of his arm. "I think they'd agree with that. Grab the last one and take dictation."

"Okay." He picked up the last poster. "I'm ready."

"We . . . Believe . . . In . . . Forever."

He faltered on the "F" and then the "V." His hand began to shake, but he finished the last word somehow. He stared at that word, remembered how it had felt, longed to know that forever feeling again. Forever. His gaze swung to Everly. She was looking at him. No, she was staring through him, and he knew it was useless to try to hide his feelings from her.

"That's a nice word," he said, his throat so tight with emotion that he could hardly get the words out. "Forever. Do you believe in forever?"

"I do," she said. "But you don't."

"I might." The poster board fluttered from his fingers as he lowered his lips to hers. She didn't pull away, but she didn't respond. He opened his eyes and saw that hers were still open. "I want to," he added, then kissed her again.

Everly moved backward and picked up a roll of crepe paper. "Here," she said, tossing it to him. "Let's see how you do with streamers. I'll tape these posters on the car."

"You don't believe me, do you?" he asked, refusing to let it end like this. "You think I'm just mouthing pretty words of encouragement, don't you?"

"I think we'd better get this car decorated before Dad comes looking for us."

"Everly!" He tossed aside the crepe paper, grabbed her arm and swung her around to face him. "Answer me."

She looked surprised for a moment, then she placed her hands on his shoulders and brought him down to her. Her lips brushed across his mouth—once, then twice. "I want to believe you. I've always wanted to believe you, Bastian. The past few days have been good, haven't they? Good for us, I mean."

"Yes. They've been wonderful."

"I don't want to rock the boat. Let's not get into any heavy discussions, okay? Let's keep it light and simple. It seems to work better that way."

"We'll have to get serious sooner or later," he cautioned. He lifted his hands and framed her perfect face. "I never thought I'd say that, but there it is."

"We're both making progress." She placed her hands over his, then turned her face to press a warm moist kiss in one of his palms. "After the wedding, we'll see how we feel about each other. Okay?"

"Okay." He released her, sighed heavily, and retrieved the roll of paper. "I guess we should concentrate on one relationship at a time. Where are Cabot and Katra going for their honeymoon?"

"The Bahamas. Katra has a beach house there."

"Where would you like to go on a honeymoon?" he asked as he played out the crepe paper.

"Oh, I don't know. Someplace . . . simple."

He began draping the paper across the front grill of the car. "Like where?"

She drew a finger along the side of the car and looked over her shoulder coquettishly at him. "A king-size bed."

The wedding day dawned bright and clear, and the wedding guests began to arrive by noon for the one o'clock ceremony. Feeling as if she were sleepwalking through the morning, Everly realized that she was running on pure adrenaline. She stood at the foot of the staircase and clutched her small bouquet of daisies and hibiscus as she waited for the signal from Miss Martha. Damselle Donner and Phyliss Jamison, Katra's friend and literary agent, stood in front of Everly. They fidgeted, giggled nervously, and rose on tiptoes to see the seated wedding guests in the ballroom.

An altar had been placed in front of the French doors at the far end of the ballroom. Guests were seated on either side of a center aisle. The minister waited along with Cabot and Sebastian. The men were dressed in morning coats and gray pin-striped trousers. Katra had ordered the women's dresses from a boutique in New York City. She'd selected simple designs of silk organza with ruffles at the top of each dress. The sleeves were sheer and ended in tight satin cuffs. Everly's dress was ice blue while Damselle and Phyliss were swathed in teal blue.

Katra stood at the top of the stairs, and Everly looked up at the woman's regal carriage. The bride wore a cream-colored satin gown with coffee-colored lace trim at the high neck and cuffed sleeves. A simple wreath of flowers had been placed in her silvery hair, which she had fashioned into a loose, feminine bundle at the crown of her head. Katra smiled down at Everly, then blew a kiss. The gesture brought sentimental tears to Everly's eyes and she batted her lashes to keep from crying.

She caught Miss Martha's signal for the procession to begin, and her heart climbed into her throat as Damselle and Phyliss began their sedate walk down the aisle ahead of her.

Everly was aware of little as she started down the long strip of white carpet. She seemed to be walking through a dream until she saw her father. His mouth was set in a quavering smile, and Everly realized that he was near tears. Such an old softie, she thought, smiling encouragement at him. Then she saw the man standing at Cabot's side and she was wide awake, no longer the numb sleepwalker.

*"What kind of guy do you want, Everly?"*

*"Tall, dark and handsome, of course."*

*"What else?"*

*"Someone who really needs me in his life."*

The adolescent banter she had indulged in with Blaire came back to her. Sebastian was tall, dark and handsome, she thought, but did he need her? She needed him. She wanted him. She loved him. Did it show? Could he read it on her face?

He only had eyes for her as she walked down the aisle, and it was unnerving to be stared at with such open fascination. It was as if he'd never seen her before, Everly thought. His gray cravat moved as he swallowed hard, almost convulsively. As she drew closer, she saw that a pulse was beating wildly in his right temple. Everly heard a collective gasp of awe, and she knew that Katra had made her entrance. At the same moment Sebastian finally tore his eyes from her to look at Katra.

Everly took her place before the altar, then turned sideways to view the approaching bride. Katra was a vision, moving down the aisle as if she were floating instead of walking. Everly felt a tightening in her throat, and she tried to fight off the impending sentiments. She always cried at weddings, but this wedding was going to be a two hanky affair. Her beloved father was taking a wife, marking an end to his bachelor-father life-style; an end to the Viverette twosome. From now on it would be a trio.

Katra handed Everly her bridal bouquet, then kissed Everly's cheek before she took Cabot's arm. The minister began the ceremony and the words rolled over Everly but barely penetrated her consciousness. What consumed her was Sebastian's nearness. She could see him from the corner of her eye and she knew by the tilt of his head that he was looking past Cabot and Katra. He was trying to catch her eye, but she was too full of emotion to look at him. She stared at the minister, watching his lips move, but hearing nothing but the drumming of her heart.

So much for mental telepathy, Sebastian thought as he straightened and faced front again. He had wanted to snare Everly's attention, but she seemed to be in a self-induced trance. Growing tired of the minister's stately drone, Sebastian leaned back a little until he could see Everly again. Her brown eyes were wide and glazed, her lips were relaxed and parted. She was breathing quickly, and the bouquet she held trembled. His heart went out to her even as his pulse quickened in response to her beauty.

That face, he thought with a broad smile. That wonderful, winsome face! In profile her nose was perky and up-tilted and her lips shone with a moist invitation. Her lashes seemed incredibly long, casting shadows across her blushing cheeks. Babies breath was sprinkled through her reddish-brown hair—glossy, thick hair that curled around the back of her neck and fell in tendrils across her forehead.

Cabot turned, nudging him with an elbow, and Sebastian realized that he wanted the wedding ring. Sebastian dipped a finger and thumb into the pocket on his vest and withdrew the simple gold band. He handed it to Cabot, noting the man's trembling fingers, and smiled. He'd never seen Cabot in such a state of nerves, and it amused him. Weddings reduced everyone to a quivering mass of raw emotion, even sophisticated mature men like Cabot Viverette.

Cabot took the ring, and turned back to his bride to slip it onto her finger. Sebastian looked past them and a warm feeling filled his chest when he saw Everly's tear-filled eyes. She blushed, smiled at him, and a single teardrop rolled down her cheek, leaving a glistening path to the corner of her mouth.

In that moment Sebastian knew that she was the most important thing in his life. He had been desperately devoted to her two years ago, and that devotion resurfaced in him. An emotional vise squeezed his chest, crowding his palpitating heart and laboring lungs. Tears burned his eyes, but it was a good feeling. A cleansing feeling.

"I now pronounce you husband and wife. May you keep to your vows. May your devotion to each other be as strong tomorrow as it is today. May the bounty of your love sustain you now and forever. You may kiss your bride, Cabot," the minister intoned.

Sebastian looked at Everly, held her gaze and whispered, "Forever."

Everly blinked twice, not believing her eyes. Had he mouthed "forever" or was it wishful thinking on her part? Sunlight moved through the French doors and across Sebastian's face. His eyes were moist and red-rimmed. Everly's lips trembled and her tears overflowed. He *had* said it! She pursed her lips into a kiss, and one corner of Sebastian's mouth tilted up into a lopsided grin.

Lilting piano music filled the room, followed by a rush of voices. Katra and Cabot embraced Everly, then Sebastian, before they turned and smiled at their other guests.

"Well, it's done," Damselle said as she linked arms with Everly and guided her down the aisle behind the new husband and wife. "You've got a stepmother now. How do you feel about that?"

"Blessed," Everly said with heartfelt emotion. She looked over her shoulder. Sebastian was shaking hands with the minister.

"Don't worry, dear," Damselle crooned into her ear. "He'll be along in a minute. Where Everly goes, Sebastian is sure to follow."

A cool, confident smile rode on Everly's lips. "That's right, Damselle, and three's a crowd."

"He's all yours," Damselle whispered confidentially. "But if you decide not to keep him, point him in my direction."

"Don't hold your breath." Everly grinned, taking the sting from her words.

"You know, I like you," Damselle said after giving her the once-over. "I approve of you." She gave Everly a little push. "Go over there and give your old man a hug."

Everly paused long enough to take one of Damselle's hands within her own. "I approve of you, too. You can take it as well as you can dish it out." She squeezed Damselle's hand, then let go and held out her arms to her father. "Congratulations, Dad. I love you."

Cabot kissed her hair. "I love you, Little Bit. Always have. Always will. Your love is something I've always cherished, but have never taken for granted."

She looked at him through a mist of tears, and a sob choked off any comment she could have made. Instead she gave him another fierce hug, then turned to Katra.

"Welcome to the family, Mrs. Viverette."

"How fitting that you should be the first one to call me that," Katra said, framing Everly's gamine-featured face in her hands. "I'm proud of the name and all that comes with it."

"May I kiss the bride now?" Sebastian asked. He draped an arm around Everly's shoulders as he leaned forward to place a light kiss on Katra's mouth. "Congratulations. I don't think I've ever seen a more beautiful bride." He looked sideways at Everly and pulled her closer, tucking her shoulder under his arm. "Or a more beautiful maid of honor."

They were all called back into the ballroom for a series of wedding pictures before the reception began in earnest. Everyone went outside where two tents had been erected. Sebastian kept Everly close to him through the agenda of cake cutting, gift opening, and champagne toasts.

Cabot removed Katra's lacy garter and tossed it to the group of single men. It was caught by a University of Miami professor who had been divorced less than two weeks. He feigned a swoon when the garter fell into his hands, making everyone laugh and joke about falling from the pot into the fire. Katra flung her bouquet toward the single women, and Damselle Donner almost broke her neck to catch it. Damselle waved it above her head as if it were a trophy, then turned toward the single men and crooked her finger provocatively. Two or three of them stumbled over each other to answer her seductive summons.

Through it all, Everly watched her father and Katra. A few months ago, Everly hadn't even known Katra Kamenski and now the woman was part of her family. She thought of her own mother, and wondered if Katra was anything like her. Katra's robust laughter rode above the din, making

Everly smile. Uncommon, she thought, recalling her father's description. Even Katra's laugh was uncommon.

The sun was low in the sky when Lewis brought around the Mercedes. The guests roared with laughter when they saw the decorated car and its hand-lettered signs. Cabot and Katra, having retired upstairs to change into traveling clothes, emerged from the house and stopped in their tracks when they saw the gaudily outfitted car. Cabot shook a scolding finger at Everly.

"You couldn't resist, could you?" he asked, coming forward and holding out his hands to her.

He looked more like her father in his dark trousers and blue sports shirt, Everly thought. She lifted one of his hands to her lips, suddenly wanting to hold onto him. She wasn't exactly giving him up; she was just sharing him. Forcing aside the pang of selfishness, she nodded toward Sebastian.

"Sebastian helped me."

"I was taken hostage and forced to take part in the scheme," Sebastian said in defense.

"I don't think there's any way we can sneak out of the Keys in that," Katra said. She walked around the car, reading the signs and laughing at each one. She had changed into an ivory-colored blouse and straight skirt, but the wreath of flowers was still in her hair. "I love the signs."

"Everly said you'd appreciate them." Sebastian opened the back door and helped Katra inside the car. "Have a wonderful honeymoon," he said, leaning down to look at her through the open side window.

Katra reached out and drew Sebastian closer. She kissed his cheek and whispered in his ear, "Be happy, Sebastian Dark."

"You, too." He straightened, looked over the top of the car at Cabot, and gave a thumbs-up sign. "She's all yours, Cabot. You're a lucky son of a gun."

"I know, I know!" Cabot eased himself onto the back-seat, then tapped Lewis's shoulder. "Let's go, Lewis. We don't want to miss our flight."

Lewis started the car and drove slowly away from the guests. The strings of cans danced behind the vehicle and the streamers sailed in the air. Everly waved until she could no longer see the car. She felt alone and deserted, but Sebastian's arms came around her and the desolation vanished. His breath warmed her cheek.

"It must feel strange to be sending your father off on his honeymoon."

"Not really," she said, folding her arms over his and leaning her head back against his shoulder. "It couldn't have happened to a nicer guy." She brushed her hands across his sleeves, thinking there was something alluring about morning coats. Men should wear them more often. Not just for weddings.

His arms fell away. "Hey, look at that! The sun's setting."

"Hmm," she hummed, glancing at the break in the trees where the orange ball was dipping into the ocean. "It's been a long, lovely day."

Sebastian stepped forward, smiled at the setting sun, then lifted his hands and applauded the show.

Everly turned startled eyes on him, but her surprise quickly gave way to pride. She applauded, too, and shared the private message in his eyes.

"That's the best way I can think of to end this day," she admitted in a husky emotion-filled voice. "I thought you didn't approve of such silly displays of human folly."

"That was before."

"Before what?" she asked, feeling a smile tease her lips.

"Before you made me appreciate it." He held her hands, swinging them between his body and hers. "Next weekend is the Key West Halloween Fantasy Fest. Want to go with me?"

She tipped her head to one side, puzzling over his transformation from an indifferent bystander to an active participant. He was turning over a new leaf, and she liked the brilliant shadings of it.

"Will you wear a costume?" she asked.

"I'll even let you help me pick one out," he promised.

"Then it's a date."

He pulled her to him and gave her a quick, hard kiss. "This will be my first Fantasy Fest. I always avoided them before."

"Mr. Dark, I do believe you're coming around to my way of thinking."

He bent down, resting his forehead against hers and looking deeply into her eyes. "Miss Viverette, I do believe you're right. In fact, if anyone can change this leopard's spots, it's you."

## Chapter Ten

The tide was in and five feet of water covered the strip of land that connected Cabot's Key with Little Bit Key. Everly untied the shallow boat and stepped into it. She picked up the long pole lying in it, and used it to push the boat through the water like a gondolier.

Things were back to normal at Cabot's Key Estate. Two days had passed since the wedding, and Miss Martha and the staff had restored order. Three writers had arrived that morning, and Everly had acted as hostess, welcoming them to the writers' colony and seeing them to their cabins. The lazy rhythm of the Florida Keys had returned and Everly was glad of it. Herons and gulls swooped overhead. Frogs croaked on the banks. Butterflies and honey bees danced among the tall grasses.

Everly stepped from the boat and secured it on the opposite shore. She stretched her arms above her head, and watched two gulls flirt with each other twenty feet off the ground. A wide path of broken shells had been added to

support the construction machinery, and Everly followed it
to the clearing where the gazebo stood. Sebastian had finished it a few days ago, and Everly loved its tranquillity. She
went inside the eight-sided structure and sat on the marble
bench that ran around it. This had become her favorite
place; it was a hideaway where she could be alone with her
thoughts and her daydreams.

She ran her hands along the cool marble, thinking of how
Blaire would love this place. Everly had spoken to her cousin
and coauthor earlier, and had told her all about the wedding she had to miss because of a flu bug.

"Are you feeling better?" Everly had asked, catching the
hoarse quality in Blaire's voice.

"A little. I'm going to live, cuz, so don't worry. I'm
staying on in Canada for another week before I head back
to New York. Did Uncle Cabot get my wedding present?"

"Yes, he and Katra loved them. Dad admitted that he'd
never slept on satin sheets, but that he was more than willing to try them out."

Blaire had laughed, then coughed violently.

"Are you sure you're okay?" Everly had asked again.

"Yes, yes," Blaire had said after she had cleared her
throat. "I'm taking my vitamins and I've been to a doctor.
You know how these flu bugs are. You just have to let them
run their course. The doctor said that I should be feeling
better in a few days."

"It's just too bad you got sick during your vacation. Why
don't you come here instead of going to New York?"

"I'd love to, but I have to speak at a writers' conference
in New York in a couple of weeks. I'll take a rain check,
though. How's the house coming?"

"It's gorgeous, Blaire."

"And how's the architect?"

"Even more gorgeous, Blaire."

Everly chuckled to herself at the memory, and leaned
back on the bench. The coolness of the marble seeped

through her white cotton shirt and knee-length pants. Falling in love with Sebastian was different this time around, she mused. She had fallen in love with him the first time in a breathless rush. No prelude. No promises. No questions. She'd been young enough to expect things, naive enough to take things for granted. Because they had lived in the same apartment, the fruition of their relationship had escalated. They had recognized their mutual attraction and consummated it in an alarmingly short period of time. Days instead of weeks, she thought.

The slow pace of the Keys had imbued her with a need to go at a sedate, experimental pace. Since the wedding, however, she was positive of her feelings for Sebastian. She loved him . . . again. Everly frowned at that last thought. Again? Perhaps she had never stopped loving him, she amended. No matter what her head had told her, her heart remained constant in its devotion to Sebastian.

She had sought his magic in other men, but hadn't found it. None of her men friends after Sebastian made her head spin. It had been difficult at first to even conceive of dating anyone, but she had finally gotten over that foolish notion. She had allowed her friends to fix her up with men whom they had promised would make her forget Sebastian Dark. None had come close to doing that.

During the months after Sebastian, she had often wondered why he had taken her, sparked a flame in her heart, then let it die. Other men complimented her and flirted with her, but they only served to remind her of the one man who had made her days golden and her nights magic. Several times, when she had closed her eyes to accept a man's kiss, she had made believe it was Sebastian kissing her. She had kept these fantasies confidential, ashamed and angry at herself for allowing such self-punishing dreams.

Sebastian had taught her how to love, and she had come to the conclusion that, should she love again, she would remember him as her patient, tender teacher. If she was a good lover, she had him to thank, and so she was forever beholden to him. No matter that he'd broken her heart, that he had been her first lover won out.

George, the resident heron, entered the gazebo and snapped Everly from her reverie. The white bird walked close to her on its spindly legs, and turned its head to look at her with one of its beady eyes.

"Hello, George. I don't have any fish for you. Sorry, old boy." She sat up, making George squawk and stumble backward. "Don't ruffle your feathers at me. I know you're a big bluffer."

George shrieked again, then ran from the gazebo when it was evident that he hadn't scared Everly.

Everly left the clearing and made her way to the construction site. The house was two-thirds finished. Only a few of the crew were working outside, while the rest were inside completing the wiring, plumbing and insulating. It was a hot day and the crew were mostly shirtless and sweaty. Several waved at her, and the foreman pointed toward the house.

"He's inside, Everly."

"Thanks." She entered through the side of the house where the louvered doors would soon be placed. The openings were covered by dusty sheets of plastic.

"No, we need at least four electrical outlets in this corner," Sebastian was saying, his voice floating to her from the office area. "She'll have a computer, printer, desk light and heaven knows what else."

"You tell 'em, Dark," Everly called, crossing the bare floor to the corner office area as Sebastian spun around to face her. "I'm glad you're looking after my interests." Everly lifted a hand in greeting to the electrician behind Sebastian. "I guess I'm interrupting, but I have to make my daily trip to check up on you guys."

"I'm glad you stopped by," Sebastian said, cupping her elbow and guiding her to a more secluded area. He pulled a handkerchief from the back pocket of his jeans and mopped his face and neck. "Why don't you come into Key West this evening? We need to pick out costumes and I'll buy your dinner while we're at it."

She nodded, letting her gaze drop from his flushed face to his shirt, hanging open and revealing a good part of his chest and stomach. Sweat glistened on him, hanging in crystal drops amid the ebony hair that was matted and damp. "What time?"

"Six is good for me."

"Me, too." She looked to one side where workmen were lugging a marble sink toward one of the two bathrooms. "How are things going?"

"Pretty good." He stuffed the hanky back into his pocket and glanced at his watch. "The energy crew should be here soon with the solar panels for the roof."

She could sense that he was impatient to get back to work, so she waved him away. "Go on. I'll show myself out."

He leaned closer to whisper, "I have to keep an eye on these guys all the time. When I arrived this morning some of the crew were fishing!"

"Ah, the tropics," Everly said with a shrug. "It's so hard to keep your nose to the grindstone when you're in paradise." She indulged in one final glimpse at his gleaming, muscled chest, then forced herself to leave him to his work.

She traversed the high water in her boat, tied it up, and went over to the writers' colony. All the cabins were occupied, and she could hear a few typewriters clacking. Lewis was fussing with some rosebushes near the recreation center, and Everly stopped to talk with him while he pruned the thorny bushes.

"When my house is finished, I'd like for you to help me landscape it," she said, examining the many-colored roses.

"Be glad to," Lewis said, clipping off one rose and handing it to her. "This one's a beauty. It's a peace rose. See the yellow shadings in its center?"

"Oh, how pretty!" Everly lifted the pale pink rose to her nose and breathed in its sweet perfume.

"You gonna live in that big ole house all by yourself?"

"Why yes." She broke off the thorns and tucked the rose behind her left ear. "It's not that big, Lewis. You make it sound as if it's a forty-room mansion."

"It's big for a little girl like you."

Everly shook her head, partly touched and partly miffed by his assessment. "This little girl likes plenty of space, Lewis. Are you going to harp on my singlehood again?"

"I'm not harping. Just making observations, Miss Everly."

"Thanks for the rose and the observations." She tugged playfully at the bill of his baseball cap, then moved off toward the main house.

Lewis wasn't the only one who'd been observing her solitary state, Everly conceded to herself. She'd thought a lot about it lately, telling herself it had been her father's wedding that had spawned her daydreams of being part of a twosome.

She went around the house to the patio and draped herself across the cushioned lounge. Staring up at the bluest sky she'd ever seen, she thought of her recent change of heart. Ever since her affair with Sebastian, marriage had not been particularly attractive. When she thought of it, she reminded herself what all the experts had said about marriage being "hard work." Hard work. Ha! Who needed it? she'd scoffed. She had enough work in her life without adding another "job." All the business of sharing bank accounts, decisions and social lives made her balk. She'd achieved her current status by the sweat of her brow, so why should she share it with someone? She loved her independence!

"Until lately," she murmured to a tuft of cloud that floated into her field of vision. "Until Sebastian Dark came rushing back into my life."

She crossed her arms over her stomach as a sense of restlessness stole through her. Her father's wedding had made her recall childhood dreams of walking down the aisle, of building a life as two, of children and grandchildren. When she outgrew her tomboy stage, she used to speak in excited whispers to her girlfriends about kissing, touching and fumbling in the dark. Marriage had seemed imminent—a foregone conclusion. *Of course* she would marry! She just didn't know to whom or when.

By the time her father had flown to the Bering Strait to pick up a young man who'd been released from a Russian work camp, Everly had begun to doubt the "foregone conclusion." She remembered heart-to-heart talks with Blaire about her own lack of sexual experience. She had worried that she might be an "old maid" since she hadn't come close to feeling lust. Maybe she was too picky, she'd fretted. Maybe she should have taken some of those guys up on their offers. Maybe it was too late! Her ship had passed her by, and she was left standing on the shore!

Blaire had laughed at her, reminding her that she was still a young woman and far from being over the hill. It will happen, Blaire had assured her. It will happen when you least expect it.

"Prophetic," Everly whispered, closing her eyes and falling into a chasm of memory. Blaire had been right on target.

Everly could recall the exact moment when overriding desire had seized her.

It had become her custom to bring Sebastian his breakfast every morning. One such morning she had tapped lightly at his bedroom door and pushed it open, breakfast tray in hand. The tray had tipped over, falling to the floor unheeded as she stared openly at Sebastian's seminude body. He had been in the process of putting on a pair of jeans and he was half-in half-out of them. He had been thinner then, but his long-limbed body was defined by stringy muscles. He had stood, statue-still, for a few moments and had stared at her, his blue-green eyes wide with surprise and his lips parted in a soft gasp.

She had mumbled an apology and backed out of the room, closing the door and leaning her forehead against it while her pulses throbbed in response to what she'd seen—but mostly from what she hadn't seen. Those hidden areas flirted with her imagination and made her blood pressure soar. Common sense had kept her from going back into the room to satisfy her curiosity.

Ten minutes later he had joined her in the living room. Cabot was away for the weekend, they were alone. Everly had quivered with sexual tension, wanting desperately for him to give her a sign—any sign—that he wanted her. Finally he had told her that he couldn't take it any longer. Their platonic relationship had broken into a thousand pieces that afternoon. They had become lovers, and Everly had never been quite the same again. She had given Sebastian something of herself and he, in return, had given her the heady knowledge of her own sexuality.

Everly opened her eyes as the memory became too poignant to bear. She sat up, feeling the throbbing need in her body. She had come full circle. From loving to hating to loving again; from dreams of marriage to appreciation of her independence to a yearning for a permanent someone.

"Forever," she said as tears built in her eyes. "Forever, Sebastian."

Gaiety was everywhere in Key West. It rattled the windows of shops along the main streets and escaped through doorways in bursts of laughter and brilliant color. It crowded the streets and sidewalks, forcing everyone to be part of it. Smelling of hot buttered popcorn and mustard-painted corn dogs, it teased the tastebuds and erupted in memories of family picnics or county fairs.

"There it is!" Sebastian said, pointing ahead to a sign above a small shop. "The Feathery. See it?"

"Yes, I see it." Everly shouldered through a crowd gathered in front of an ice cream store and followed Sebastian inside the mask shop.

The twelve-by-twelve foot room was cramped and full of elaborate masks. A man, who looked like Santa Claus in jeans and a plaid shirt, sat behind a counter and worked on a partially completed mask that stood on a wire stand.

"Hello," he said, glancing up and smiling at them. "Happy Fantasy Fest!"

"Hi. I guess you're Martin Farmer," Sebastian said, leaning one elbow on the counter.

"That's me."

"I read about you in the newspaper," Sebastian explained. "We decided to shop for masks and costumes to match them."

"Great idea." Martin spread out his arms to envelop the small shop. "Who needs an elaborate costume when you're wearing one of these beauties?"

"What do you think?" Sebastian asked, turning back to Everly.

"They're fabulous!" Everly turned in a complete circle, taking in the colorful masks that hung on the walls. They were made from feathers, shells, bones, fur and sequins. "How long have you been doing this?" she asked the craftsman.

"Ten years. I travel between New Orleans and Key West." Martin picked up a long green feather and fitted it onto the mask before him. "Masks free the spirit." His blue eyes twinkled as Everly and Sebastian took his bait and moved closer to him and his current creation. "Normally, you're responsible for your own actions. When you put on a mask, the mask becomes responsible."

"That's a dangerously appealing theory," Sebastian said with a crooked grin. "Where do you get all these feathers?"

"From hunters and from firms that specialize in dying feathers." Martin sat back, eyed his creation, then selected a black plume. His hands were big and beefy, but he worked with swift, pure skill. "I glue them onto cardboard forms that fit over the eyes, nose and front portion of the skull." He stroked his bushy white beard and examined Sebastian carefully. "You'd look good in black, I'd think. And you—" he squinted his merry blue eyes at Everly "—you'd look great in crimson and bright yellow."

Everly looked above his head. "Like that one?" she asked, pointing to a mask behind him.

Martin turned around and located the mask. "Yes. Why don't you try it on?" He lifted it off its peg and handed it to Everly. "There's a mirror down there at the end of the counter."

Everly took the mask from him and located the mirror. She fitted the fanciful creation over her face and adjusted it until she'd lined up her eyes with the corresponding holes. Crimson satin formed the mask and short plumes of red and yellow fanned back from it. Longer feathers draped down along the sides of her face, framing it perfectly. A few rhinestones were scattered throughout, adding sparkle and stardust. She looked like an exotic, rare bird.

"How's this?" Sebastian asked, drawing her attention from her own reflection.

He had chosen a head-hugging mask of black feathers. It made Everly think of Poe's mysteriously elusive raven. The color of his turquoise eyes added to the mystique.

"It's you," she said, grinning at him. "We're birds of a feather."

Sebastian removed the mask with a flourish. "Let's flock together." He wrapped an arm around her waist and pulled her against him.

"Wait!" Everly laughed, glancing over at the smiling craftsman. "Let's pay for these masks before we do anything rash."

They purchased the masks and decided to improvise the rest of their costumes from their own wardrobes.

"Remember," the craftsman said as they started to leave his shop, "once you put on these masks you're different people. Enjoy the chance to toss aside your inhibitions. You can blame it on the masks the next day."

Everly glanced nervously at Sebastian, catching his cunning smile. He liked the idea, she could tell, and she found herself intrigued as well. Maybe it would take something like hiding behind masks before they could really open up to each other, she thought as Sebastian guided her from the shop.

"Where do you want to have dinner?" Sebastian asked, walking beside her.

"Someplace that has key lime pie. I'm craving it for some reason."

"Key lime pie..." He thought for a moment. "How about Mrs. Minever's? She makes a mean pie."

"Great. It's only a few blocks from here, isn't it?"

"Yes, just up the street." He squeezed closer as the sidewalk grew more congested. "These crowds! The Fantasy Fest hasn't begun, but this place is already in the party spirit."

"Years ago Blaire and I came to the Fantasy Fest dressed like Tweedledum and Tweedledee."

"How appropriate," Sebastian deadpanned, then smiled when Everly poked her elbow in his side.

"Anyway, it was the most fun I've ever had. This place is wild and wonderful during Fantasy Fest. It's sort of like Mardi Gras, but more homespun. Are we going to the Pretender's Ball Saturday night?"

"Of course. We'll take in the sights, see the parade, go to the ball then we'll end up dancing in the streets like everyone else. I might not be as fun as Blaire, but I'm going to try."

Everly linked her arm in his, feeling as if they might be on the brink of something wonderful and, perhaps, lasting. "You've always been good company, Bastian. In fact, I'll tell you something if you promise not to get bigheaded over it."

"Well, that's a tall order," he admitted, stroking his chin reflectively. "Okay, I think my ego can handle it. What?"

They were at the entrance of the restaurant. Everly stepped in front of him and made direct eye contact.

"Seriously," she prefaced, wiping the grin off his face. "You're the only man I've been with who has always held my interest. You never bore me." She laughed to lighten the mood and took him by the hand to pull him inside the restaurant. "You infuriate me at times, but you never bore me."

His smile was as golden as the setting Florida sun that spilled deep orange light through the windows of the restaurant. A hostess led them to a table and handed them menus when they were seated. After some discussion, they decided to share a seafood platter with key lime pie as dessert.

"Miss Martha makes key lime pie," Everly said after taking a long, refreshing drink of the lemonade she'd ordered. "But she hasn't made it since I've been back home."

"Back home," Sebastian repeated softly. "Do you really feel as if this is your home?"

"Yes. Why should that surprise you?"

"Cabot has four homes that I know of. Cabot's Key, the penthouse in New York, the beach house in Malibu, and the château in Gstaad. What made you decide that this one was 'home'?"

"It always has been to me. The penthouse is convenient for our work, and as for the others, I haven't been in them but a few times in my life. The Keys have always been home base for Dad and me.'' She paused, debating whether or not she should continue, then decided it was time to pull out all stops and speak her mind. "The only reason he brought you to the penthouse when you were released was because we just happened to be living there at the time. We both had publishing contracts.''

"Oh, I see.''

She regarded his slight scowl before asking, "What made you decide to come to the penthouse instead of going to your own home?''

"My home had been an air force base. By the time I was out of prison, I was no longer in the air force.''

"I meant your parents' home,'' she said, then hoped he wouldn't close her out. It seemed that any mention of the penthouse made him clam up. When he didn't answer after a few moments, Everly wished she could take back the question. "Never mind. I shouldn't have asked. It's really none of my business.''

"No, it's not that,'' he said quickly. "I was just trying to think of a way to explain how I felt back then. I was probably more than a little paranoid and I figured most people would doubt my innocence. I was arrested for spying, and even though it was a trumped-up charge, I was worried that my family might think there was a grain of truth in it. What I didn't expect was my father's attitude. He was glad to see me, but he was . . . well, cautious.''

"How do you mean?'' Everly asked, glad that he was trusting her with this information.

"I told you about how he couldn't understand why I'd sign a confession of guilt.''

"Yes.''

"Well, that's it. I felt uncomfortable around him, and I knew that he felt uncomfortable around me.''

Their food arrived and they lapsed into silence as each selected their favorites from the platter.

"You'd have to know my father to really understand, I guess," Sebastian said after a few minutes of sampling the shrimp and fried clams. "He goes by the book, especially in military matters. Everything is black or white with him. He was disappointed that I'd sign something when I was trained not to do that under any circumstances. In that regard, I felt that I'd failed him. On the other hand, he wasn't successful in obtaining my release. It took Cabot to pull the right strings. Therefore, my father felt as if he'd failed me."

"But you've resolved all of this, haven't you?" Everly asked, but knew by his grimace that he hadn't. "It's still an issue between you and your father? After all this time?"

"I'm discussing these things with you," he explained, "but I've never talked about it with Dad." He nodded at her baleful expression. "Yes, I know. It's stupid to keep this stuff bottled up, but Dad was hurt when I talked to Cabot first about my experiences in the work camp."

"For the book," Everly said, then realized it was unnecessary. It was Sebastian's father she should be telling this to, she thought.

"Yes, but he doesn't understand that. He feels betrayed." Sebastian shrugged and waved his fork as if dismissing the problem. "The strain on my relationship with my father is a casualty. We still love each other, but we're not as close as we used to be." He buttered a slice of bread and smiled at his own thoughts. "Cabot was exactly what I needed at the time; he was sympathetic, calm, reasonable, willing to give me the benefit of the doubt. I was grateful to him for taking an interest in my welfare and I felt that collaboration on a book would, in some small way, pay him back for his trouble."

"But it's a shame that your relationship with your father was damaged," Everly said. "Why don't you open up with him, Bastian? Why keep all this hurt deep inside of you where it can't do any good?"

"I know, I know." He sighed deeply, sadly. "I'm beginning to see the folly in that. For a long time I thought that insulation was the best defense, but I guess I was wrong."

His admission was a blessing to Everly. She wanted to reach across the table, frame his handsome face in her hands and give him a big kiss, but she refrained from it. She pretended to enjoy the seafood, but she didn't even taste it. Her mind whirled with the possibilities. Was this stubborn leopard really changing his spots or would a celebration be too hasty?

"You know, I'm the only black spot on the Dark family's military service."

She frowned, not liking his implication. "I wouldn't call unjust imprisonment a black spot," she corrected firmly.

"No, but it's not a medal of honor, either." He grinned lopsidedly. "However, looking on the bright side, I inadvertently ended my family's rule that every Dark male must serve in the air force before he thinks about a career."

"I don't think being in the air force should be a prerequisite before one can embark on a profession."

"My grandfather was an ace flyer, but the air force *was* his career. My own father served twenty years, received a few ribbons and worked in an airplane factory when he retired from the air force. My younger brother is a pilot with an airline. My family is really big on traditions of all kinds. Christmas, Thanksgiving, the Fourth of July, birthdays, you name it!" He rolled his eyes to punctuate his meaning. "They go all out. Each holiday has certain ceremonies that must be followed with no deviation. I think my grandfather started all this stuff. He was a rigid man who wanted everything done his way and on schedule. Christmas dinner was served at three o'clock exactly. We pulled taffy at five o'clock and opened presents at seven o'clock. Nine o'clock was caroling time. At ten grandmother recited Christmas poems." He smiled, wickedly. "I bet Granddad even made love to Grandma on schedule."

Everly smiled, but sobered quickly. "Did you like all that regimentation when you were growing up?"

"I didn't think much about it one way or the other. But while I was in the work camp, I thought about it a lot. I realized that too much importance is put on a bunch of stuff that doesn't amount to a hill of beans. Who cares if dinner is an hour late? Why should someone be expected to enter a certain arm of the military if it serves no purpose other than to continue a pattern that holds no rhyme nor reason? I swore that if I ever got out of Russia, I'd live my life more freely." He glanced up from his plate, caught her accusing glare, and shrugged his defeat. "I know what you're thinking."

"What? Read my mind," she taunted.

"You're thinking that I haven't lived up to my pledge. I guess it's easier said than done."

"We all have our defense mechanisms. I guess you have a right to be guarded, but you might have taken it too far for your own good. You must know that I'd never hurt you, Bastian. Especially back in New York."

"I didn't think you'd hurt me, Everly. I thought I'd eventually hurt you."

She dropped her gaze to her plate, unable to keep the words from spilling out and unable to look at him when she said them.

"You did," she whispered.

"Yes, I know, but it would have hurt more if I'd stayed." He held up a hand when she started to speak. "No, let me say this and then let's be done with it, okay? I was running scared. I admit it. When we started our affair, I didn't think ahead. I *was* living day to day, but it caught up with me. I realized that you had your life together and you didn't need to play nursemaid to an emotionally insecure wreck of a man."

"You weren't—"

"I *was*," he insisted. "I might not be a shining example of maturity today, but I'm a sight better off than I was then. You have to admit that."

"Yes, you're more stable, more in control," she conceded. "But there were things that I loved about you then that are missing now."

"Like what?"

"Trust, for one. I never did anything to make you not trust me. And another thing," she said, shoving aside her plate. "I can understand your being a little jaded, but you seem to scowl at love and devotion and all those sweet human emotions."

"I used to, but can't you tell that I've changed?" He reached across the table to take one of her hands. "I'm changing for you, and for me. You've made me *want* to reach out again."

Emotion wedged in her throat, and she would have told him that he couldn't have said anything more wonderful, if the waitress hadn't spoiled the moment by clearing off the table. Sebastian let go of her hand and leaned back to give the waitress and busboy room to work.

"We're ready for your famous key lime pie now," he told the waitress.

"I'll be right back with it," she promised, then left them alone again.

When the dessert was brought to them, Sebastian laughed as Everly took her first bite and feigned a swoon.

"That good, is it?"

"Mmm," Everly mumbled, nodding her head vigorously. "Heavenly. A wish come true!"

He was so pleased by her reaction that he insisted on buying a whole pie for her to take home. After paying the check, he was handed the pie while the cashier went into the kitchen to find a box for it.

"You really didn't have to do this," Everly said as they waited for the cashier to return, "but I fully intend to take advantage of your generosity. I'm going to take that pie up to my room and pig out!''

They were standing near the entrance when several noisy customers entered and filled the reception area. One of the young women, who seemed to have had one drink too many, stepped back into Sebastian and jostled him off balance.

Everly only had a moment to react when she saw the pie wobble in Sebastian's hands. She reached out, but was too late. The pie tipped backward, even as Sebastian made a desperate attempt to right it, and slid down the front of his shirt and slacks before it landed with a soft plop on the linoleum.

"Ooops!" The young woman whirled around, saw the globs of whipped cream and lime that decorated Sebastian and made a distasteful face. "Oh, yuck! What a mess you've made!"

"*I've* made!" Sebastian barked at her as he pulled his handkerchief from his back pocket and made a futile attempt to mop off the whipped cream. "You made me do this! You backed into me and squashed this damn pie all over me!"

"Don't blame it on me!" the woman shot back, then moved off with her friends, who had located a vacant table.

"Why, you little—" He shifted his attention from the culprit to Everly, who was doubled over with giggles. "You think this is funny?"

"Y-yes! You should see ... see yourself!" Everly managed between hiccuping giggles.

"Here, share in the fun." Sebastian scooped up some cream and aimed it at her nose, but Everly raised her hands and it smeared across her palms.

"Bastian!"

His aim was better the second time and she found herself looking cross-eyed at the dollop of white cream on the tip of her nose.

"Bastian, you . . . you!"

"Oh dear," the cashier said, returning with a large white box. "You dropped it!"

"It was knocked out of my hands by one of your tipsy customers," Sebastian corrected her, but he was grinning from ear to ear. He licked his fingers and made a discerning face. "Tastes better this way." He looked down at the pie filling that had smeared across the front of his trousers, then back up at Everly. His lips parted, but he shook his head. "I could make a racy suggestion, but I won't."

"Thank you." Everly took a damp rag from the cashier and tried to wipe the gooey mess from Sebastian's shirt.

"Let me get you another pie," the cashier offered.

"No, no." Everly laughed, handing the rag back to her. "I've had enough pie for one night, but Sebastian might want another one."

"No, thanks." Sebastian seized Everly by the hand and pulled her toward the door. "This pie goes great with my shirt. I don't want to push my luck and get one that clashes."

Outside they pried their sticky hands apart and laughed until they were weak and aching. Everly wrapped her arms around her sore rib cage, trying to control her laughter.

"Let's get back to my place so I can change out of this mess," Sebastian suggested, holding his arms out from his sides as if he were afraid they might stick to him. "You're the one who wanted the pie, so why am I wearing it?"

"It looks good on you," Everly said, giving him a thorough once-over. "Lime is definitely your flavor."

"I'll remember that next time I want to wear one," he wisecracked, then leaned toward her and licked the cream off her nose. "It might look good on me, but it tastes better on you."

She felt herself blush, but she was more aroused than embarrassed. "*I* could make a racy suggestion, but I won't.'' She put an arm around his waist, and they set off for his apartment.

When they arrived, Sebastian excused himself and left Everly in his living room while he washed and changed clothes. She thought of the spilled pie and smothered a laugh. It felt good to laugh with him again, she thought as she wandered aimlessly around the room. She heard him moving about in the bedroom as a thought struck her.

"Bastian, the least that cashier could have done was to refund your money since we didn't get to enjoy—'' She sucked in her breath, realizing she'd walked boldly into his bedroom and had caught him with one leg in and one leg out of his jeans. "Oh, I'm sorry. I—''

"That's okay. You've seen the merchandise before.'' He grinned and, holding out his arms, he beckoned her. "Would you like to take advantage of the situation?'' His amusement dissolved when he saw a faraway expression cover her face, draining it of its color. "Everly?'' he asked softly, wondering why she was looking through him instead of at him. He glanced down at his T-shirt and jockey shorts and déjà vu swept over him. The feelings he had felt the first time washed over him. He felt a tremor of awareness in the pit of his stomach that mushroomed into a remembered desire. He reached down and pulled up his jeans, fastening them with shaking fingers.

"It seems we've done this before,'' he said, then shook off his inexplicable shyness and went to her. He placed his hands lightly on her shoulders and bent his knees to stare into her slightly dazed eyes. "You have a knack for catching me with my pants down.''

She smiled, but didn't feel like it. She wanted to go back, back two years when things were less complicated and feelings were strong and intact. It had been so wonderful then. Being in love was the most precious thing in life, and she wanted it again.

"Oh, Bastian," she said, sighing his name. "What happened to us? Why did we have to say such ugly things to one another? Why did we have to change?"

He pressed a warm kiss to her lips as his hands moved over her shiny cap of hair. "Love makes fools of us all."

"Did you love me back then?"

He straightened and reached for his clean shirt. "Of course. I loved you enough to let you go." He jerked the shirt into place and buttoned it.

She shook her head, puzzling over his answer, then brought herself up. She'd stayed too long. It was late and there was nothing more to say.

"I'll see you Saturday bright and early," she said, forcing a cheerfulness to her voice as she moved from his bedroom and crossed the living room.

On the threshold leading into the office area, she turned and leaned back against the door frame. Sebastian filled the bedroom doorway. His hands were propped high up on the frame, taking his weight. He seemed shadowy and remote. She could tell by his brooding expression that he was still thinking of their past.

"It was a fine time, wasn't it?" Everly asked after a few moments.

His smile lifted the moodiness from his face. "The best time I've ever had." He glanced down at his bare feet, then back up to her. "See you Saturday. I'll pick you up."

"A real date?" she teased.

"It's about time, isn't it?"

She laughed at the irony in that. "We do everything backward. First we have an affair, then we break up and then we go on a date. No wonder we're so confused!" Turning away, she left him with the memories they had stumbled over.

## Chapter Eleven

My feet are killing me!"

Everly removed her sandals and examined the red lines the straps had left on her feet.

"I should have worn tennis shoes like you," she said, gingerly massaging her tender arches.

"Here, let me see to them."

Sebastian lifted her feet into his lap, swiveling Everly around on the bench. She leaned back on stiff arms and stretched her legs, sighing when Sebastian's gentle hands began rubbing her tired feet and calves. She lolled her head forward to relieve the weary muscles in her neck and shoulders, and looked around at the others who had drifted to Mallory Square after the Grand Parade. Most of them looked as tired as she felt.

"Are you going to be able to make it to the Pretender's Ball?" Sebastian asked, glancing at his watch.

"Yes. What time is it now?"

"Eight. You've got an hour to catch your second wind."

"You mean my fourth wind," she corrected. "I'm feeling my age. The last time I attended Fantasy Fest I went from one dawn to another with no let up. Blaire and I tore up and down the streets, ate tons of junk food, danced until the wee hours of the morning and were going strong when everyone else was dead on their feet." She bit her lip when his kneading fingers touched a particularly tender area at the back of her ankle. "Look at me now! After a few hours of sight-seeing, having lunch, and watching the parade, I'm drained!"

Sebastian smiled indulgently. "So let's take a few minutes to repair our tattered bodies before we go back to my place to change for the ball." He reached out one hand to tip up the brim of her sombrero-style straw hat. "Feeling better after my expert massage?"

"A little. Are my feet going to blister?"

"What kind of shoes did you bring to wear to the ball?"

"High heels."

He arched one brow in speculation. "Your feet are going to blister."

She shrugged and swung her feet to the ground. "Who cares? I'll live, and I'm not missing the Pretender's Ball just because I'm a tenderfoot." Resting her arms on the back of the bench, she crossed her ankles and gazed at the ocean, golden now in that time between sunset and twilight. "Remember when we'd spend a whole day in Central Park? I hardly ever venture into the park anymore."

"Remember that day we spent on Coney Island? That was fun."

Everly turned her head to see his nostalgic expression. He was looking at the ocean, but she didn't think he was seeing it. She had a hunch that he was watching a replay of their madcap times in New York. He blinked, glanced at her, and seemed to snap from his reverie.

"The parade was great, wasn't it? Which float was your favorite?"

"The Time Machine," she said. "Which was yours?"

He gave some thought to it before answering, "The hot-air balloon, I guess. No, the pirate ship." He chuckled. "All of them. I haven't been to a parade since I was a kid when Dad would take the family to the Fourth of July parade because he always marched in it. This one was better. 'Fantastic Fantasy Voyages,'" he said, repeating the theme of the Key West parade. "What a great idea. I felt like a kid again when the clowns and floats passed by."

"Me, too." She watched him closely, enjoying the lightheartedness in his voice and the excited look in his eyes. She liked him this way, easygoing, companionable, unguarded. He'd been like that all day, and her love for him had grown with each burst of laughter and every uncensored smile. On impulse, she covered one of his hands with her own then laced her fingers through his. "I like us when we're like this. It's like old times."

He met her gaze and his turquoise eyes widened. "You're not going to cry, are you?"

"No." She wiped away her sudden tears. "Well, maybe a little. It's been such a wonderful day—blisters and all."

"And we've got a wonderful night ahead of us," he reminded her, giving her hand a squeeze. "What kind of outfit did you decide on?"

"It's just a red dress. Nothing fancy. What about you?"

"I rented a tux."

"You did?" she asked, her voice rising incredulously.

"You told me once that you couldn't resist a man in a tux." He brought her hand up to his lips for a lingering kiss. "I hope that still holds true."

The weight of an impending decision settled within her, a decision she'd been pressing to the back of her mind all day. From the sparkle in Sebastian's eyes, she knew that she wouldn't be able to postpone the inevitable much longer. From the moment he picked her up that morning, she could tell by the affection he had shown toward her that he didn't expect the evening to end at the stroke of midnight. This was no fairy tale, this was reality, and the reality was that she was a woman and he was a man and the payoff for his patient courting was at hand. His lips pursed again to place another kiss in the palm of her hand, then he closed her fingers around it for safekeeping. Her stomach muscles tightened, making her aware of her own weakness.

A tuxedo! her mind wailed. You know you won't be able to resist him in a tuxedo! What's more, *he* knows it, too!

He reached down and picked up her sandals. Dusting the sand off her feet, he put the shoes back on her, buckling them slowly as his fingers brushed across her ankles and toes. His gaze lifted to her, held there, and sent a sexual message that made her skin tingle.

"I've been thinking about what that mask-maker told us," he said in a low seductive voice. "You remember. That stuff about masks being held responsible for our actions?"

She could only nod.

"I think he might have a point. When I was a kid and used to trick-or-treat, I took on the personality of whatever mask I wore. The year I was a vampire, I flew down the street like a bat out of hell, and the year I was a pirate, I swaggered and waved my plastic sword. Instead of asking for candy, I demanded it."

Everly forced herself to speak. "What are you this Halloween? Your mask makes me think of a raven."

"A raven," he mused, glancing up at the darkening sky. "Mysterious, illusive, brash, cunning." He smiled absentmindedly. "I wonder how a raven will react to a fire bird?"

"Smoke and flames," Everly whispered, feeling the warmth of passion in her soul.

"Yes," Sebastian agreed. He stood up, took her hands in his and pulled her up to her feet. "A powerful combination. Can you stand the heat?"

Her sense of mischief rose to the occasion. "I don't know. I might melt."

"Oh, I hope so."

His mouth molded over hers. He swept off her hat and tossed it aside onto the bench, then, suddenly, she was pressed against him, his hands cupping her hips and fitting her against his stomach and thighs. His lips moved to the side of her neck, seeking out her pulse and the sensitive places there. Everly closed her eyes and leaned back her head, giving him free rein. His hands moved to the small of her back, then around to her waist. She gasped softly when he hoisted her up off the ground. Wrapping her arms around his neck, she held on as he raised her higher until she found herself looking down, instead of up, into his eyes. She laughed, recalling how he used to lift her up like this and then bring her down, down until her mouth met his—just as he was doing now.

She closed her eyes as her mouth made contact with his. Her entire being seemed to center on the kiss as his tongue added that extra something that made her heart leap in her breast.

It was like his kisses of old, more than a meeting of lips and tongue—it was a pledge.

Happiness added fuel to her flames of desire. Everly opened her mouth to receive his tongue caresses that were silken and heartwarmingly familiar. The pain, the disappointments and the anguish dissolved in the light of joy, in the tenderness of the once-in-a-lifetime passion he had given her. In a stirring moment of clarity, she knew that she had dwelled too much on the gloomy side of their love affair when she should have remembered the ecstasy of it all.

His feverish kiss brought all of that back to her, making the decision that had seemed so traumatic a few minutes ago, a simple matter of doing what came naturally.

Her feet touched the ground again and she opened her eyes. Sebastian kissed her tender lips once more before he straightened and stepped back.

"We're good together," he said matter-of-factly, then he picked up her hat and fitted it onto her head. "I've never met anyone like you. You're so many things...so many conflicting things."

Everly adjusted the hat on her head and gave him a winning smile. "Like what?"

"Stubborn and flexible. Understanding and obstinate. Half woman and half waif." He cupped her chin in one hand and smiled. "Sometimes when I look at that face I see a childlike quality, then in a blink of the eye, I see a woman of passion. It's a stirring combination." He looked at his watch, and dropped his hand from her chin. "It's getting late. We don't want to be the last ones to arrive at the ball, do we?"

"No, I suppose not." She sighed, realizing that his heartfelt confessions had come to an end. He had given her insight, making her realize that she puzzled him as much as he puzzled her. "One thing about us," she said, taking one of his hands as they began to walk in the direction of his place, "we're two complex, baffling individuals."

"I can honestly say that there's never a dull moment around you. Sometimes I'd like to shut you up, but I've never found myself nodding off," he said.

"Shut me up? When, for example?"

"When you're dredging up all that awful stuff we went through right before I left New York. I swear, I've never known anyone who enjoys dwelling on the painful past more than you."

"No more." She let go of his hand and settled an arm around his waist. His arm circled her back and he massaged the muscles in her neck tenderly. "I know I've lashed out at you, but I wanted to make you suffer as I've suffered. No more," she said firmly, reminding herself of Katra's advice to let go of the past and the pain. "I'm taking a page from your book, Bastian. I'm going to live in the present. I told you that, remember?"

"Yes, but do you mean it? Can you really put it behind you? A clean slate is easier said than done. I know that from experience."

She looked up into his eyes, eyes that had always held a special appeal for her. "This leopard has changed her spots, too," she promised. "I mean it. We both made mistakes and we're both to blame. You're right; I expected too much of you. I'm right; you could have let me down easier." She gave an indifferent shrug. "But that was ages ago and shouldn't interfere with what's going on between us now."

It was only when he smiled and visibly relaxed, as if he'd suddenly been released from a ball and chain, that she realized the extent of his own regret for having ended their affair so badly.


Everly rummaged through the nightcase she'd brought with her and located her perfume. Spraying it lavishly on her pulse points, she smiled at her reflection in the bureau mirror. She replaced the perfume bottle in the case, then stepped back until she was pressed against the foot of Sebastian's bed. She turned slowly, taking stock of the red satin dress with a slit up one side that reached to mid-thigh. Her red heels and smoke-colored nylons did wonders for her legs, she thought. She presented her back to the mirror, admiring the draped fabric that exposed the curve of her spine, then she faced front again and plucked at the large white off-the-shoulder roses.

It was her favorite gown, and she'd packed it on a last-minute whim although she'd told herself she wouldn't have an occasion to wear it. Thank heavens for whims, she thought with a smile. Miss Martha had pressed it that morning, hung it on a padded hanger, then covered it with sheets of protective plastic. Sebastian had eyed the hidden dress, but Everly hadn't offered to show it to him. She wanted to surprise him. She wanted to see his expression when he saw her in it.

Everly lifted the feathered mask from its hatbox and placed it carefully over her eyes, then tied its long red ribbons at the back of her head for a snug fit. The effect it had on her was magical. She peered through the eye holes, and felt seductive and alluring. She spread out her arms as if they were wings, and her imagination soared.

A tap sounded on the bedroom door, and Everly dropped her arms to her sides. Her heart pounded furiously as she made herself respond in a nonchalant voice, "I'm decent. Come in."

Sebastian opened the door, took one step over the threshold, and stood frozen to the spot. His eyes, behind his mask of short black feathers, seemed to bulge. His throat moved as he swallowed—no, gulped.

*"Just a red dress?"* he said, his voice breaking. "That's what you call that?" He let out a low whistle and moved closer. Taking her hands in his, he positioned her arms out to her sides as his lambent gaze raked over her. "No wonder you had it all covered up and wouldn't let me see it! I don't know if I should let you out on the streets in that. They might arrest you for being too sexy."

She laughed in response to his kidding; however, her attention was not on what he was saying, but on how he looked in his black tux, pearl-gray shirt, red cummerbund and black tie. It occurred to her that he'd added the cummerbund to match the colors in her mask, and his thought-fulness touched her.

"If anyone gets arrested, it will be you," she said, giving him an appreciative smile.

"Am I irresistible?" His hands tightened on hers, pressing for the right answer.

"Irrefutably," she said, tugging him closer for a whisper-soft kiss. When he moved in for more, she leaned back with a laugh. "You'll smudge my lipstick."

"So?"

"So I don't want to go to the ball with smudged lipstick." She let go of his hands and swept her evening bag off the bed. "I trust your carriage is waiting?"

"It is," he said in a moderate tone as he crooked his arm to receive her hand there. "Shall we, milady?"

He escorted her to his car, and she liked his gallant mood as he handed her inside, closed the door, and walked proudly around to the other side. He gave her a knowing look before starting the engine and driving toward the hotel where the Pretender's Ball was being held. It seemed that every car they passed was filled with costumed merrymakers. The streets were clogged with traffic and the sidewalks were teeming with trick-or-treaters. Everly could barely take it all in as ghosts, goblins and witches competed with queens, kings and other members of royalty.

Martin Farmer's feathery masks were everywhere, but each was distinctly different. Everly didn't see any that were exactly like theirs. It made her feel unique for the first time in her life.

The hotel was ablaze with light and color. Sebastian left his car to a valet and escorted Everly inside the busy lobby. Signs pointed the way to the ballroom, but they weren't needed. One had only to follow the music and laughter. The ballroom was on the mezzanine, but the sounds of merry-making filtered down to the first floor lobby. Sebastian gave the doorman their tickets, and Everly went in ahead of him.

It was almost too much for her eyes. Colors whirled as dancers circled the floor in an eddy of movement. Around the pool of dancers, others stood or were seated at tables, their laughter and voices lifting above the tinkling of fine crystal meeting in toasts. The ceiling was obscured by thousands of balloons, with streamers attached to them. The streamers waved in the air, which was redolent with perfume, after-shave and champagne.

And she was about to become a part of it all!

She smiled, thinking of the last Pretender's Ball she'd *almost* attended. She and Blaire had tried to sneak past the doorman, but had been caught and sternly chastised by the uniformed man. They had stood back, watching the costumed couples glide past them on their way to an evening that she and Blaire could only fantasize about.

*"It must be the most wonderful feeling in the world to be in the arms of a man—a masked man—and be whirled around that big ballroom floor."* Blaire tried to see past the doorman and into the lavishly decorated room.

*"Oh, Blaire! Look at them! Look how they dance. They don't seem to be touching the floor!"*

*"I wish we could go in and just watch them, don't you, Everly?"*

*"I wish we had dates. Dates with tickets to the ball."*

*"Someday we will."*

*"You really think so, Blaire?"*

*"Why not? Anything can happen, especially on Halloween."*

"I think we're the last ones to arrive," Sebastian said, cupping her elbow in one hand and dispelling her poignant memories.

"I can't believe I'm really here!"

The throbbing excitement in her voice arrested Sebastian. Everly's eyes were glittering with pleasure, and her lips were parted in wonder as she stared in awe at the finery before her. A bemused smile curved his lips and he shook his head at the complexity of women.

"Do you want to dance or would you rather stand here and drink it all in?"

"No, I mean, yes. I want to dance." She laughed, and it had a nervous, flighty edge to it. "I've always wanted to dance at the Pretender's Ball. As long as I can remember..."

"Then you shall." Sebastian took one of her hands and guided her through the crowd that edged the dance floor. Her hand trembled slightly, and he was amazed that something as ordinary as a Halloween dance could warrant such strong emotion. He'd had no idea how much this ball had meant to her, but he knew for certain as soon as he took her in his arms, and saw her sparkling eyes and sweet smile.

He circled her waist with one arm, bringing her closer to him, and pressed her captured hand to the front of his shirt. Her lashes fell demurely, triggering a desire in him to make this an evening for her to remember. Her steps were so graceful, so fluid, that he felt as if he were dancing with an apparition. If not for the glitter of her eyes and the feather-light touch of her fingers in his hand, he would have sworn he was dreaming.

The white roses on her shoulders enticed him, and he dipped his head and nuzzled one with his nose. Her laughter enveloped him, encouraging his playful streak. The roses smelled of her, lightly scented but long on the memory. His lips touched silky skin and moved up along the curve of her shoulder to the length of her neck. The pulse just under her ear beat frantically. His mouth moved on, across a silken cheek to the moist invitation of her lips. He kissed her lightly, aware of the aftertaste of her lipstick on his mouth, which he gathered with the tip of his tongue. It tasted good so he took a second helping, removing a generous portion this time. After the third kiss, her lips were almost bare. She smiled and rubbed her thumb across his mouth.

"You're wearing more lipstick than I am," she said, her voice husky with laughter.

"I don't mind. I like the taste of it."

Her thumb moved across his lips again. "There," she said. "It's all gone now." She swayed back against his arm. "You know, it's amazing what the mask does to you. I know you're behind there, but I have to keep reminding myself that it's you and not some masked stranger."

"You'd let a masked stranger kiss you like this?" He captured her mouth again, parted her lips with his tongue, and plundered the sweetness within. She shivered in his arms, bringing an answering quiver through him.

"Oh, Bastian," she whispered, leaning her feathered forehead against his shoulder. "I remember this feeling."

"What feeling?"

"Being quivery and full of emotion. Irrational thoughts are flitting through my head. Anything seems possible..." She brought her head up, met his gaze, then stepped back from his arms. "Let's get some of that champagne."

"Champagne?" he asked, thrown into confusion by her sudden desire for drink instead of for him.

"Yes. I'm ... I'm overheated."

"Well, so am I, but—" The rest of his sentence was left hanging as she took his hand and pulled him from the dance floor.

Everly spotted a tray of drinks being passed around by one of the waiters, who were costumed tonight as jockeys in colorful silks. She motioned to the waiter and took two glasses of champagne from his tray, handing one of them to Sebastian.

"Hold on!" Sebastian said, catching her wrist on its way up. "Let's have a toast before this champagne disappears."

She acquiesced and waited for him to think of a tribute. Her throat was dry as if it were stuffed with cotton, and her nerves were all aflutter. On the dance floor, held tightly by Sebastian, she had experienced a wave of longing so powerful that it had frightened her. Should she tell him that she wanted him more than anything or should she keep such shocking revelations to herself? It was wonderful to feel it again—this consuming desire that made her alarmingly aware of her own femininity and the needs of it.

"I've got it."

"What?" she asked with alarm.

Sebastian's eyes narrowed behind the mask. "You said that as if you'd been shot!"

"Go on," she said with a measure of irritation. "Make your toast."

"Your charm underwhelms me," he drawled, one corner of his mouth lifting in a sarcastic grin. He raised his glass and touched it to hers and the ping of fine crystal sang out. "May the night fulfill its promise."

She looked at the champagne, needing it to quench her thirst but apprehensive of the strings attached to it. Her gaze lifted, finding the glint of his eyes amid the black feathers, and she smiled at the yearning that wafted through her. She brought the rim of the glass to her lips and drank deeply. The champagne cooled her parched throat and spread warmth through her body.

"Delicious," she said after taking another drink. "I'll have to go easy on it. I've never developed a tolerance for alcohol."

"Don't worry. You're among friends."

Everly enjoyed his flirtatious smile for a few moments before a movement behind Sebastian caught her attention. A woman, wearing a pompadour wig and an emerald-green gown, stopped beside him and placed a tentative hand on his sleeve.

"Hello, old friend," she said, and it was her high-pitched voice that Everly recognized.

"Maribelle!" Sebastian covered her hand on his sleeve. "How have you been lately?"

"Fine." Maribelle looked at Everly and extended her hand. "I don't know if you remember, but we've met."

"I remember," Everly said, shaking her hand. "Maribelle Aimsley. Nice to see you again."

"I almost didn't recognize you two," Maribelle said, running a finger down the side of Sebastian's mask. "I watched you on the dance floor for a few minutes, but I still wasn't sure. I decided to sneak up behind you, and it wasn't until I heard Sebastian's voice, that I was sure it was him."

"That's what the Pretender's Ball is all about," Sebastian said. "You're not supposed to recognize us." He stepped back to examine Maribelle's costume. "You look great. Who's your date?"

"Bill Curtain. I don't think you've met him. He's one of the Conch Train tour guides." She looked behind her, scanned the crowd, then turned back to them. "I've lost him. He's wearing a scarlet overcoat. He's supposed to be Bach."

"Then you might find him near the harpsichord," Sebastian kidded her, making her laugh.

Maribelle shrugged and squeezed Sebastian's arm. "I'd better go find him. You two make a great-looking couple. I really mean that. Have a good time," she said, including Everly with another smile.

"Bye, Maribelle. Good to see you!" Sebastian raised a hand in farewell, then finished his champagne. "Let's dance again."

"You haven't seen her in a while?" Everly asked, giving him a coy look.

"No, I haven't." He led her to the dance floor again and took her into his arms. "I haven't seen much of anyone since you blew into town."

"I like the sound of that," she admitted, following his lead as he whirled her in a tight circle. She flung back her head, laughing at the sensation. It was almost like flying!

"Oh, Everly!"

She gasped when his lips flamed down her throat, then moaned as the rough velvet of his mouth and tongue became almost too much to bear.

"I want you," he murmured against her skin. "More now than ever before."

Someone bumped into her from behind, jolting her back to her senses. She met Sebastian's gaze and nodded slowly.

"And I want you, but the night is still young. It isn't even midnight!"

"Oh, Everly..."

She kissed his pouting lips. "It's the Pretender's Ball! You know how much this means to me, Bastian. I want to dance until dawn!"

"Dawn," he moaned, then smiled indulgently. "Until midnight, at least. After that, I can't make any promises."

She accepted that and nestled closer to him. It felt good to have their desire for each other out in the open, but it felt better to dance with him. He moved like a dream, and she closed her eyes and let him be her guide.

"How are your feet holding up?" he asked with a chuckle in his voice.

"I'm floating. I don't need feet."

One song drifted into another as minutes formed hours. The room became less crowded as couples moved on to other parties, but Everly remained in Sebastian's arms.

At midnight the balloons were released and drifted lazily from the ceiling. Sebastian caught four of them for Everly, then kissed her into the next day.

A new day, she thought, enjoying his tender, probing kiss. A new beginning.

She didn't resist when he led her from the dance floor to the front lobby and outside into the dark cool evening. The fat full moon sailed across a sea of stars; a Halloween moon of pale orange with a jack-o'-lantern face.

Once in the car, Everly started to remove her mask, but Sebastian stopped her.

"No, not yet," he said, seizing her wrist and bringing her hand back down to her lap. "Let me . . . later."

His request sent shivers through her. She balled her hands in her lap, feeling her palms grow moist as her heart beat in double time. She stared straight ahead, blinded by visions of their past lovemaking. Would it be as good as it had been back then? Had she changed, physically? She glanced down at the low bodice of her dress and felt the stirring of insecurity. Sometimes memory played tricks, she thought. Imperfections are erased and perfection takes their place. Would he be disappointed when she stood before him?

She had no such qualms where he was concerned. If anything, he was better looking than he had been two years ago. He had added some weight and muscle. She had no doubt that she would be pleased by the changes in him.

Sebastian glanced sideways at her, wondering what thoughts were scurrying through her mind. Self-doubt surfaced, making him feel a little queasy. He shouldn't have had that third glass of champagne, he thought belatedly. He needed a clear head. He had to be at his best. He couldn't disappoint her. He'd put on about ten pounds in the two years since he and Everly had parted. Worry tackled his self-confidence and he rolled his eyes in disgust. Too late for evaluations, pal, he told himself. It's the witching hour.

He looked up at the moon and rubbed his chin reflectively, feeling the scrape of his beard's stubble. Should he shave before...? No. That would make it seem too practiced, too cut and dried.

"You just passed your apartment," Everly said, slicing into his thoughts.

"I did?" He whipped his head around and saw the light outside his office building wink at him. "Oh, hell! I had my head in the clouds." He steered around the corner, feeling like a complete idiot. He looked at Everly's pixie smile and told himself to ease up. It wasn't his first time, so why was he acting like it was?

"You're not nervous, are you?" she asked.

"No!" His voice soared up to a grating register and he felt his face redden under his mask. "No, of course not," he said in a more manly baritone. "Are you?"

"No more than I was the first time I was considering this," she said, angling a grin at him. "And I was a basket case then."

He parked the car, but didn't get out. Instead he turned toward her, sliding one knee onto the seat. "You could have fooled me. I thought I was the nervous one then."

"You? Mister-Cool-As-A-Cucumber?" She laughed, leaning forward and touching her forehead to his. "You were wonderful. I never thanked you for being so gentle with me that first time. Thank you, Bastian. Thank you for making it so wonderful, so magical."

"Thank you, Everly."

"For what?" she asked, the feathers on her forehead still mingling with his.

"For being my savior. I never thanked you for that, either."

"Savior? Me?"

He fell back against the door and his eyes glinted in the dim interior of the car. "Men are vain creatures, Everly. When we don't have sex for, say two or three weeks, we begin to wonder if we can do it again. Can you imagine my doubts after being deprived for more than fourteen months?" He whistled and his head moved slowly from side to side. "I was petrified." His smile was wide and radiant, his teeth white in contrast with his black mask. "Until there was you."

"Bastian, I never knew that you had any... any doubts in that department."

"Well, it's not something a man likes to discuss with his prospective lovers. I knew you were a little nervous about making love, and I didn't think it would help if I told you that I was doubting my own abilities." He chuckled and it was a warm, deep sound. "But I'll confess, when I felt that first stirring you-know-where, it was all I could do not to shout for joy!"

"When did you... feel that stirring?" she asked, burning with curiosity.

He reached out to stroke one of the long red feathers that ran along her cheek. "The first morning you brought breakfast in to me."

"That soon?" Her lips parted in surprise. "Why, that was the first day you were with us!"

"Yes, it was. You came in—I remember exactly what you were wearing. Blue jeans—tight and sexy—and a Columbia University sweatshirt—loose and tantalizing. You set the tray on the bed and I could smell your perfume. That did it. That's all it took. I caught the proverbial scent and I was back on the trail again!" He laughed at her obvious embarrassment.

"Then why did it take you so long to follow through?" she asked after a few moments.

"It was the 'follow through' that made me doubt myself. I didn't want to come on like a semitrailer. Not with you. I had to be sure that you wanted me as much as I wanted you, but you were hard to read. Of course, I was a little out of practice, but you were a puzzle. At times I thought you really liked me, but I wasn't sure you liked me in *that* way.''

"Until I walked in on you that day." She grinned mischievously at him. "Caught you with your pants down, so to speak."

"Exactly. The way you looked at me, I knew." His gaze moved slightly, taking in her partially hidden features. "Like you're looking at me now." He gripped the back of the seat with one hand and pulled himself forward. His mouth covered hers and her lips trembled beneath his. "Do you think we should go in now?"

Her breath was warm on his face as she laughed softly. "I think we'd better."

He reached across her and unlatched her door, then he opened his own and unfolded himself from the M.G. and locked it. She stood at the front door, waiting for him, looking for all the world like a cardinal sitting in a rosebush. He shook his head as the cockeyed fantasy overtook him.

*Heaven knows what I look like to her,* he thought as he fumbled with his key and finally managed to unlock the front door. *Probably like a clumsy penguin.*

Pushing open the door, he extended an arm in a gallant sweep. "After you. Welcome to my humble abode. It might look like an office, but if you'll go straight through, you'll find a charming apartment."

"I know my way," she said over her shoulder. "I've been here before. In fact, my clothes are scattered all over your bed."

"Already?" He slipped his keys into his pocket and followed her through the dim office area. She turned on the light in the living room and tossed her purse onto the coffee table. "Make yourself at home," he said. "Want a drink?"

"No, I've had enough drinks for one evening." She wandered over to the window and looked up. Moonlight spilled across her face, giving it an otherworldly cast. Sebastian could see her lashes peeking out from the mask.

"I've never made love to a bird before," he said, wanting to ease the tension that seemed to quiver within him like plucked strings on a harp—many-colored and sweetly tuned.

"How do birds make love?" she asked, angling a sly glance at him.

"Too quickly for my taste," he teased back. *Like old times,* he thought. *We made beautiful, whimsical music together then and now.*

Passion stroked the taut strings within him again, and the music swelled, making him move in time with it until he was behind her. He placed his hands on either side of her neck. She didn't move a muscle. His hands moved down to the gentle swelling of her breasts above the tight bodice. Her head tipped back against his shoulder. His fingers moved inside the bodice, and she turned slowly in his arms and sought his mouth.

Her lips clung to his, moist and pliant. Sebastian thought he would die from the pleasure of her. His fingers found the bow at the back of her head and he pulled it slowly until he felt that last tug of resistance. Leaning back, he caught the mask in one hand and looked upon the face behind it; the face that had been behind every good thing in his life since he'd first laid eyes on it. His gaze caressed the freckles across her pert nose, the bloom of color in her cheeks, the dark umber of her enormous eyes.

He reached behind his head, untied his mask, and threw it aside.

"No more masks for us, Everly." He took her hands and walked backward toward the bedroom, letting memory guide him around the coffee table and chair. "I won't hide behind anything tonight."

"Neither will I," she vowed, then laughed when he backed into the bed and stumbled. "Dis must be de place," she said in an exaggerated Bronx accent. She leaned sideways to view her scattered clothing. "Let me fold those clothes and get them out of the way."

"No, allow me." He let go of her, whirled around and, in one giant swing, swept the clothing off the bed and onto the floor. "There," he said, turning back to her. "Where were we?"

"They'll wrinkle!" she protested, then surrendered as his hands smoothed down her arms and left goose bumps in their wake. She shrugged indifferently. "Right. Who cares?"

"I'd like to pluck these roses," he murmured as his hands closed on them. He dipped his nose into one as his hands moved behind her and found the zipper. He slid it down in one quick movement that brought a gasp from her. He slipped his hands up her arms again, grasped the white fabric roses and pushed them down her slim arms.

It was his turn to gasp.

The sight of her bare breasts sent a spasm of desire through him that settled in his loins.

She'd never in her life fainted, but she came close to it as his lips tugged at her and his teeth scraped against her sensitized flesh. She was faintly aware of him shoving her dress over her hips until it pooled around her ankles. By rote, she stepped out of it. By rote, he removed her half-slip, but was foiled by her panty hose.

Laughing lightly, she sat on the bed and wiggled out of the filmy black nylons, while he shrugged out of his tux jacket and untied the bow at his throat. Feeling self-conscious, she crossed her arms over her breasts and couldn't bring herself to remove her panties, even though they were brief and covered precious little.

Sebastian unbuttoned his shirt, removed the cuff links that Everly had given to him, and carefully placed the links on top of the bureau. The shirt was flung haphazardly toward a chair, missed it, and fell to the floor. He unsnapped his cummerbund—*why the hell did you wear so many clothes!* his mind screamed—and unbuckled his belt and trousers, then he noticed how woebegone she looked, sitting there on the edge of the bed, all folded up in herself.

"Who are you hiding from, angel?" he asked, dropping to his knees before her. "Not from me, surely."

"I'm having a bout of 'why am I here and where's my clothes' second thoughts," she said, trying to smile.

He shook his head in a stern reproach. "We'll have none of that. You're here because it's right." He grasped her wrists, pulled through her resistance, and uncrossed her arms. "Unfold those wings. Don't hide from me. I want to see you." His gaze moved slowly across her small breasts. "You're beautiful."

She sighed. "I wish that were true."

"Don't argue with me. If I say you're beautiful, then you are! Case closed."

"When God handed out breasts, I must have been the last in line." She looked down at her small bosom and frowned. "I got the meager leftovers."

Sebastian grinned, but kept himself from laughing aloud, afraid that she might think he was laughing at her instead of with her. He pressed her back until she was lying flat, then slid onto the bed beside her.

"If I'm not complaining, why should you?" He brought one of her rosy nipples to his lips and kissed it, then stroked it with his tongue. She writhed next to him and put her arm around his neck to pull him across her.

With his chest shielding her nakedness, Everly felt invincible. She moved her breasts up and down, loving the friction of his chest hair against her turgid nipples. His mouth was relentless, rubbing against hers and growing hotter and hotter. His tongue probed the inside of her lips, then delved into her mouth. She answered it, stroke for stroke, tasting the champagne and the emerging tang of arousal.

His back was smooth, and muscles writhed beneath her wandering hands; muscles that hadn't been as powerful and as evident before. His shoulder blades weren't as sharp, his ribs not as easy to count—other than that, he was the Bastian she remembered.

"Bastian, Bastian," she whispered between hungry kisses, enjoying the feel of his name on her lips.

"Bastian," he said with a short laugh. "You're the only one who's ever called me that." He lifted himself up on his elbows and looked down into her face. "When you first called me that, I wasn't sure I liked it, but then I realized that that's how I felt when I was with you."

"How you felt?" she asked, running her fingers through the sides of his silky straight hair and thinking that it was a lighter shade of brown than it used to be. The Florida sun had done a wonderful job on him.

"Bastian. You know, like a bastion of strength. A strong fortress."

She wrinkled her nose. "Yes, but that's spelled differently."

"I know, but it sounds the same. That's what I thought when you called me that. I thought, 'Yes, I'm strong now. I'll shelter her from all the pain and cruelty in the world. It won't scar her, not like it scarred me. I won't let it.'"

His face blurred before her as tears welled up in her eyes. "That's beautiful. You thought that when you were with me?"

"I still do." He buried his face in the side of her neck and his voice was muffled against her skin. "I'm sorry I hurt you, Everly. I am. I'm truly sorry."

She wrapped her arms around his waist and held him to her, rocking from side to side in mute elation. The tears ran down her cheeks and one splashed onto his ear. He raised up, smiled, and wiped the tears away with his fingertips.

"My dear, I think you're on the verge of a crying jag."

"No, I'm okay," she said, sniffling. "I'm just happy."

"Sure?" he asked, tipping his head to one side.

"Yes." She held his face in her hands and rose up to kiss his mouth. "No more tears. No more wasted time." Her hands moved between their bodies and unzipped his trousers. Slipping one hand inside, she found him, straining and fully aroused. She smiled into his eyes, moving her fingers ever so slightly, but it brought a deep moan from him, and he pushed himself off the bed.

The light from the living room fell across the floor in a pyramid of pale yellow, its apex stopping at Sebastian's feet. Within a minute, he had shed the rest of his clothing. He stood beside the bed, gazing at her until she wanted to cover herself with him again.

"Bastian, come here," she said, lifting her arms to him. "Don't keep your distance."

He grabbed one corner of the navy blue coverlet and gave a mighty jerk, laughing heartily as she shrieked and jumped to her feet at the other side of the bed. The satin quilt floated to the floor as Sebastian pulled down the top sheet, plumped up the pillows, then sprang onto his knees in the center of the bed.

"Come back here," he said, catching her wrist and pulling her off balance. She fell to the bed, half-on and half-off it. Sebastian wound an arm around her waist and positioned her in the right place, then eased her head down onto one of the soft pillows. His fingers combed through her reddish-brown hair, letting the curls wrap around them.

He slipped over her like a sheet, his legs framing hers, his hands framing her face. His lips flirted and teased, running across her cheek and down her neck, leaving a moist trail over her shoulder to the inside of her elbow. Stopping there. Nuzzling. Licking. Moving on. Sideways now to her stomach, his tongue dipping into the inviting crevice of her navel. Making her shiver. Quick strokes of his tongue below her navel where muscles fluttered invitingly, but her inner thighs were a stronger invitation. Swift kisses against the soft, white skin, white where the sun rarely touched. Suckling the back of her knee, finding a sensitive spot and biting it gently.

He was all over her. Locating pulse points, secret places, forgotten pleasures. Everly closed her eyes, trying to keep up with him through her senses, but he was too quick. Like a bandit. Striking in a blinding flash, then gone, leaving only his shadow behind. Her hands grabbed the air, then his shoulders. Then his muscled, rock-hard biceps.

This man feels so good, she thought. So strong and solid. Like a bastion. Bastion, Bastian.

"Sebastian Jefferson Dark," she whispered, smiling.

"Present," he answered, laughter threading through his voice.

"Such a noble name."

"Such a mouthful of a name," he amended.

She opened her eyes and found that his face was poised above hers.

"Everly Suzanne Viverette," he murmured, his voice clear of all humor.

"In the flesh," she said, recognizing the flickering light in his eyes, pulsating like an inner flame.

He looked from her face to her right shoulder, then bent his head and kissed it. His teeth nipped her lightly, playfully, then he turned his head and pressed a passionate kiss against her neck. At the same moment his hot urgent shaft of desire parted her inner sea and drove upward until it filled her cavity of longing. Her legs came up and her heels locked against the small of his back. The wonder of him rushed back to her, pulsating slowly and rhythmically, moving within her like a restless tide. It swept her away, set her adrift in her own private passion, then brought her back to share it with him.

She cried out his name and his mouth covered hers. His tongue joined in with the movement of his body, slipping into her mouth and sliding out again.

For Everly it was recitation of the love she had given him two years ago. Achingly familiar, but made sweeter with the passage of time and the healing of old wounds.

For Sebastian it was a blending of heart and soul. Unfelt until this moment, but perfectly timed because now he was strong enough to acknowledge it, and man enough to appreciate it.

## Chapter Twelve

Everly opened her eyes and stared at the gold eagle that rested in the hollow of Sebastian's throat. She raised up on one elbow and kissed it, then let her lips wander across his chest, awakening him to arousal.

Making love to him in the bright light of morning seemed more permanent than it had with the cover of night hiding their bodies and facial expressions. They lay on their sides, stomach to stomach, breasts to chest, legs scissored, and gazed openly at each other. Their love climaxed in soft moans and wavering smiles of fulfillment.

Everly pressed her lips against his shoulder as her hands moved up and down his back.

"I love you, Bastian," she whispered, the words falling from her lips as naturally as rain falls from clouds. Moments passed before the void struck her. "Bastian, I love you," she said more loudly, more distinctly.

His hands skimmed down her back to her hips. His fingers tightened in an unsatisfying response.

Anger rumbled through her like thunder and she was out of the bed like a streak of lightning.

"Everly?" Sebastian called after her when she stomped from the bedroom into the living room. He tipped his head to one side, listening to the sounds of her dialing the telephone. He strained to hear her conversation, and his eyes widened when he realized that she was calling for a taxi. "Everly, come back in here!"

She came into view again, all tanned skin and tumbled hair, which she pushed back from her forehead. Without a word, she began dressing, and he'd never seen anyone dress as fast. Panties, shorts, top, shoes, hat.

"Everly, where the hell are you going?"

"Home. The party's over." Her voice was stinging, lashing out like the tip of a whip.

"Everly, don't be this way," he complained, propping up on his elbows. He sighed heavily at her pouting expression. "Everly, honey, I loved last night and this morning. I love being with you."

She delivered a sickly sweet smile. "Close, but no cigar, *honey*." She threw shoes and other accessories into her overnight case and snapped it shut, then grabbed her red dress and shoes.

"Let me take you back to Cabot's Key and we'll talk this out on the way there."

She ignored him and headed back into the living room. Sebastian swung his legs over the side of the bed, gathered the top sheet around him, and followed her. She had her purse, dress, and nightcase in her arms, and was making her way to the office and the front door.

"Everly, will you listen to me?"

"No!" she shot back over her shoulder.

"Everly..." He pressed his lips together, hearing the whining quality in his voice and despising it. His gaze fell on her red-and-yellow mask and he snatched it up and hurried—as much as the sheet would allow—after her. She was opening the front door as a taxi stopped at the curb.

"For pity's sake, Everly!" When she kept walking, he shouted, "Here's your mask!"

She stopped, spun to face him, and her eyes narrowed to dangerous slits. "Keep it," she said in a fierce whisper. "You're into masks more than I am. I only wear one on Halloween, but you wear one all the time!"

"Don't be this way. Let's discuss this." He held the sheet gathered at his waist in one hand, and leaned the other against the door frame.

"There's nothing to discuss," she said, opening the back door of the taxi and throwing her things inside it. "Your silence spoke eloquently for you." She sat in the back seat and slammed the door behind her.

Impotent fury careened within him as he leaned out the open door and yelled, "Do you always pick a fight after you make love to a man?"

Too late, he noticed that he had an audience. A smartly dressed business woman stood only a couple of feet from him. She stopped in her tracks and stared, somewhat amused, at the man wearing the sheet and glaring at her as if he expected an answer.

"No, I don't," she said, her voice light with laughter. "Do I win a prize?"

Sebastian felt heat rise to the roots of his hair. "I—I wasn't talking to you." He looked at the taxi and Everly's stern profile. "I was talking to that woman in the taxi."

"Oh, I see." The woman shrugged and walked past him, glancing over her shoulder one last time for a final look at his sheet-draped body and flushed face.

"Are you satisfied?" Sebastian shouted at Everly, still mortified from the encounter with the passerby.

Everly kept the smile from her lips as she brought her gaze around to his. "I know you love me, Bastian," she said through the open window. "But it doesn't mean a damn thing unless *you* know it." She leaned forward and spoke to the driver and the taxi shot forward.

"Everly!" Sebastian slammed the side of his fist against the door frame. Damn it, he *did* know it!

He whirled around and almost fell over his own feet. His gaze darted wildly around the room while his mind searched for a plan of action. Why did that woman always catch him with his pants down? he wondered, closing the front door and stumbling over the sheet as he hurried back into the bedroom for his clothes. It seemed that at every crucial time in their relationship, he was either half dressed or completely naked!

He put on the first things he could find—tuxedo trousers, tennis shoes and the fancy pleated shirt. Leaving the gray shirt unbuttoned, he ran from the building and got into his car.

Driving ten miles faster than the speed limit allowed, he cursed himself for being so thickheaded. Why hadn't he told her he loved her? She had every right to leave him. All she wanted was the truth, the simple, clear truth. What had gotten into him? That was a hell of a time to get cold feet!

He ran a hand down his face, felt his sandpapery whiskers, and glanced into the rearview mirror. His reflection scared him. Red-rimmed eyes, hollow cheeks, bristling stubble, brown hair falling in negligent disarray.

"Boo!" he said, then focused his attention on the stretch of highway and searched for the turnoff to Cabot's Key. He saw the Key West cab whiz past him on its journey back to town, having deposited Everly.

He jerked the wheel, tromped down on the accelerator, then braked in a squeal of rubber in front of the main house. Leaping from the car, he ran up the steps and flung open the front door. Miss Martha placed a hand over her heart and her dark eyes widened in alarm.

"Sebastian! You scared me half to death!"

"Where's Everly?" he asked, moving to the foot of the stairs and looking up at the second landing. "Is she in her room?"

"No, she's not here. She came in, dumped her things in this chair, and went back out." Miss Martha picked up Everly's overnight case from the chair in the foyer. "She was in quite a snit."

"I know, I know." He put a hand at the back of his neck and massaged the tense muscles there. "Did you see which way she went?"

"Toward Little Bit, I think."

"Little Bit. Of course." He strode toward the front door, paused to plant a kiss on Miss Martha's cheek, and broke into a trot toward the neighboring Key. He skidded to a halt at the shore, his tennis shoes slipping in the wet grass.

The tide was coming in and there was a good four feet of salt water between him and Little Bit Key. Sebastian shaded his eyes with one hand and could see the flat-bottom boat tied on the other shore.

"Damn it!" Looking down at his rented clothes, he shrugged and waded out into the cold water. He lifted his arms above water level and felt his tennis shoes sink into wet sand, then he felt one slip off his foot, then the other.

"Great, just great!" he bellowed to the clear blue sky, his hands waving frantically as he tried to keep his balance. The water lapped at the center of his chest, occasionally splashing in his face.

Sloshing up the opposite bank, he made a face at his soaked clothes and bare sandy feet. Dodging clumps of grass burs, he picked his way to the gazebo.

She wasn't there, naturally.

He looked ahead, recalling sharp rocks and plenty of sticky burs. Sucking in his breath, he charged forward, watching for hazards. He was almost to the house when he stepped in a clump of grass and felt needles sting his bare foot.

"Ouch!" He hopped on the other foot and plucked a bur from his instep. "Everly!"

She didn't answer, naturally.

"You'd better be here if you know what's good for you," he muttered darkly as he hip-hopped to the louvered doors. One stood partially open and he stepped inside, thankful for the smooth polished floors.

She was sitting in the middle of the living room. Just sitting there, waiting for him.

Sebastian sighed, propping his hands at his waist. Hell's bells, she knew him better than he knew himself!

"You knew I'd come after you, didn't you?" he asked.

She crossed her legs, Indian fashion. "Yes, but you got here much faster than I thought was possible." Her gaze moved over him, taking in his soaked clothes and bare feet. A grin overtook her. "You swam over?"

"I didn't have much choice. You took the boat." He removed the wet shirt and dropped it to the floor. "This stuff is rented, you know."

She laughed, rocking back and forth, and the sound of her laughter echoed in the empty house. "Serves you right. What were you yelling about out there?"

"I stepped on a sandbur! It hurt like hell!"

She wrinkled her nose. "If you can survive life in a Russian prison camp, I think you can survive a sandbur."

He paced toward her and sat down in front of her. Reaching out, he swept the hat from her head. "I guess you're right. Are you listening to me?"

"I'm all ears."

"I love you."

Instead of jumping for joy, smothering him with kisses and telling him that she was the happiest girl in the whole U.S.A. as he expected her to do, she stared at him, sad-eyed, looking like a little girl who'd been told that her favorite rag doll had disintegrated in the washer.

"Now what's wrong?" Sebastian asked, his shoulders slumping in defeat. "That was supposed to make you happy."

"Why didn't you tell me you loved me before? Why did you make me force a showdown? I had to *make* you say it!"

"I don't know." He ran a hand through his hair, remembering how terrible he looked. "Why am I soaking wet and half-dressed? Why couldn't I be clean-shaven, dressed fit to kill and waxing poetic? I look a fright. I nearly scared Miss Martha out of ten years of growth." He peered at her through his lowered lashes. "I'm not answering your question, am I?"

"No, but you're good at that."

Only a foot separated them, but it seemed like a mile to Sebastian. He recalled the night and the morning and some of the distance was erased.

"I should have told you earlier that I loved you. I've made myself so isolated.... I've been so careful not to get myself into a situation where I might hurt another woman as I hurt you, that it's difficult to break down my cell walls." He chuckled, but it sounded sad to his ears. "That's what Katra said. She said that I was in my own prison cell of sorts. She's right. She *was* right," he corrected himself. "Katra made me see a lot of things. I owe so much to her and to you." His lashes lifted and his eyes took on a fever- ish intensity. "I'm free, Everly. Free, at last."

She reached across the space and her fingers stroked his cheek, lightly and lovingly. "I can see that. How does it feel?"

"Wonderful."

"And a little scary?"

"A little." A shiver shook his shoulders and tingled down his spine. "I guess I was afraid to be happy."

"Afraid that it would be taken away from you again?"

"Yes." He captured her hand and held it between his. "But I want you in my life. I want to be loved by you."

"Forever?"

"Oh, yes. Forever." He lifted her hand and kissed the back of it. "I want a family. One of my own. I want to be happy again. I want everything that this life offers." His expression hardened with fierce determination. "I can't forget what happened to me, no more than I could forget you, but I want to move ahead. I want to live instead of just exist."

She tugged her hand from his and stretched out on her back, flinging her arms over her head. "I want to remem- ber this moment forever and ever because I've been waiting to hear you say those things for so long. There was a time when I thought I'd never be able to reach you again. Never be able to love you again." She sighed with exaggeration. "A moment of silence, please."

He couldn't resist her allure. Her body beckoned him; her love awaited him. Sliding onto his stomach, he draped an arm across her and kissed her. Her tongue outlined his lips and she giggled.

"You taste of salt water." She licked her lips, then his again. "You *are* a mess." Her hands touched his wet trou- sers. "You've got seaweed all over you! I feel like I'm being seduced by the Creature from the Black Lagoon!"

"It's your fault. If you hadn't flown off the handle and left me high and dry I wouldn't be wet and fishy now!"

Her fingers combed through his hair and came to rest at the back of his neck. "Don't blame me. You had your chance and you blew it."

"You didn't give me a chance!" He raised up to sit beside her prone body. "I was barely awake!"

"You were awake enough to make love to me," she pointed out with irritating perception.

"That's different. I can do that in my sleep."

"Well, that's a sweet thing to say. You're so romantic, Bastian!"

"You know what I mean," he grumbled.

"If you mean that you respond to a warm body—*any* warm body—then I guess I do." She sat up and glared at him, and there was a challenge in her eyes.

"What I mean is that I was still a little…well, hazy from making love. I was getting around to telling you that I love you—"

"Getting around to it? That makes it sound like a chore!"

"So I'm not good with words. You're the writer, not me."

"We're not writing. We're speaking aloud. There's a big difference."

"The important thing is that I have said it. I love you!" He stood up, angry that this wasn't going well. Why was she so stubborn? She should have fallen into his arms the moment he spoke the words! "What's more, I want you to marry me. It's up to you now. I've done everything I can do, short of getting on my knees and begging forgiveness, which I will *not* do," he said, slicing her with a warning glare, "so don't waste your breath!"

She tipped her head back and smiled up at him. "Bastian?"

"What?" he snapped, glancing at her, then doing a double take when he realized she was pulling her blouse over her head. Desire pulsated through him, quick as lightning. All it took was one look, one smile, and he was ready for her. He shook his head, amazed at his shameful weakness.

"Do you always pick a fight before you make love to a woman?" she asked, smiling lazily, confidently.

His anger played itself out, leaving him feeling stupid and petty. Looking down into her sweet face, his love for her poured through him like sun through the skylight overhead. He dropped to his knees, holding her tightly against him until he could feel the beat of her heart.

"No. Do I get a prize?" he asked, grinning ear to ear.

"Yes," Everly said, framing his face and kissing him with complete abandon before she let his mouth slide down to her breasts. "You get me."

# The Silhouette Cameo Tote Bag Now available for just $6.99

Handsomely designed in blue and bright pink, its stylish good looks make the Cameo Tote Bag an attractive accessory. The Cameo Tote Bag is big and roomy (13" square), with reinforced handles and a snap-shut top. You can buy the Cameo Tote Bag for $6.99, plus $1.50 for postage and handling.

Send your name and address with check or money order for $6.99 (plus $1.50 postage and handling), a total of $8.49 to:

**Silhouette Books**
**120 Brighton Road**
**P.O. Box 5084**
**Clifton, NJ 07015-5084**
**ATTN: Tote Bag**

SIL-T-1R

The Silhouette Cameo Tote Bag can be purchased pre-paid only. No charges will be accepted. Please allow 4 to 6 weeks for delivery.

N.Y. State Residents Please Add Sales Tax

Offer not available in Canada.

# COMING NEXT MONTH

**MISTY MORNINGS, MAGIC NIGHTS—Ada Steward**
Recovering from a recent divorce, Carole Stockton had no desire for
another involvement. Then politician Donnelly Wakefield entered her life
and he was determined to be a winning candidate.

**SWEET PROMISE—Ginna Gray**
At eighteen, Joanna fell in love with Sean Fleming. But he only considered
her a spoiled child. Could she convince him of the promise of a
woman's love?

**SUMMER STORM—Patti Beckman**
When political cartoonist Leida Adams's sailboat capsized, she couldn't
tell her handsome lifesaver, Senator Grant Hunter, that he was the target
of her biting satire. Would the truth keep their love from smooth sailing?

**WHITE LACE AND PROMISES— Debbie Macomber**
After high school, Maggie and Glenn drifted apart and suffered their
private heartaches. Years later at their old friends' wedding, they fell in
love. They were determined to bury their pasts and trust their rediscovered
happiness.

**SULLIVAN VS. SULLIVAN—Jillian Blake**
Kerry and Tip were attorneys on opposite sides of a perilous case. The
situation was getting hotter by the minute. They could agree to a
compromise, but only if the verdict was love.

**RAGGED RAINBOWS—Linda Lael Miller**
Shay Kendall had grown up overshadowed by her actress mother's faded
Hollywood fame. When exposé writer Mitch Prescott convinced her to
collaborate on her mother's biography, she knew that he would free her
from her haunting past and share her future.

---

## AVAILABLE THIS MONTH:

**NOBODY'S FOOL**
Renee Roszel

**THE SECURITY MAN**
Dixie Browning

**YESTERDAY'S LIES**
Lisa Jackson

**AFTER DARK**
Elaine Camp

**MAGIC SEASON**
Anne Lacey

**LESSONS LEARNED**
Nora Roberts

# Take 4 Silhouette Intimate Moments novels
# FREE

Then preview 4 brand new Silhouette Intimate Moments® novels —delivered to your door every month—for 15 days as soon as they are published. When you decide to keep them, you pay just $2.25 each ($2.50 each, in Canada), *with no shipping, handling, or other charges of any kind!*

Silhouette Intimate Moments novels are not for everyone. They were created to give you a more detailed, more exciting reading experience, filled with romantic fantasy, intense sensuality, and stirring passion.

The first 4 Silhouette Intimate Moments novels are absolutely FREE and without obligation, yours to keep. You can cancel at any time.

You'll also receive a FREE subscription to the Silhouette Books Newsletter as long as you remain a member. Each issue is filled with news on upcoming titles, interviews with your favorite authors, even their favorite recipes.

To get your 4 FREE books, fill out and mail the coupon today!

# Silhouette Intimate Moments®

**Silhouette Books, 120 Brighton Rd., P.O. Box 5084, Clifton, NJ 07015-5084**